CRUISING TOWARD DEATH

CRUISING TOWARD DEATH

Lesley St. James

For my parents, Jerry and Lana.
Thanks for all the books.

PROLOGUE

A bead of sweat trickled down Detective Mike McCall's back, and he shifted in his seat nervously.

"Relax, McCall. I'll have this up and running before he gets here. We have plenty of time." Detective Karen Rollins's fingers flew across the screen of the tablet.

"It was working a few minutes ago. I don't know why it stopped," complained Mike.

"The Bluetooth on the tablet connected with a different device for some reason, but I've got it under control. Listen."

Mike could hear Finn and Mary talking behind the bar. The wire was working. Mike breathed a sigh of relief, and Karen smirked at him.

"O ye of little faith."

Now all they could do was wait there in the storage room for the bar to clear and events to unfold. Mike never found waiting a problem. He had been on so many stakeouts that he had perfected the art of being still and alert while at the same time allowing his mind to wander. Unless he could occupy his mind, he would fall asleep. So, while his ears listened, his mind thought about all the great times he'd had at Meehan's Pub. It was his local bar, and he often spent the evening there having dinner, listening to music, and talking to friends, especially Finn and Mary, the proprietors. The pub was an anchor for the neighborhood and helped to make that small corner of the Upper West Side feel like a small village rather than just another few blocks of the sprawling, teeming island that was Manhattan.

That's why this was personal.

Mike groaned internally. A good cop didn't let the job become personal. A good cop let other cops handle the cases close to home.

Except no one else would touch this case, for whatever reason. Mike had his suspicions and a long list of nos from colleagues and supervisors. So what else could he do? Thank goodness Karen hadn't forsaken him. She was the best partner he'd ever had. He offered up a silent prayer that everything would go according to plan, that nothing would happen to hurt Karen, Finn, or Mary. If he got hurt, he could live with it...or not. But if anyone else got hurt...

"Mary, it's time you headed home," Mike heard Finn say. Mary started to protest, but he cut her off.

"No arguments!"

"Well, I'm not going home. I'm going to church. I'll be lighting candles at St. Columba's. Come find me when it's over."

The microphone popped and cracked as Mary and Finn embraced, at least that's what Mike assumed. The next thing he heard was Finn whistling, and he could imagine the barkeep wiping down the bar as he did so. Mike heard the scrape of chairs, the thump of footsteps, and a door open and close. Hopefully, the last customers were calling it a night.

"The bar's empty," whispered Finn in confirmation. Mike

heard the odd sound as the proprietor went about his end-of-the-night tasks.

"He might not show," whispered Karen.

He was Tomaso Giovanni Gaudiano, a.k.a. Tommy Tantrum, a mid-level gangster who had been squeezing businesses in this neighborhood for the past year. He was trying to move up, thought Mike, and he was getting more aggressive. When things didn't go his way, as in someone resisted, Tommy blew his top. The last time Mount Tomaso had blown, a third-generation baker had lost his life. No one could prove that Tommy had made the baker's wife a widow, but she had quickly sold the business to a real estate investment firm that was a front for the mob. Then she moved to Florida.

"He'll show. He thinks he's getting what he wants."

"That's no guarantee. He likes to set meetings on his own—"

Mike and Karen tensed at the sound of a door opening.

"Mr. Gaudiano," announced Finn. "So good of you to come."

"Hello, Tommy Tantrum," whispered Karen.

"I had a feeling you'd make contact, what with how dangerous the neighborhood is becoming," replied a soft masculine voice. The wire was only just picking it up. Mike swore softly. Gaudiano was doing it on purpose. Was he normally this cautious, or did he suspect something?

"Well, my beer distributor got mugged right out front, and someone broke in and smashed all my well liquor. Left my best whiskeys alone, though. Didn't even steal 'em. Then he cut the cord on my freezer, and I lost all my meat."

"I told you the neighborhood was going to hell."

"Prophetic."

"You obviously need some protection."

"Obviously."

"How about you pour me a glass of the O'Sullivan's Reserve, and we'll talk terms."

"Your friends want some?"

"They don't drink."

Friends. Gaudiano wasn't alone. Mike and Karen looked at each other. This situation had just become more dangerous. Finn was outnumbered. Mike knew he kept a sawed-off behind the bar, but that was only two shots, and he didn't want Finn to have to defend himself anyway. Finn going to jail for illegal firearms or worse, manslaughter, was not the point of this operation. Gathering evidence to put Tommy Tantrum behind bars and end the protection racket in the neighborhood was.

Mike and Karen could hear Finn place a glass on the bar.

"So where's Mary tonight?" asked Gaudiano.

A soft *thunk* sounded over the headphones as Finn uncorked a bottle.

"She's at home."

"Or is she at St. Columba's? A spiritual woman, your Mary."

Karen gasped, and Mike's heart pounded in his chest. What was Gaudiano playing at?

Finn filled the glass and set the bottle on the bar. Mike wondered if the older man's hands were shaking, but he doubted it. Finn was a cool customer and had seen the likes of Gaudiano before.

"Bring the drink to my table."

Mike flinched, and Karen set a steadying hand on his arm. She mouthed the word "no" and reinforced it by firmly shaking her head. Every atom in Mike's body wanted to charge into the bar. He knew Finn was in trouble, but Karen was right. Two cops bursting in would end in a firefight for sure. Left alone, Finn might be able to talk his way out of it.

But what if he couldn't?

They could always sneak out the back and come in the front door as if they were a couple stopping for a drink. That would break things up nicely. Gaudiano wouldn't want witnesses, and he might balk at killing three people instead of one.

Whatever they heard next would determine their course of action.

Movement, as Finn came around the bar with the drink and set it on the table. Then a scuffle, and nothing else. The wire went dead.

"Front door?" asked Karen as she sprang to her feet.

"No time. Call it in," bit back Mike as he drew his weapon and headed for the door to the bar. Before she could stop him, he was gone.

"NYPD! Drop your weapons!"

Finn was kneeling on the floor, and one of Gaudiano's thugs had a gun pressed to his forehead. That gun immediately swung in Mike's direction, a tactical error because Finn took the opportunity to roll under a table. Mike and the gunman stared each other down. Gaudiano, on the other hand, sat at his table and calmly sipped his single malt.

"This place is about to be swarmed by cops," said Mike through gritted teeth. "So I suggest you put down your weapon."

"I don't think so," smiled Gaudiano. "I doubt your partner had time to call it in." He gestured toward the door to the storage room, but there was no way Mike was turning around to look. Instead, he began to edge sideways so he could see. The thug mirrored his every move. Soon Mike saw the doorway and Karen with her hands in the air, held at gunpoint.

"I'm sorry, Mike. It happened so fast."

"Don't worry about it, Karen."

"It looks like it's lights out for us," she said as her body shook convulsively.

"A realist," smirked Gaudiano. "I admire that."

"No way, Karen! This isn't over!"

"It's lights out, Mike!" she cried again, shaking even more violently. Mike realized what she was doing right before her elbow struck the light switch next to the door.

When darkness descended, Mike crouched instinctively and rolled to a new position. He could hear grunts and breaking glass from behind the bar, running footsteps, and a door opening. Gaudiano was getting away. Mike sprang out of his crouch to pursue the gangster just as a gun discharged. He felt a ball of fire tear through his leg and a seismic shock as his whole body collided with the floor. And then he felt nothing else.

CHAPTER 1

*A*nd there went my hat. A gust of frigid February wind swept it off my head, and I watched the stunning creation, white straw with a huge black and white bow, drift gently down to land in the Hudson River. It floated for a moment before sinking into the murky brown water like a doomed ocean liner. If I believed in omens, I would have turned around right then and there, marched down the gangway, and hailed a cab for home. But I didn't believe in omens.

I believed in money well spent, and that hat had cost a small fortune. I could have held onto it if it wasn't for my rolling suitcase, which had a wonky wheel and liked to turn over unexpectedly. Already it had caused me to stumble several times as I made my way up the gangway, and I was failing miserably at looking as graceful as Rose in *Titanic*.

Rose didn't have to manage her own luggage.

Now my Rose hat was gone. (*Sniff.*)

With a hard yank, I righted my bag and continued the climb up the long walkway to the boarding area amidship. In front of me, my good friend Liz Gordon loped gracefully while carrying an overstuffed duffel bag with ease. Liz was toned, and her cocoa skin glowed with health, set off by the yellow t-shirt, tropical print summer skirt, and sandals that she wore effortlessly. I, of course, had opted for a linen suit and pumps. I was overdressed as usual, but it was my first cruise, and I wanted it to be special, like a great voyage on an ocean liner of old. I'm an idiot.

This might be a good place for introductions. The idiot is Jill Cooksey, senior account executive at a public relations firm called Waverly Communications. A native Virginian, I moved to New York six years ago to begin a career in PR, and it had been quite an adventure. That adventure was about to take to the high seas, but this wasn't going to be a pleasure cruise. It was work.

Seaswept Cruises, a brand-new cruise line, was considering retaining Waverly Communications to help it achieve household name status, which was a tall order. Waverly, a beauty PR firm, had no travel clients, and the big boss, William Waverly, wanted to diversify. Because I was angling for a promotion to account manager or (dare I dream?) vice president, I had scouted Seaswept Cruises on my own and had laid the groundwork, but the contracts weren't yet signed. My mission was to get firsthand knowledge of the ship and to impress the owner of the company. If everything went according to plan, Seaswept would be my client when we returned in a week.

Fun was also on the agenda. I hadn't had a real vacation since I started at Waverly, and I had recently used my vacation days to moonlight with another company to pay off some credit cards. When I approached Seaswept, they invited me on their inaugural cruise to the Bahamas to get a better sense of what the line had to offer and to make my final pitch. What a hardship! And since the rooms were double occupancy, I decided to bring along my good friend and sports enthusiast Liz. She also worked in PR, but that's not why I brought her along. Well, not altogether.

Seaswept Cruises' flagship, The Lady Luck, was the largest casino afloat, something I planned to promote heavily. She was also packed with extreme sports opportunities that would appeal to a young clientele. That meant rock climbing, bungee jumping, rappelling, parasailing, cliff diving, and something called The Keel Haul. Now I was mentally and physically prepared for the casino—and the pool, the yoga classes, the gym, and the spa—but a thrill seeker I am not. Thus Liz. She jumped at the chance, and I was sure she would be doing a lot more jumping once we were on board.

Since the sum total of my knowledge of cruise ships came from *Love Boat* reruns, *The Poseidon Adventure*, and *Titanic*, I had some preconceived notions that I was certain would not pan out. Was I going to meet my soulmate? Probably not. Would I lead my fellow passengers to safety after a maritime disaster? Hopefully not. Would a vagabond artist draw me like one of his French girls? Decidedly not. But I did hope for drinks in pineapples, salsa dancing, and sunshine.

As we crested the gangway, passed into the ship, and emerged into a large space ringed with gold and glass elevators surrounding a huge ice sculpture of a giant wave (sweeping us to sea?), I suddenly felt that all my fantasies would come true.

I looked around for the cruise director. Sure enough, a perky brunette in a blue and white naval uniform, complete with epaulets and a name tag that read "Cindy," was directing folks to the elevators that would whisk them up to the main lobby for check-in. The elevators moved quickly, efficiently ferrying passengers and making room for more to board.

I was still taking in my surroundings when I heard mutters and cries from passengers around me, but it wasn't until something crashed into me that I really paid attention. I was knocked to the floor, and I heard and felt the back seam of my linen pencil skirt give way. Unbelievable.

"Why don't you watch where you're going?" I snapped, and

then I looked up to see an elderly man on a red mobility scooter. He had to be in his eighties despite the jet-black toupee that roosted atop his pate. Below that shock of fake black hair, his bushy white eyebrows perched like fuzzy caterpillars above his rheumy eyes and jaundiced complexion. This man looked ill, and I felt terrible for snapping at him—until he opened his mouth.

"I'm a disabled senior citizen! You have to watch out for me!" he yelled and then motored on his way. I watched as he rolled up behind Cindy and sounded a bicycle horn attached to his scooter to get her attention. She almost jumped out of her pumps, and annoyance briefly crossed her face, but she swallowed it and forced a smile.

I was distracted by two hands thrust in front of my eyes. One belonged to Liz and the other to a male crew member. Taking both of them, I hauled myself upright.

"Are you okay?" asked Liz.

"I'm fine, but who is that guy?" I asked.

"Casimir Koblinsky, the mattress king of Piscataway, NJ," said the crewman. In addition to his uniform, he sported a combination cap with gold braid over equally golden hair and green eyes the color of the ocean.

He was tall. Very tall.

And fit. Very fit.

He spoke with a faint accent that sounded vaguely German or Scandinavian. The question of his origin was settled when he introduced himself.

"Lieutenant Gunnar Halvorsen, at your service. And may I recommend, ladies, that you steer clear of Mr. Koblinsky? He is notorious in the industry for being a nasty fellow who spends most of his life aboard ship harassing the crew and other passengers."

Liz and I introduced ourselves in garbled speech that I hope did the job. I was glad to see that she was as tongue-tied as I was in the face of this Norse hero.

"You're the PR people." He beamed a smile our way. (Okay, he beamed a smile at Liz.) "We were told to expect you. Where is the rest of your party?"

"We're the only ones," she smiled back at him.

"That's funny," he said. "We were told to expect four of you."

How odd. I had liaised with the cruise company and booked one suite for two people. I supposed someone had made a mistake. Maybe Lieutenant Beowulf was confused.

The gallant officer took Liz's duffel bag, hooked his other arm through hers, and escorted her to the promenade deck. My wonky suitcase and I brought up the rear, which was just as well. Liz hadn't dated anyone in a while, and it was nice to see her get her flirt on. And even though Thor was a hottie-and-a-half, I had absolutely no interest in romance.

We emerged from the elevator onto the promenade deck to find it bustling with guests waiting to check in. Gunnar snagged two glasses of champagne for us from a circulating waiter. It was crisp, bubbly, and delicious. Then he guided us to a VIP line, and soon we were handed bracelets and a small tablet computer apiece. Immediately, the tablet began speaking to us, introducing itself and offering us directions to our cabins. High tech! The interface was user-friendly and elegantly designed, and I added it to the list of things to promote about Seaswept Cruises.

Distracted by the technology, I nearly bumped into someone as I turned to go, a woman with a nautical scarf tied kerchief-style over her head and huge sunglasses. I tried to apologize, but she just about ran in the opposite direction, leaving behind a cloud of perfume that I knew quite well—Fall Fantasy by Eshellon Cosmetics, one of my clients. Another satisfied customer.

"Liz, did you recognize that woman?"

"Do you think it's someone we know? A celebrity maybe?" she asked. I shrugged my shoulders, and we headed for the elevator, where Gunnar bid us adieu.

"Alas, I must attend to my duties."

"Of course, you must," breathed Liz, lashes aflutter.

"But I will certainly see you at dinner. May I be so bold as to sit with you this evening?"

Liz simpered. She actually simpered.

"Until then." Gunnar raised her hand to his lips, clicked his heels together, and was gone in a flash of gold braid.

Oh my!

Liz and I looked at each other and burst into giggles.

"I'll swan, Liz. That very fine man is positively smitten with you."

"Forget Mr. Darcy. I'll take Captain Wentworth!" Liz was flushed, and her eyes were bright. She looked like she had a fever, a clear sign of love according to most novels. Well, love or consumption.

"Can we talk about his eyes, hair, chiseled chin, and muscles, in that order?" I enumerated his finer points on my fingers.

"Don't forget that smile!"

After riding down four decks, giggling all the way, we exited the elevator to be confronted by a rabbit warren. Narrow hallways extended in every possible direction. Thank heaven for the tablet, which quickly guided us to our cabin and even unlocked the door. We paused before entering our suite for a moment of drama.

"Are you ready for the vacation of a lifetime?" I asked Liz.

"Is that you talking or a press release?"

"Both." I pushed open our door to reveal...a closet. It had twin beds in it, but it had to be a closet. A tiny door off to the side might have been a bathroom. Across from it was a lighted vanity with little shelves all around it and three small drawers under it. I had been assured by my contact at the cruise line that we would have a suite with a balcony. All we had was a tiny porthole.

"This has to be a mistake," I moaned.

It wasn't. Ten minutes later, I was back upstairs at the check-in desk.

"You are in the correct cabin," said the clerk. "The other members of your party are in the suite on the windjammer deck."

"There are no other members of our party. We are the whole party from Waverly Communications."

"So Mr. and Mrs. William Waverly aren't part of the Waverly Communications group?"

My heart sank. Was it possible? Was Mr. Waverly aboard? But he wasn't married. Wife number three had left him the year before, and I was pretty sure he was too old to try again. But maybe not.

Defeated, Liz and I trudged back down to steerage and our cupboard under the stairs.

"You know, it's really not bad," said my ever-chipper friend. "If we were paying for this ourselves, this is exactly where we would be staying."

Liz was right, as usual. There ended up being a closet behind the door, and the bathroom, once we ventured into it, was not as tight as I had imagined. It had a lot of shelves and very good lighting. So the space between Liz's bed and mine was about a foot and a half. No big deal. We wouldn't be spending a lot of time in the cabin anyway.

Before she would let me unpack, Liz insisted that we clean the room and bathroom.

"Norovirus is rampant on cruise ships. Who knows what the last passengers left behind."

"But we're the first passengers."

"The cleaning crew then. You can't be too careful." With

that, she produced a packet of sanitizing wipes, and we went to work. It didn't take long thanks to the size of the cabin. When we finished, Liz, a veritable Mary Poppins, pulled a spray bottle from her bag and spritzed the pillows. Lavender.

"We want sweet dreams on this trip so we return home rested and refreshed."

I waited to see what else would emerge from Liz's duffle. Burning sage? A Himalayan salt lamp? But she was finished, so we went about unpacking our suitcases and soon had our little room to rights. The first rule of Carefree Cruising, according to my favorite YouTube cruising expert, Carol, was to unpack completely and immediately and to stow your luggage so it wouldn't be underfoot. Carol the Carefree Cruiser was right.

In no time we were heading up the elevator again toward the lido deck where we would wave goodbye to New York and hello to the Bahamas. I had visions of confetti, streamers, noisemakers, and drinks in pineapples and coconuts—a real New Year's Eve at noon. When we arrived at the lido level, the deck was already crowded with passengers three deep at the rail. There was no sign of confetti or streamers, but I did see someone drinking from a pineapple.

"I want one of those!"

"Here you go," smiled a handsome waiter as he offered us a tray of pineapples decked out with umbrellas, orchids, and elaborate straws.

"Thank you!" Liz and I crooned in unison as we claimed our drinks. Behind the waiter came a happy young woman in a Hawaiian shirt handing out leis. Soon we were festooned with flowers. Liz and I looked at each other and clunked pineapples (because no matter how hard you hit two pineapples together, you'll never get a clink).

"To a 168-hour tour!"

"To escaping New York in February!"

Indeed, while the mood aboard the ship was warm, as was

the lido deck thanks to outdoor heaters, New York looked gray and dreary. I suddenly felt giddy. Liz and I were on our way to hot temperatures and azure water. So what if I had to sweet talk the owner of the company, finish my research, and give a stunner of a presentation to win the client? I was headed for the Caribbean in February! It was a small price to pay for a vacation just when I needed it.

I had foregone my vacation back in December when my boyfriend, cop-turned-reporter Mike McCall, had dumped me. I had opted to use my vacation days to moonlight at a children's television show, which had turned into a lot more work than I'd bargained for, what with murder and all. With only a couple of days off for Christmas, I had been working nonstop since then with my beauty PR clients and in my small role on the kids' TV show. (It's a long story.) This working vacation was a godsend.

I nearly jumped out of my skin and came perilously close to jettisoning my pineapple when the ship's horn sounded. And then we were moving away from the Manhattan cruise terminal.

"Sayonara, suckers!" I yelled at New York in general.

"Yeah, try to stay warm!" cried Liz, and we giggled furiously.

The sound of sirens cut short our giggle-fest, and a police cruiser came tearing down the pier, lights flashing. It screeched to a halt right at the end, and a uniformed cop and a plain-clothes detective sprang from the vehicle. But there was nowhere else for them to go. This ship had sailed. The detective punched the air with his fists, and if we had been closer, I'm sure we would have heard a string of profanities. Then the fight seemed to go out of him, and he stood, hands on his hips, and watched us sail away.

"I wonder what that's all about," murmured Liz.

"I don't know, but does that detective look familiar to you?"

"Detective Donato? It couldn't be." Liz squinted to get a better look at the rapidly shrinking police officers.

"You're right. There are probably hundreds of police detectives in New York. What are the odds?"

Detective Donato and I had been thrown together on a couple of murder cases, and by "thrown together" I mean I had solved them for him. The first time it happened, he had begrudged my involvement, but my PR campaign and my friend's life, not to mention my livelihood, were on the line. The second time, he had asked for my help, so we had come to a place of mutual respect. Even so, a murder investigation was the last thing on my agenda. I was interested in pineapple drinks, warm weather, and a promotion, in that order.

"Ladies and gentlemen, on behalf of Seaswept Cruises, welcome aboard the inaugural cruise of the Lady Luck!" boomed a familiar voice over the speaker system, blowing away all thoughts of the police. Liz and I turned toward a multi-level stage that was positioned between two spade-shaped swimming pools. A familiar perky brunette stood in the middle of the stage and held a microphone. "I'm Cindy Helms, your cruise director. Now to get this party started. Here she is, our very own siren, the incredible Novette!"

Cindy exited the stage just as the opening synthesizer strains of Lady Gaga's "Poker Face" had us looking all around for the band, which we soon located on a large balcony above the swimming pools. A tall woman with luxuriant blond curls cascading down her back mounted the stage. She wore an electric blue, sequined mermaid gown and rhinestone-crusted stilettos that probably required a permit to operate. Without further ado, she launched into Lady Gaga's classic with gusto, and in a matter of moments, the crowd was caught up in the performance.

"She's terrific!" cried Liz.

"She's just all right," sneered a familiar voice. Caz Koblinsky had rolled up on his scooter, which was festooned with leis he had probably demanded from the crew. Two pineapple drinks perched precariously on the double cup holder on his scooter, and he held a third in his left hand, presumably so he could steer the scooter with his right. I had a feeling Caz was the kind of cruiser who was determined to get his money's worth. He slurped his drink while he watched the show intently, but his disdainful expression revealed his ugly feelings about it. Liz and I edged away from him before he could bring down our mood.

Novette was soon joined on the stage by a bevy of handsome male background dancers in electric blue sequined pants and white silk t-shirts festooned with sequined hearts, spades, clubs, and diamonds. They leaped and gyrated around Novette as she belted out the song and danced in place, while the crowd sang along and danced with their pineapples held high.

Then two of the dancers knelt in front of and behind her.

"What are they doing?" whispered Liz.

They were manipulating two cleverly hidden zippers at the front and back of the mermaid dress. When they were unzipped, Novette's mermaid dress was transformed into a sequined pants suit, and then she really got busy. The crowd roared in response. She joined the male dancers in their complex hip-hop-style routine. Then they lifted her, swung her, passed her around, and her voice never faltered. When she hit the last note, standing atop a pyramid made of hot men, the crowd went wild.

Novette jumped from the top of the pyramid and landed in the arms of the dashing Lieutenant Gunnar Halvorsen, while the pyramid disassembled itself efficiently and transitioned to the next number. Soon a tuxedo-clad male singer ascended the stage and began crooning "Luck Be a Lady Tonight." I sensed a theme.

Gunnar escorted Novette over to us, but slowly as so many passengers wanted to congratulate her on the performance.

"Do I look okay?" asked Liz, straightening her skirt and top.

"Perfect as always." I smiled at my friend, and she smiled back in an utterly adorable embarrassed way. "He's really cute."

"The cutest," she sighed. Of all the Avengers, Thor had always been Liz's favorite, so Gunnar made complete sense. Actually, he made sense in any context. Note to self—visit Norway.

When Gunnar and Novette finally made their way to us, I noticed that he made a point of standing next to Liz. Excellent. Our Viking friend made introductions, and we all shook hands.

"Novette is the best entertainer I've ever seen on board ship," gushed Gunnar. "We were so lucky to steal her from a competitor. You might want to feature her in the PR campaign."

"He's too kind," said the singer. She was older than I, but I couldn't tell how much. It could have been five years or fifteen. Novette was one of those women who would remain ageless no matter how many candles were on her birthday cake. She was the kind of woman cosmetic companies abhorred.

Her speaking voice was soft and gentle and carried a hint of magnolias and blackberry cobbler. She didn't have a Virginia accent, but she was certainly southern.

"Not at all," I replied. "You're fantastic."

"I remember Lady Gaga's Super Bowl halftime show, and you were just as good if not better," added my friend.

"You call that entertainment?" Caz Koblinsky was back. As he muscled into our group, he ran over my toes with his scooter.

"Ow! Watch it!" I cried as I hopped up and down on one foot. Caz paid me no mind.

"You did that same number aboard the Circe of the Seas," he spat at Novette. "It was mediocre then, and it's mediocre now."

"It's a completely new number, Casimir, as you well know," replied Novette, unruffled. Clearly, the singer and the grouch had history.

"Mr. Koblinsky, you need to apologize," muttered Gunnar between clenched teeth.

"What'll you do if I don't?" challenged Caz. "Nothing, that's what." The crusty curmudgeon laughed bitterly and rolled on through, making the others jump out of his way. Novette wasn't quite fast enough, and the ruffle at the hem of her sequined pantsuit got sucked into the scooter's wheel. I heard a rip that left one leg of her pantsuit without a ruffle. "Buffoons!" I heard Caz cry as he motored on, sequins trailing behind him.

"What a jerk!" spat Liz. "He should be tossed overboard."

"Oh dear," sighed Novette as she surveyed her ravaged hem. "I'm on again in a minute. It'll just have to do." She saw the outrage in Liz's face and patted her hand gently. "It ain't nothing but a thing." And then she was gone. She mounted the stage just as the music transitioned from "Luck Be a Lady Tonight" to the Juice Newton classic "Queen of Hearts." Novette dove into the song as if nothing had happened and soon had the audience clapping along. She struck me as a woman who rolled with the punches, and from what I'd learned in my twenty-eight years of life, that ability was earned through hard experience.

"Caz has had a thing for Novette for years," Gunnar informed us. "I think he's asked her to marry him ten times, but she always turns him down. He's bitter."

"Caz thought he had a chance with Novette? Really?" I said before I could stop myself.

The thwarted suitor in question bulldozed through the crowd, causing a wave among the startled, bruised, and insulted passengers, like a fox running through a wheat field. His wave of destruction came to an abrupt halt at the cruise director.

"Oh no," muttered Gunnar, and he loped off to intercept the snarky senior. Liz and I hurried to catch up, but by the time we did, Cindy's face was beet red, and Gunnar was on the verge of cold-cocking a disabled senior citizen.

"You call that entertainment?" yelled Caz. "I want her gone!"

"Mr. Koblinsky, Novette is one of the most respected performers in the industry." Cindy was struggling to keep her cool. The little fringe hanging from her epaulets was quivering. "We're fortunate to have her aboard the Lady Luck."

"We'll just see how fortunate everyone is when Faraday gets here!"

"What are you trying to say?" demanded Gunnar. "That sounds a lot like a threat."

"There's no threat about it!" smirked the outrageous octogenarian. Then he turned his scooter one hundred and eighty degrees and zoomed off to invade new lands.

"That man needs taking down a peg," I said as I watched Caz's hideous toupee retreat into the distance.

"He's despised in the industry," explained Gunnar. "He wreaks havoc on every ship, and he has sailed on just about all of them."

"Why doesn't the industry ban him?" asked Liz. "If everyone knows who he is, it shouldn't be hard to deny him entry."

"Because he's a big spender," explained Cindy. "He always books the most opulent suites, orders the finest meals, spends money like it's water, and he loves to gamble. The ships make too much money off him. They'll never say no. Especially this ship."

"Why?" I asked.

Gunnar's strong, muscular shoulders actually sagged, which I hadn't thought possible. "Casimir Koblinsky owns Cashmere Dreams."

"The mattress company?" chirped Liz. "I have a Cashmere

Dreams mattress. My chiropractor recommended it. It's heavenly."

"I still don't follow," I said.

"Cashmere Dreams has the contract for all the mattresses in all the staterooms aboard this ship and any other ships in the Seaswept line," sighed Gunnar. "He's a business partner with the owner, Aton Faraday. We'll never be rid of him."

"And if he complains to Mr. Faraday," added Cindy as her eyes rapidly filled with tears, "we could lose our jobs."

"Well that just burns my bacon!" I wondered why some people had to be so nasty. We were all embarking on a magical vacation with memories to be made and luxurious amenities to be sampled. How could anyone want to ruin the experience? It just didn't make sense. Who had put a burr under Casimir Koblinsky's saddle? Could his industry-wide misanthropy be the result of something as simple as unrequited love?

"Don't you worry," offered Liz. "We'll speak up for you. We saw the whole thing. We'll vouch for Novette's incredible performance and for how you remained professional despite that…that…"

"Snake in the grass?" I provided.

"Exactly! And when I get home, I'm getting rid of my Cashmere Dreams mattress!"

Gunnar looked at Liz with dreamy eyes and a soft smile. *Love, exciting and new…* Cindy swallowed her tears and pasted a smile back on her face. I had mastered that move myself, so I felt for her.

"It's nothing for you to worry about," she fake-smiled at both of us, although she did it very well. "You just worry about enjoying your cruise." With a little salute, she turned on her heel and marched off with her head held high.

Just then, Novette finished her song to tremendous applause. She tripped off the stage as Rod Stewart ascended from the other side.

Wait a second! Rod Stewart?

No, not really. The thirty-something man was attempting the Rod Stewart look with a leopard print shirt and frosted hair. Unfortunately, he hadn't shaved his mustache, so he came closer to resembling the Tiger King. One poor choice… Still, he sounded a lot like Rod as he belted out "Some Guys Have All the Luck," and the Gen-Xers and Baby Boomers were buying in. So was Liz, who was now dancing with Lieutenant Siegfried. Oh my stars! We had been on the ship for one hour and already we'd had a cabin mix-up, been accosted twice by a scoundrel, scored pineapple drinks, watched a fabulous show, and one of us had fallen in love. All in an hour! The ship was magic, and anything could happen.

The voice of our cruise director interrupted my musings. Did I hear a bit of a lump in Cindy's throat?

"Ladies and gentlemen, if you will direct your attention to the port side of the ship, we are about to pass the Statue of Liberty."

Immediately, all the passengers stampeded hard to port to catch a glimpse of Lady Liberty. And yes, for a moment, I wondered if the ship would lean to one side. Do not judge me. I was a cruising neophyte.

"And, ladies and gentlemen, if you will direct your attention to the crown of the statue, you will see something quite extraordinary."

While Tiger King Stewart continued to croon, we all peered up at Liberty's crown.

"Is that Ironman?" asked a little boy.

"What's going on?" asked a nervous lady.

"What am I looking at?" I asked Liz, who was holding hands with Leif Erikson.

"It appears to be a man in a space suit sitting on top of the Statue of Liberty," replied my friend calmly.

"Well, okay then."

Suddenly, several plumes of smoke erupted from the suited figure.

"He's on fire!"

"Someone help him!"

But then the figure rose, floated even, above Lady Liberty's head, past her torch, and toward our ship. As he or she came closer, I began to make out details. The individual seemed to be wearing a pilot's flight suit and helmet, along with large metal boots and gauntlets, like armor. Streaming from the boots and gauntlets were blue flames, the source of the smoke.

"It's a jet suit!" breathed Liz in wonder. "I've been dying to try one."

"You have?" Gunnar and I asked in unison, Gunnar in rapture, me in shock and dismay. I liked my friends alive.

Just as the singer again crooned "Some guys have all the luck," Cindy broke in over the speakers.

"And here he is, the guy with all the luck. The man of the future and your host...Aton Faraday!"

Some people clapped, some people gasped, and a few even screamed, as the man of the future swooped down upon the ship. Watching a human being fly free through the air like a superhero was certainly impressive, and all the amazing PR opportunities were flooding my brain...until Aton Faraday swooped too close to a canvas awning providing shade for pool-goers, and it burst into flames.

Afterward, when we analyzed the physics of what took place over another pineapple drink, Liz, Eric the Viking, and I determined that the force expelled by Faraday's jet boots actually ricocheted off the canvas awning, throwing him off balance and ass-over-teakettle into the swimming pool.

It's unfortunate that the lifeguards were so mesmerized by the spectacle that it took them a moment to react and to remember that metal boots probably won't float. Faraday might then have emerged from the water conscious. Mouth-to-mouth mightn't have been necessary, and the man of the future might not have upchucked profusely. And all of that might not have been captured on hundreds of cell phones and uploaded to countless social media accounts.

It was at that moment I realized having Aton Faraday for a client might not be a pleasure cruise.

CHAPTER 2

So this was how the other half lived.

After the fire was extinguished and Aton Faraday was revived, Gunnar, Cindy, Liz, and I followed the medics as they carried the cruise line owner by stretcher to his suite in the bow of the ship. While the medics tended to Mr. Faraday in his bedroom, the rest of us were left to wait in the opulent living room. I would have been happy to wait there for the rest of the cruise.

Aton Faraday's suite had the best view on the entire ship. The glass-fronted suite presented an unobstructed view of the prow and the ocean beyond. The only things missing were Jack and Rose playing at being the king of the world. I imagined what the view would be like in rough seas as the ship climbed large waves and descended into troughs, the water crashing over the prow and coating the glass wall with spray. Thrilling! I half wished we could encounter a small storm right then and there.

Instead, I sat on the white sectional sofa that faced the glass wall, sipped cucumber water, and nibbled from a cheese and fruit board provided by Mr. Faraday's personal assistant,

Joseph, a mildly handsome man of medium height and build with brown hair and brown eyes. The most striking thing about him was his outfit-a Nehru jacket and matching trousers in navy blue. It was futuristic, but it blended in with Aton's suite perfectly.

After all the commotion, it was nice to sit in peace and quiet. I think Cindy, sitting beside me, felt the same way. The lovebirds, however, were talking quietly. Gunnar looked worried, and Liz, true to form, was taking care of him. She had ordered some chamomile tea from Joseph, which she pressed Gunnar to drink.

"I'm sure he'll be all right," soothed Liz. "He was talking while they carried him here."

"Oh, I know he'll be fine," replied Thor Heyerdahl. "It's not Mr. Faraday I'm worried about." Gunnar raked his hands through his hair, causing his attractiveness quotient to rise, something I hadn't thought possible. Unconsciously, Liz's hand flexed, and I knew she was itching to run her fingers through his hair. Who wouldn't be?

"Then what's troubling you?" she asked.

Gunnar hesitated, studying his immaculate fingernails.

"He thinks it's a bad omen," pronounced Cindy. "Don't you, Gunnar?"

"Don't you?" he replied, finally looking up.

Cindy sighed and massaged her brow. I could sense a headache coming on.

"Look," Gunnar continued. "Caz Koblinsky is on board, thanks to Mr. Faraday. The ship suffered a fire on its way out of port, thanks to Mr. Faraday. And the owner of the ship nearly drowned himself. What if...?"

"What if what?" I prompted.

"Just say it," moaned Cindy as she began massaging her temples.

"What if...?" Gunnar paused to make sure Joseph wasn't in earshot. "What if the owner of the cruise line is...a Jonah?"

"I thought his name was Aton," said Liz.

"Jonah the biblical prophet," I explained.

"Oh, the one who tried to run away from God."

"And fled on a ship, which almost sank in a storm until the sailors threw him overboard," I added.

"A Jonah, according to the superstitious," Cindy looked pointedly at Gunnar as she spoke, "brings bad luck to a ship. The only way to restore a ship's luck is to remove the Jonah."

"So you want to throw Mr. Faraday overboard?" Liz smiled as she said it, and Gunnar had to laugh.

"Of course not. But would it be so bad if he had to be helicoptered off the ship...for his health?"

"I don't see why Mr. Faraday has to be the Jonah," I put in, fully aware that I was joining in the superstition but unable to resist. "You have a much better candidate on board."

Cindy hooted and clapped her hands. "Caz Koblinsky. I second the motion." Cindy's face was splotchy and she looked worn out, even though we'd only been sailing for an hour.

"Yeah, let's throw him overboard!" cried Liz.

"And his scooter." My toes were still tender.

"It's certainly tempting," admitted Gunnar.

"But seriously," said Cindy. "You can't mention a Jonah around the crew, Gunnar. You just can't. It'll spread like wildfire."

"You think it hasn't occurred to them already?" he countered.

"I pray it hasn't," sighed the cruise director. "Otherwise, it's going to be a long voyage."

What would rumor of a Jonah do to the crew? Would they believe it so wholeheartedly that they'd act on it? Did such things occur in the twenty-first century? I thought back to my research on cruise ships, specifically on the things that could go wrong on board. One of the key tasks for PR is mitigating bad publicity, so I wanted to be fully prepared. I was surprised by the number of people who go missing on cruises. Some, I was certain, were accidents. Some were suicides. But some had to be murders, probably prompted by infidelity, the promise of insurance payouts, and too much alcohol. But were some of the victims perceived as Jonahs?

I didn't have a chance to ask the experts because the Jonah in question chose that moment to make his entrance.

Preceded by the medics, who quietly scurried from the suite, Aton Faraday appeared fully recovered from his accident. Of medium height and very slender build, he sported a set of green silk pajamas with a mandarin collar, white socks, and wooden Japanese sandals. His large head was completely bald and, dare I say, polished to a high gloss. His eyebrows were black and thin, possibly waxed or tweezed. He had a long thin nose and a small mouth, but his eyes were incredibly large and green. In short, he resembled an alien.

When Faraday entered, Cindy and Gunnar jumped to their feet and rushed to his side.

"Sir, I'm so glad to see you're all right." Gunnar bowed stiffly from the waist. Cindy did the same.

"Are you truly well, sir?" she asked.

"I am perfectly well, my friends. Thank you." Faraday smiled beneficently at them and briefly touched their shoulders. They both relaxed.

The dynamic was…interesting. Cindy and Gunnar didn't come across as sycophants. More like disciples of Faraday the guru. Curiouser and curiouser.

Gunnar introduced us. Liz followed the crew's example and bowed briefly, so I had to bow too, but I felt like a fool. Did Faraday refuse to shake hands? He did bow in return, so the weirdness wasn't one-sided. Thank heaven for small favors.

"You came highly recommended by a good friend, Ms.

Cooksey." Faraday gestured to the sofa, and we all sat down again. "Hoss Buckworth sends his regards."

Hoss was the owner of Eshellon Cosmetics, my primary client. He owed me a favor, and it looked like he had paid up. Good ole Hoss.

"It has been a pleasure to work with Eshellon Cosmetics, and I want to assure you, Mr. Faraday—"

"Call me Aton."

"Aton, that I will give Seaswept Cruises the same level of personalized care and attention."

Aton tented his fingers and shot a piercing look my way.

"Does that include solving any crimes that come our way?" He smiled knowingly.

I laughed nervously.

"So, you heard about that."

"Hoss's lips get quite loose when he's been drinking bourbon, and even looser when he's playing poker. Let's just say, Ms. Cooksey—"

"Jill, please."

"Jill, that level of dedication to a client is quite impressive. If your proposal on Thursday is solid, I will feel quite comfortable moving forward with Waverly Communications."

If only the bane of my working life, Pamela (think Miranda Priestly but inept), could hear Aton. Or the big boss, William Waverly. I couldn't wait to see Pamela's face when I secured this client. She would turn positively green with envy, bless her heart. And Mr. Waverly might remember my name for once! Wait a second. Mr. Waverly was aboard the ship at that very moment! I wondered if we'd ever bump into him and if I could get Aton to repeat his words to the company owner. *Promotion, here I come!*

Aton suggested a tour of the ship, so we rose to leave.

"I hate to say goodbye to this suite," I remarked casually. "The view is out of this world."

"Yes," said Aton. "I like to be at the front of the ship facing forward, into the unknown, into the future. I never want to go backward."

"Unless the ship is going in reverse," quipped Liz, "no matter where you are on board, you're technically moving forward." She had a very literal mind.

"Er, quite," muttered Aton as he ushered us from his suite.

Cindy and Gunnar said goodbye and went back to work, Gunnar with a promise to see us at dinner and a kiss on Liz's hand.

Mr. Smooth.

We were joined by Joseph, who carried his own tablet computer. I soon learned that it was connected to the ship's central mainframe because Joseph could control just about anything with it. He unlocked doors, summoned staff, placed an order for sushi (because Aton was feeling peckish), and even directed the captain to increase the ship's speed so we could see just how fast she would go. The boat could scoot!

We began our tour in the engine room at the aft end on the lowest deck and worked our way up the ship. Along the way, Aton pointed out the futuristic tech he had incorporated into the ship's design. Every system that could be improved with advanced technology was, from energy-efficient engines with supplemental solar power to retinal scans for cabin safes. Aton Faraday had attempted to design the ship of the future.

By the time we reached the uppermost heights, the Crest Club, an invitation-only nightclub and poker venue perched above everything but the radar antenna and accessible only by private elevator, we had walked ten miles. Liz and Aton seemed unfazed, but I was feeling the exercise. It felt wonderful to sink into a plush divan and to be handed a chilled mocktail comprised of assorted fruit juices. Aton admitted he never touched alcohol. I didn't care, and neither did health-conscious Liz. The combination of pineapple, passion fruit, and mango delighted my tastebuds, and the sugar soon perked me right up.

From our aerie, we could see the entire ship from bow to stern. Now that we had seen all the pieces, Aton was ready to talk about it holistically, including his vision for Seaswept Cruises. I had been recording our tour with my phone, with his permission, and I knew the philosophy behind the business would inform our PR decisions. There's nothing like a lofty statement of purpose to elevate a press release.

"I believe in taking risks," Aton Faraday began. "Everything humans have accomplished has required them to take risks."

This was standard futurist boilerplate that I'd heard from a hundred different TED talks, but I plastered an interested look on my face and hoped he'd eventually get to something original.

"I embrace risk in my life. I take great scientific risks that have fortunately paid off. Those have required great financial risks that have paid off as well. But I've found that it's important to cultivate risk-taking as a character trait or a virtue, if you will, to maintain the level of risk needed to push my business, and thus humanity, forward."

Okay, so he was conflating his business and the fate of humanity (ego much?), but he still had my attention.

"To nurture my inner risk-taker, I've made myself take risks in all areas of my life. From bold architectural choices for my residence to extreme sports in my leisure time. And it's the latter that inspired Seaswept Cruises.

"I want to provide people with the opportunity to engage in risk at every level of the vacation experience. Where they sleep. Did you know you can sleep in a hammock above the ocean? It's the equivalent of a mountain climber's tent except that it hangs off the ship instead of off a cliff. What they eat. You'll find fugu—that's pufferfish—on the menu, along with a host of foods that, while not dangerous, are not for the faint of heart.

Personal care. Have you ever had a snail facial? What they wear. We have a clothing-optional pool. And recreation. We've amassed the largest concentration of extreme sports opportunities on one ship AND the world's largest floating casino.

"At every turn, guests can cultivate risk-taking, and when the vacation is over, they will carry their newfound courage and adventurousness into their everyday lives. Think of how transformative it could be!"

Whoa, Nelly! Aton Faraday had drunk his own Kool-Aid, but I had to admit, the concept would be a moneymaker and would inspire countless copycats. His challenge would be to perpetually innovate to stay ahead of the pack. I'd have to cover that in my proposal.

I turned to Liz to get her take and found her with eyes shining and a wistful expression.

"It sounds wonderful!" she breathed. "Who couldn't come away from such an experience a changed person?"

"Exactly," beamed Aton. Now I had two Kool-Aid drinkers on my hands, but I had a question that might irk the true believers. Nevertheless, I had to ask.

"What happens if something goes wrong?"

Aton, luckily, wasn't thrown.

"An excellent question, Jill. An important question."

Oh, good.

"As I said, I believe in taking risks…"

Yeah, yeah.

"…but only acceptable risks. Therefore, we have put the strongest safety measures in place for every experience. Sleeping on the side of the ship? There are safety nets and twenty-four-hour monitoring. Trying fugu? Our chef was specially certified in Japan in how to prepare it safely, and if he's sick and can't come to work, fugu is off the menu. All our extreme sports utilize the most up-to-date equipment and safety measures in the industry. I've even pioneered some safety equipment myself where I thought improvements could be made. What is the use in cultivating your inner risk-taker if you don't make it off the ship alive?"

Now that was an excellent question, and I liked his attitude toward safety. Maybe Aton Faraday, who was a leader in so many technological areas, would also become a leader in the cruise industry. One could but dream.

"What about the casino?" asked Liz.

Aton's face, so full of enthusiasm and pride, fell.

"You have stumbled on our Achilles heel."

He sighed heavily.

"I believe in taking risks…"

Enough already!

"But not everyone can be a billionaire. There are acceptable risks and unacceptable risks. Betting one's house or a child's college education is not an acceptable risk, so I wanted to make the casino cashless. My vision was to provide every passenger with credit in the casino, Monopoly money if you will. They could enjoy the thrill of gambling without the danger of financial ruin. But my investors didn't see it my way. Only Hoss Buckworth took my side. There's too much money to be made in gambling, so I had to give in."

"Pardon my curiosity, but if you disagreed, why didn't you fund the cruise line on your own? You certainly…" I paused before I crossed a line.

"Have plenty of money?" He finished my question. "I do, but, you see, exploring this world's oceans is only phase one for Seaswept Cruises. I needed to keep resources in reserve for phase two—Spaceswept Cruises."

Say what?

"We'll start with what the industry calls a 'cruise to nowhere,' circling the planet and the moon, as well as exploring a small portion of the vast space between Earth and Mars. Once I establish a resort on the moon, we'll have a port of call.

Eventually, I'll build a series of space station resorts between here and Mars until we reach the red planet and establish a station. I know some people want to go directly from Earth to Mars without these incremental steps, but really, it's untenable. As I said, Ms. Cooksey, I believe in taking acceptable risks."

I looked carefully at Faraday's face for any trace of a smile, but the man was completely serious. Space cruises? Was it possible? Scenes from *Dr. Who* and *The Fifth Element* sprang immediately to mind.

"Fhloston Paradise," I whispered unconsciously. Faraday grinned.

"Exactly! I'm so pleased that you grasp my vision."

Oh, the vision was certainly clear. But the Fhloston Paradise of Luc Besson's most excellent film, along with the space Titanic from *Dr. Who*? Well, let's just say nobody made any YouTube videos about their awesome experiences aboard those ships. And taking into account Jennifer Lawrence's experience in *Passengers* and Sigourney Weaver's torment in *Aliens*, the only way I was ever going to board a space liner and head out into the cosmos was if a band of Cylons was hot on my tail. Yes, I liked my science with a heavy dose of fiction, but cautionary tales were created for a reason.

With difficulty, I wrenched my mind back into the present to find Aton Faraday smiling at me like a pleased parent.

"The possibilities are dizzying, aren't they?"

"That's one word for it." I forced a smile, not wanting to alienate my potential client. "Just so we're clear, do you have a timeline for, um, Spaceswept Cruises?"

"We'll have cruises to nowhere up and running in five years. The first space station resort in ten. Mars in twenty-five to thirty."

Oh, thank heaven. The way the PR industry worked, I'd most likely be working for another company in five years.

There was little chance I'd have to take a space cruise for my job.

"But we should be offering our first day trips into the exosphere in the next six months."

Hellfire and damnation!

35

*A*fter climbing all over the ship and receiving an info dump from Aton Faraday, I was plum tuckered out, so I headed back to the room for a little nap before our first dinner aboard the Lady Luck. Liz, that dynamo, went off to explore on her own, but as soon as my head hit the pillow, I fell fast asleep…and dreamed. Maybe it was a premonition, but I dreamed of my ex-boyfriend, Mike.

"Just get on the door, Mike," I yelled in exasperation. I was soaking wet and clinging to a door in the middle of the North Atlantic. Freezing didn't begin to cover just how cold I was. Ice crystals frosted my hair, and the color of my skin was somewhere between glacier and robin's egg.

"There's not enough room for two," he smiled up at me from the water as he gripped the edge of the door. His spiky brown hair was crusted with ice. "I'll be fine in the water."

"You'll die in the water. Get on the door. There's plenty of room. This thing is huge and made of oak."

"It will tip over."

"Not if you're careful, and if it tips, we'll just crawl back on at the same time from opposite sides. It can be done."

"I don't want you to get wet again."

"Too late. Already wet and cold. Stop being noble, and get on the daggone door."

"No."

"Then let go."

"Pardon?"

"You heard me. Let go."

"Um…"

"If you're going to be a jackass about this, then just let go, float away, and die. You're going to freeze to death anyway. Get it over with and stop wasting my time."

"Hold on. I'm getting on the door."

Rose didn't have a clue about how to handle men, but I did. I felt very self-satisfied…until I woke up. Then I sat straight up in bed and gripped the sheets.

Why was I dreaming about Mike?

I had been in a relationship with cop-turned-reporter Mike McCall, but he had dropped me out of the blue. That wasn't unusual in New York where men often disappeared out of your life without warning. With so many people available in the city, both men and women tended to treat dating like an all-you-can-eat buffet. I've never been one for the buffet myself. I'm more of a sit-down-meal person, five courses at least.

Mike's sudden disappearance from my life was painful, though, because we had made a connection and forged a bond during a particularly stressful part of my life, the launch of a new perfume for Eshellon Cosmetics that had led to a murder. We had worked together to bring a killer to justice and to save my client, dear Hoss, from ruin.

Well, I thought we had made a connection.

After a few weeks of serious dating, however, Mike dropped off the radar without a word. Well, that wasn't quite true. I received a bouquet of red roses with a card that simply said, "Cooksey, See you soon. Love, Mike."

Lies!

Weeks later, I saw him again in Central Park with his new girlfriend, and he pretended not to know me.

The dirty dog!

But then I received a Christmas present from him, a poster for one of our favorite movies.

Mixed messages much?

To my credit, I resisted the urge to cyber-stalk him. Mike McCall's whereabouts were a complete mystery to me, and my pride was very much intact. My heart, however, had some missing pieces. Well, I mean, not anymore. I was totally over him. Totally.

Then why was I dreaming about him?

"Dreams are never literal," explained Liz as we made our way to dinner that evening. "Mike is a symbol for something. You just have to figure out what for."

What for, indeed. Clearly, it was something I wanted to save, but if it caused too much trouble, I was willing to let it go.

The elevator reached the windjammer deck, and Liz and I made a detour to the suite that should have been ours in the hope of running into Mr. Waverly. A DO NOT DISTURB sign hung on the door. Maybe Mr. Waverly and his new missus were on their honeymoon. I was of two minds about it. Part of me was delighted that he could find love again at such an advanced age. Another part of me just thought *ew*!

From there we headed to the promenade deck, which was devoted to myriad dining experiences. As we walked through the lobby toward the main dining room, I caught a glimpse of the two of us in the mirrored wall. Liz, as always, was stunning. She wore a long, pink, organza sundress with platform sandals and carried a white pashmina so we could walk the deck after dinner. Her tight jet curls were studded with pearl hairpins.

I, on the other hand, had opted for a dove gray, calf-length coat dress with narrow lapels and a cinched waist. I was going for polished and professional since I was here to win a client. I had followed a YouTube video and put my hair up in a chignon, but there was one hairpin that kept trying to go rogue. I checked it again. Yep! I pushed the little rebel back in line. No way was a hairpin going to detract from my capable image.

The dining room was over-the-top but in such a good way. Navy blue and gold were the predominant colors of the carpeting, wall hangings, and table linens, but the glint of mirrors, crystal chandeliers, and candelabras festooned with blue, white, and yellow flowers filled the space with reflected light. The maître d'hôtel led us past large family parties, couples dining in romantic solitude, and strangers making friends, until we reached the captain's table, which was elevated and inhabited a corner of the dining room. From her table, the captain could survey her domain.

Captain Martha Staggs rose to greet us, as did the gentlemen at the table. Tall for a woman and solidly built, the captain had a powerful presence. Her black hair, streaked with silver, was styled in an angled bob that fell to just below her chin. Her dress uniform of navy blue with gold buttons and epaulets was well-tailored to her figure. She wore a gold band on her left hand, a very complicated watch on her left wrist, and a pair of diamond studs in her ears. She wasn't flashy, but she oozed quality and confidence. Liz sat to the captain's left, with Lieutenant Halvorsen next to her (big surprise) while I was seated to the captain's right. A youngish man was seated next to me, and beside him was the very talented Novette.

"Hey, sugar!" smiled Novette. "Jill, right?"

"Jill Cooksey. That's right. How are you, Novette?"

"I'm right as rain. I even fixed my costume." She winked at me.

The man seated beside me turned to me and offered his hand.

"How do you do? I'm John."

We shook hands, and I was surprised at how soft his was. John was a moisturizer. I wondered what product he used.

More people arrived at the table, and once all the seats were full, Captain Staggs stood to make a speech of welcome.

"Ladies and gentlemen, welcome to the inaugural dinner seating and captain's table aboard The Lady Luck. May it be the first of many."

The captain's voice was slightly husky and velvety smooth. She didn't have to raise her voice to get everyone's attention. I wondered what that must feel like. Her arresting voice coupled with her significant stature conveyed confidence and inspired it in those around her.

"I look forward to getting to know each of you, and if I or my crew can do anything to make your voyage more memorable, you have only to ask. Now, please charge your glasses."

There was a glass of champagne at every place, and we all raised them.

"To luck!" said Captain Staggs with a cheeky wink.

"To luck!" we replied in unison and clinked glasses on all sides.

Then we were invited to take turns introducing ourselves to the group. It felt a lot like the first day of school or a business meeting, but such is life.

The gentleman next to me turned out to be Mr. John Gowdy, an investment banker from New York. While our waiter took our orders, I took a discreet inventory of the man. I estimated he was between thirty and thirty-five years old and about six feet tall. He had dark brown hair and whiskey-colored eyes with heavy but not overbearing brows. His face was lean with prominent cheekbones and chin in that sculpted way some male models have. The rest of him, clad in a black suit with a contrasting gray waistcoat, looked lean, as well, and strong if his broad shoulders were any indication. He was no pretty boy, despite the soft hands, and I found myself appreciating the view.

I was so caught up in nature's bounty that I didn't hear the waiter when he asked for my order. That's how John caught me looking at him. He smiled knowingly, the stinker. He knew how attractive he was.

I quickly stammered out my order, and the waiter moved on to John. That's when Captain Staggs leaned over for a quiet word.

"It's fun to be the captain of The Love Boat. You have good taste." And then she winked. I could feel myself blushing, so I looked hastily in the other direction, toward Novette. Big mistake. She wiggled her eyebrows at me in "Hubba! Hubba!" fashion, and I felt my face get even hotter. I tried to catch Liz's eye for some sympathy, but she was busy listening to a saga as told by Thor Odinson. I was on my own, and I just wanted to scream "I'm not interested!" Because I wasn't. Really.

I could appreciate John Gowdy's good looks, but my interest stopped there. As I've already stated, my priorities were pineapple drinks, a promotion, and a vacation. Men didn't make the list. My last date ended up deceased, so I was more than a little gun shy, no pun intended. I had decided to focus on living my best life as a single woman with fabulous friends and a career on the rise. For the time being, and maybe forever, that was enough. Unfortunately, my appreciation of the male form had everyone thinking I was crushing, which would add nothing good to the calm and capable image I was trying to project. Even when I avoided men, they were determined to trip me up.

By now, the waiter had moved on to Novette, so there was no help for it. I pasted my best PR smile to my face and turned to face John Gowdy.

To his credit, he didn't try to make me feel more embarrassed. He asked where I lived. I told him Queens, he said

Staten Island, and we moaned about our commutes for a little bit.

"So, Jill, where are you really from?" he asked. "I know you weren't born in Queens. Not with that accent."

"I'm from a little town in Virginia called Luthersburg. It's close to the mountains."

"I knew it!" cried Novette. "I just knew you were a southerner. I'm from Memphis, myself. They make sweet tea in the kitchen specially for me. You want a glass?"

"Yes, please!"

"Wait, what just happened?" asked John bemusedly. "You're ordering more tea?"

Then I turned to John and explained that Novette was getting me a glass of *sweet* tea.

"So iced tea with sugar in it?" He pointed to the glass of unsweet tea in front of me and then to the cut crystal dish full of sugar packets.

"Yeah, it's not the same."

Novette and I smiled at each other, and a silent conversation passed between us that went something like this.

Novette: Yankees!

Jill: Bless their hearts!

"So, tell me more about Luthersburg," said John.

"You really want to hear about it?"

"Yeah, it kind of sounds like the setting of one of those Hallmark movies. I didn't think those places truly existed."

Did he watch Hallmark movies? I loved Hallmark movies! So I told him all about my hometown, and he listened, although heaven knew why.

"And your family still lives there?"

"Just my mom. My dad passed a few years ago."

"I'm sorry to hear that."

I thanked him and changed the subject.

"So what brings you aboard The Lady Luck? Business or pleasure?"

"A bit of both. I'm considering investing in the company, but I also haven't had a vacation in quite some time. And I love to play poker."

"So why not visit the world's largest floating casino?"

"Exactly. Do you play poker, by any chance?"

I did. My dad had spent hours teaching me the game he loved so well. Daddy was an incredible poker player, so good that most of the men in town refused to play with him. He'd sometimes travel out of town to play in big games in Charlottesville, Richmond, and Washington, DC. He had even gone to Atlantic City and Las Vegas a time or two. Yes, I knew how to play poker. I played it well.

"No," I lied. "I've never played."

"Maybe I can teach you."

I just smiled and nodded. I wasn't going to play poker with him, but I wasn't going to alienate a potential investor either.

The first course arrived, putting a halt to the conversation, for which I was grateful. John had made me think about things I'd been avoiding for a long time, and I didn't want the first time I faced down those memories to be in the midst of a group of strangers. Luckily, it was time to eat.

During the main course, I took the opportunity to peruse the dining room. From the captain's table, I had the perfect vantage point, and I loved people-watching. Most everyone seemed to be enjoying dinner. People ate and talked and laughed. The servers buzzed from table to table answering the needs and whims of the diners.

As I scanned, I caught sight of the lady in the scarf who had bumped into me earlier. How could I tell? Because she was still wearing a scarf over her head and huge Jackie O. sunglasses. I assumed she must be a celebrity and made a note to take a closer look at some point.

Then I caught sight of that scoundrel Casimir Koblinsky. He was haranguing his waiter about something while a pretty young woman with long red hair suffered in silence next to him. Wife? No way. Daughter? Possibly.

"Captain Staggs, who is that young woman with Casimir Koblinsky?"

"That's his daughter, Mira. Poor child. She's completely under his thumb and has lived most of her life aboard one ship or another."

I felt for the girl. With Caz for a father, she likely spent much of her life feeling embarrassed. And a life spent on cruise ships must have been strange indeed.

I forked up another bite of steak au poivre and continued my survey of the dining room until my eyes came to rest on a striking couple. I could only see the man from the back. He had blond hair cut very short, almost in a buzz, and he was wearing a midnight blue suit. His dinner companion, seated opposite him, had silky black hair almost down to her waist, pale skin, and the longest eyelashes I had ever seen. She wore a white halter dress accented with silver bugle beads, and diamonds glinted from her ears and her neck.

Out of nowhere, the man clasped her hand and raised it to his lips. So romantic!

Then the waiter approached their table with the next course, and the man turned toward him. I saw his profile and dropped my fork on my plate with a huge clatter. Sauce spattered the tablecloth, my water glass, my napkin, and probably my dress, but I wasn't concerned. The man in question had turned back toward his dining companion, but I needed, *needed*, to see his profile one more time. I stared at him, willing him to turn again.

"Jill!"

I jumped in my seat and once again became aware of my

immediate surroundings. All nine of my dinner companions were staring at me as if I'd lost my mind.

"Jilly," soothed Liz as she peered around the captain. "Are you all right?" The concern on her face forced me to pull myself together.

"I'm fine." I tried to laugh. "I just thought I saw someone I knew, but I was mistaken. Sorry to alarm everyone."

Then I saw the mess on the table.

"Oh dear!" I grabbed my napkin and began blotting sauce off my water glass and the table cloth.

"Well, you never know who you're going to meet on a cruise," boomed Captain Staggs to cover my awkwardness. (Calm and capable image torpedoed and sinking fast.) "I once met a passenger who had flown all the way to Miami from Wisconsin to take a cruise to South America, and lo and behold, her next-door neighbor was on the ship! And she and the neighbor couldn't stand each other!" Everyone laughed, and I finished cleaning up, or so I thought until Novette was suddenly by my side and whispering in my ear.

"Sugar, you have a little something on your dress."

I looked down. The "little something" was a silver dollar-sized spot of cream sauce.

"Don't panic. I have a Tide pen in my purse. Let's go to the ladies' room."

As unobtrusively as possible, I rose and followed Novette. At least I intended to follow Novette, but when I realized that the path to the bathroom would take me right by the mystery man with the shocking profile, my eyes fixed on his table, and my steps slowed to a crawl. For some reason, it became harder and harder to breathe the closer I got to the man. And when I got close enough to read the cute little "Just Married" sign hanging from the back of his chair, probably placed there by the servers to celebrate newlyweds, I stopped breathing altogether.

Slowly, I moved past the table until I could see his profile, and then more than his profile, and…

I was confused.

Blond hair, not brown. Blond mustache, not clean-shaven. Green eyes instead of bright blue. Full, almost chubby cheeks.

It wasn't Mike. Why had I thought it was Mike?

That brow. That chin.

It wasn't Mike. A brow and a chin do not a person make. I was deluding myself. Why I had no idea.

Because you still love him.

Sick of myself, I turned on my heel to head for the bathroom and collided with a waiter carrying a tray of flaming baked Alaska. I saw it all happen in slow motion, although it must have only taken a second. As the tray tipped, the fiery desserts slid off and were launched into the air. They were beautiful, flames streaming behind them like the tail of a comet, as they carved a graceful arc on their way to crashing on the brand-new rug of the brand-new dining room of the brand-new ship. The rug had barely caught fire when an agile waiter smothered it with a spare tablecloth. I don't know what happened next because I moved faster than the time a copperhead got into the house, and the next thing I knew, I was in the ladies' room.

"I wondered where you'd got to," Novette said as she handed me a stain removal pen.

I burst into tears.

"Oh, sugar, it's okay. It's just a little spot. We can get it out."

"It's not that," I sobbed. "I thought (sob) I saw my exboyfriend (sob), but it wasn't him."

"Oh, sugar."

While I cried, Novette went to work on my dress. Then she ran cold water in the sink and gently pulled my wrists under the stream. It seemed to help because I stopped crying except for the occasional hiccup. Then she dried my tears with a tissue, wiping away the mascara that had run down my cheeks.

"There," she pronounced as she turned off the faucet and handed me a paper towel. "All better."

"Thank you, Novette," I replied with a much steadier voice. "I don't know what came over me."

The singer smiled sadly at me, which told me she knew exactly what had come over me.

"How long ago did you break up?"

"Three months." If you could call it a breakup. Mike had dropped me, ghosted me, pretended like I never existed.

And then he sent me a Christmas present. Men!

"Well, of course, it still hurts. But you've come to the right place to get over him. You need a rebound guy, and, honey, there's no better place to find a rebound than a cruise ship."

I didn't tell her that I'd already found a rebound guy, sort of. I went on a date. It was awful. And then he was murdered.

Some stories don't need to be told to recent acquaintances.

"I've sworn off men, Novette, for the foreseeable future. I'm here on business, and that's it. No hanky-panky, no shipboard romances. Business, pure and simple."

Novette gave me a pitying look. Then she patted my arm and led the way back to our table. I kept my head down as we passed through the dining room, so I didn't see the newlywed couple again, but I did see the small scorch mark on the rug. I really would have to find that waiter and apologize.

CHAPTER 4

No one at our table mentioned the baked Alaska incident, so they either hadn't seen it or they were very polite. My money was on good manners. I made a supreme effort not to embarrass myself further and to make interesting conversation to make up for my earlier faux pas. I was succeeding, too.

Not gonna lie, I played the *Mr. Snicklefritz* card. I currently had a small role on that famous children's television show, a thank-you from the producers for solving the murder of a puppeteer. When people find out you've worked on an iconic television show, your cool quotient goes way up, and they have lots of questions. I wasn't planning to mention it to anyone, but then I tried to burn down the ship with flaming desserts. Desperate times…

Still, I avoided baked Alaska for my own dessert, opting instead for the very safe vanilla bean crème brûlée. It was delectable and very much not on fire. All social equilibrium was restored by the time the after-dinner coffee arrived. John Gowdy and I were listening to Novette tell us about a nightmare ship she once worked on when a flash of red scooter caught my eye.

Casimir Koblinsky was on the move, but he didn't get very far before he crashed into a table. He corrected, hit the gas too hard, and crashed into the back of someone's chair. He corrected again and nearly ran over a waiter. This progression continued across the dining room until patrons had enough and became vocal.

"Why don't you watch where you're going?"

"Don't you need a license for that thing?"

"Go back to your table!"

"I'm going for a smoke! Lighten up!" yelled Caz as he brandished a cigar in one hand and attempted to steer with the other.

"I think someone's had too much to drink," murmured John.

I looked to the captain. Would she step in? Her face was grim, but she made no move. I wondered if she had been instructed by the company to keep Koblinsky happy at all costs.

After a painful interlude, Caz finally made it to the sliding glass door that opened onto the promenade that encircled the ship. The room breathed a collective sigh of relief as his scooter disappeared into the night.

That's when I decided to make friends with Casimir Koblinsky. In a matter of hours, he had shown himself to be a PR nightmare, and if no one was going to call him out on his bad behavior—behavior that could easily be captured by a cruising YouTuber—I needed to find another way to curb his outrageous ways. If I had to extend the hand of friendship to coax him to join Team Seaswept, so be it.

Calmly, I gathered my purse and told my dinner companions that I would be back in a moment. Then I headed across the dining room toward the sliding glass door.

Before I had taken ten steps, Mr. Newlywed rose from his

chair, buttoned the top button of his suit jacket, said something to his bride, and began to walk toward the same door Caz had exited.

And he didn't limp.

Mike had been shot in the line of duty during a stand-off with a gangster who was trying to extort money from a bar in his neighborhood. The bullet had torn through his thigh doing all sorts of damage, leaving him with a slight limp. Recovery had taken a long time, and that long road, coupled with the censure he received from the police department for an unauthorized sting operation, had convinced Mike to leave policing behind and pursue his other love, journalism.

Mr. Newlywed didn't limp, and now I could also see that he was thicker around the middle. More proof not only that he wasn't Mike but also that I needed to get over my ex-boyfriend.

Soon I was at the door. I hesitated for a split second, took a deep breath, and stepped outside.

The first thing I noticed was the frigid air, which stung my face and caused me to gasp. Second, I saw the moon. It was large and not quite full, but it lit the scene clearly. A tall, thin man, a crew member on break from the look of his clothing, was standing at the rail, his back to me, smoking a cigar. To my left, the dining room's wall of glass continued for about fifteen feet until it was interrupted by a steel bulkhead that protruded outward. A metal cigarette receptacle was attached to this wall, and that's where I found Mr. Newlywed smoking a cigarette and chatting amiably with Caz Koblinsky, who was puffing away on his stogie.

Dang! I hadn't expected to find Caz engaged in conversation. Deploying my southern charm would be difficult if I had to butt my way in, and I took a moment to strategize. Should I emphasize his role as an investor or play on his sympathy for—

"What do you need, doll? Who you looking for?" Caz's

harsh voice broke my train of thought, and I quickly regrouped.

"Mr. Koblinsky, I wanted to introduce my—"

I heard the click of a stapler followed immediately by a sharp ping as something struck the wall near Caz.

"Get down!" someone yelled. It might have been me.

Mr. Newlywed and I hit the deck, while the man on a smoke break fled down the promenade. Caz, trapped by his scooter, slumped over it trying to make himself as small as possible.

I waited for another…what exactly was I waiting for?

When nothing else happened, I raised my head.

"What just happened?"

"Gunshot," said the terse groom as he climbed to his feet. I slowly followed, my ears pricking up and listening for another staple gun sound.

"If so, it's silenced," I said.

"Casimir," said Mr. Newlywed, but Caz wasn't moving. He remained slumped over his scooter. I rushed to him and felt for a pulse. It was faint and sporadic. I put my hand in front of his mouth. He wasn't breathing. I looked for blood, but I couldn't find any.

"I think he had a heart attack! Go get help!" I cried, and Mr. Newlywed took off running.

Thankfully, my Girl Scout training kicked in, and soon I had lowered Casimir Koblinsky to the deck and was administering mouth-to-mouth resuscitation.

Yes, you should pity me because it was gross, but a man's life was on the line, so let's all get some perspective.

Paramedics arrived shortly and took over, thank heaven, because administering the kiss of life to mister cigar mouth was one of my least favorite experiences ever—right up there with cleaning fish and bathing a dog with diarrhea. Once the professionals took over, I was free to notice the crowd that had gathered and had watched me try to revive Caz. His daughter was there, supported by fellow passengers as she looked on in horror. John and Novette were also there, and I stumbled toward them.

"Vodka!" I cried.

"Will whiskey do?" asked Novette as she pulled a small flask from her evening bag. The woman was prepared for every eventuality. I took a large swig from the flask, swished it around my mouth, gargled, and spit it over the side and into the ocean.

"Thank you," I coughed as I handed the flask back to its owner. "Caz enjoys a good Cuban."

"Enjoyed," said John, and he nodded toward Caz, whom the paramedics had now covered with a blanket from head to toe.

Casimir "Caz" Koblinsky, the mattress king of Piscataway, New Jersey, was pronounced dead of cardiac arrest at 9:47 p.m.

The party started at 9:48.

CHAPTER 5

The crew bar was packed, the liquor was flowing, and the bass was pumping. The staff of The Lady Luck was whooping it up in honor of the passing of the most notorious passenger in cruise ship history.

"When I was on The Mystic of the Seas, he peed in his bed every night just so we would have to clean it up. Once he even laughed at us and said, 'Have fun, ladies!'" recounted a maid named Daisy.

"He sent back fifteen *piña coladas* to my bar one time," recalled a bartender whose name tag read Tom. "He said my rum to juice ratio wasn't exactly to his liking. Then he complained to management, and I was put on probation."

"That's nothing," interrupted Sarud, a server from the dining room. "You know Cindy the cruise director? Well, he got her fired from her last ship. I don't know the details, but I know for a fact he did it."

"Good riddance! I can't abide a Jonah!"

"Yeah, at least we should have smooth sailing from now on."

"To Caz Koblinsky!" yelled Tom, and everyone in the bar raised their glasses. "May he rot in Davy Jones's Locker!"

I lowered mine quickly. As awful as the man was, celebrating his death felt worse. My eyes met Liz's, and I could tell she felt the same.

Then the DJ changed the song to "Goodbye Earl" and a collective screech of laughter rocked the bar. Everyone high-tailed it to the dance floor except Liz, Gunnar, and me, although I caught Gunnar looking longingly at the party from time to time. Everyone was dancing and singing along, except they substituted Caz for Earl. When they got to the chorus and the whole room shouted that "Caz had to die," Gunnar joined in.

"Everyone's so happy!" he laughed and took a swig of his beer like a Viking in a mead hall celebrating a vanquished foe. Yes, everyone was happy—for now—but that could change once security started to ask questions.

While Gunnar saw a room full of friends, compatriots even, celebrating their good fortune, I saw a room full of suspects. Every one of them had a Caz Koblinsky horror story to tell, which meant every one of them might have pulled the trigger. And this wasn't the whole crew! Many of them, like Cindy and Novette, were on duty. There was no telling how many people aboard the Lady Luck had it in for Caz. For all I knew, they had all chipped in and hired a hit man.

Another roar of laughter from the frenzied crew had me standing up to leave. It was all too blood-thirsty for my taste.

"I'll see y'all later."

"I'll come with you," said Liz. I nodded and left her and Alexander Skarsgård

to say their goodbyes. She caught up with me a moment later in the hallway.

"What do you want to do?" she asked.

"I want to sleep."

By the time we made it to our room, I was falling down tired. While Liz conscientiously followed her beauty routine, from makeup remover to silk bonnet, I yanked the pins from my hair, stripped, threw on a t-shirt and sleep shorts, and collapsed on the bed.

And then I couldn't sleep. The events of the day swirled around my overstimulated brain: rocket men, sequins, red scooters, mustaches, and baked Alaska.

"Do you want to talk about it?" Liz carefully folded back the covers, plumped her pillow, and settled down to sleep. Then she turned her kind brown eyes my way.

What could I say? I'm so hung up on my ex-boyfriend that I'm seeing him everywhere I go? I wasn't ready to go there. I'm making a fool of myself right, left, and center when I'm supposed to be impressing a new client? Too depressing. I stuck with the most obvious elephant in the room.

"I can't believe Mr. Koblinsky died."

"It was horrible, but you did your best."

"I can't believe everyone's so happy about it."

"That's not your fault. He brought it on himself."

"Yes, but how can everyone be so callous?"

Liz sighed.

"I don't know."

Maybe Liz and I were friends precisely because we didn't know. I tried to think of someone, anyone, whose death I would celebrate, but I couldn't think of anyone.

Not even Mike McCall.

CHAPTER 6

I wasn't surprised when Aton Faraday's assistant, Joseph, called me the next morning to request my presence at a meeting at nine. Aton probably wanted to hear about the events of the previous night from an eye—not to mention lip—witness.

Sticking to the theme of calm and capable, I donned a navy blue skirt suit and low pumps and wrangled my hair into another chignon.

"How do I look?"

"Very executive," enthused Liz, who was comfortably attired in yoga pants and a hoodie. As we had a full day of sailing ahead of us, she was planning to try all the extreme sports. First stop, the ropes course.

"If I get out of this meeting quickly, I'll come to watch you on the ropes."

"They may have trouble getting me to come down." Her eyes sparkled. "Supposedly, most of the time you walk on lines extended over the ocean. It's going to be thrilling!"

"I'm really glad you're here, Liz." I wiped my suddenly sweaty palms on my skirt.

When I reached Aton's suite, I discovered the captain was joining us.

"We'd like to hear your version of events," explained Captain Staggs while Joseph poured me a glass of cucumber water.

I took them through it, beginning with my trip out to the promenade deck and ending with trying to keep Casimir alive. Oddly enough, no one took any notes during my statement, but then I thought perhaps they would have me type something up for their official records. When I finished, they had questions.

"And why did you head out to the promenade deck in the first place?" asked Aton.

"I wanted to befriend Mr. Koblinsky. He is—was—a PR liability, and I hoped that I could make nice with him and bring him onto the team. After all, he was in business with the cruise line. I wanted to convince him that bad publicity would hurt him as well."

"And the sound you heard," began Captain Staggs. "You said it sounded like a stapler."

"The gun must have been silenced."

"If there was a gun," remarked Aton.

"Come again?"

"You say it sounded like a stapler, but no one saw a gun," he clarified. "And we have no bullet."

"Because it ricocheted. Why do you think Casimir Koblinsky had a heart attack? The bullet scared him to death."

"He might have had a heart attack because he was an eighty-year-old smoker," said the captain.

"What about the other guy?" What was his name? I couldn't call him Mr. Newlywed. "When we hit the deck, he said it was a gunshot."

Captain Staggs consulted a small notebook. "When the head of security spoke to Mr. Robin Shelby earlier, he said he wasn't sure what had happened. He said he thought it might have been a gunshot, but he admitted he has no experience with firearms."

"Well, I do," I cried. "Someone shot at Casimir Koblinsky—"

"With a staple gun," smirked Aton.

"With a silenced weapon. The shot went wide and ricocheted off the steel bulkhead, triggering Mr. Koblinsky's heart attack. Don't you care that someone has died?" Or were they among the hundreds of people on this ship ecstatic that Casimir Koblinsky was dead?

"Of course, we care," said the captain with a frown. "But it looks like he died of natural causes, which happens aboard ship all the time. Even if you think someone fired a weapon, that doesn't mean someone did. We have no evidence."

"What do the authorities think? Doesn't the FBI have jurisdiction over crimes against American citizens?"

Captain Staggs bristled. "The captain of the ship has jurisdiction first and foremost. If the captain determines a crime has been committed, then the FBI is contacted. As we have no evidence of a crime—"

"But the gunshot!"

"No evidence of a gunshot," she continued through clenched teeth, "we are not going to waste the FBI's time."

"And to insist that a shot was fired, in the face of a complete lack of evidence, would be tantamount to slander." Aton steepled his fingers and scrutinized me. "Correct me if I'm wrong. Protecting a client's image, including fighting any attempted slander, is your job."

"Absolutely," I replied because it was true. Aton's message was clear. If I wanted Seaswept Cruises for a client, I would have to let it go.

But could I let it go? If there was a maniac running around the ship with a gun, someone had to do something about it. And, even though he was a complete jerk, someone needed to get justice for Casimir Koblinsky. But I could tell these two would be of no help. I couldn't come up with a motive for Aton Faraday to kill his business partner, but a seasoned cruise ship captain might have run into Caz before and might very well hold a grudge.

"Excellent," pronounced Aton, assuming I was completely on board, no pun intended. "Then I think it's time Waverly Communications and Jill Cooksey, senior account executive, had a trial run."

I WAS FUMING as I made my way to the ropes course on deck fifteen. This was the deck devoted to extreme sports, and all around me, folks were indulging in adrenaline. Me, I didn't need bungee jumping, rock climbing, or rappelling. My adrenaline was up thanks to the meeting and the resulting to-do list. I was now in charge of celebrating the life of Casimir Koblinsky, staunch supporter of the cruise industry, and putting the best possible spin on his demise, which inconveniently occurred on the first day of the inaugural voyage of Seaswept Cruises. Meanwhile, I also had a mighty large personal to-do list item—find out who killed Caz. I wasn't ready to tell Aton Faraday to take his cruise line and shove it, but I also couldn't ignore the fact that a crime had been committed. I would have to tread very carefully if I wanted to win the client and see justice done.

Familiar territory for me. *Sigh.*

"Jill!" I heard Liz's voice and looked around. Where was she? "Up here!" I looked up—and out. Liz was high above my head and out over the ocean. She was perched on a narrow board extended over the open sea, like a balance beam on steroids. Thank goodness she was wearing her harness and safety rope. I tried to get closer to my friend.

"They call it walking the plank," she laughed. "Watch!" Liz turned and crept out to the very end of the board, her toes hanging over the edge. Then she spread her arms as wide as they would go. Her safety rope, while attached, was slack, and Liz certainly couldn't feel its reassuring tug. She was balanced all by herself and embracing the abyss.

How utterly terrifying.

"Wheeeeeeee!" she trilled. Then a gust of wind threw her off balance, and suddenly she was hanging by her safety rope over the water, laughing hysterically. She wasn't even making a move to get back on the board.

My palms broke out in a sweat, and the bottoms of my feet cramped up. I would have screamed "Someone save her!" if Gunnar hadn't arrived at that moment.

"It's the most incredible feeling," he smiled. "You should try it."

When pigs flew and bacon was no longer delicious.

Liz found her way back onto the board and continued with the rest of the ropes course while Gunnar and I watched. He was enchanted by her courage while I was appalled by the dangers.

When she arrived back on terra firma, or rather decka firma, Gunnar greeted her with a kiss that had my toes curling for a different reason. The Atlantic Ocean in February suddenly felt unseasonably warm. Had Liz met her soulmate on The Lady Luck?

When their lips finally parted company, we decided to go for lunch, but we avoided the Extreme Eats Café on deck fifteen and instead headed for a taqueria on the promenade deck. Gunnar joined us even though he supposedly had a job on the ship. Watching the lovebirds canoodle over tacos didn't bother me, but I needed to speak to Liz alone. I couldn't very well announce to a ship's officer that I was going to flout the cruise line's request to leave Caz's death alone. What if he told the captain? So, I tried to be patient and focus on my scrumptious shrimp tacos.

Eventually, Gunnar made his excuses and departed.

"Finally!" I breathed. Liz looked hurt.

"You don't like Gunnar?"

"I do! I just really need to talk to you. I have a problem."

While Liz addressed her tacos, I told her about the meeting and Aton's veiled threat.

"And you're sure you heard a gunshot?" she asked through a mouthful of food. Luckily, I speak taco.

"Yes. It was silenced, but it was definitely a gunshot. Even Robin Shelby agreed."

"Who's Robin Shelby? The name is familiar." Liz wiped some salsa off her fingers.

"The man who was out on deck with Caz. The one who ran for help."

"He said it was a gunshot?"

"That's what he told me, but he told the head of security that he wasn't sure." Just like a man to waffle.

"It's too bad there weren't any other witnesses."

But there was! I told Liz about the crew member taking a smoke break.

"And you're sure he was a crew member?"

"What man wears white pants if it isn't part of a uniform?"

"Did you get a name?"

"His back was turned. All I know is he wore white pants and a navy blue polo shirt. He was tall and trim but not skinny. He had sandy brown hair. That's all I know."

"It's not much to go on, but I can ask Gunnar about him."

"That's tricky. Gunnar can't know that I'm poking around about Caz's death. If it got back to the captain, I'd lose the client for sure."

Liz shot me an *Oh, please* look.

"I got this."

CHAPTER 7

*A*fter lunch, my friend had rock climbing and rappelling scheduled, so I left her to chase the adrenaline dragon and went back to the room to work on a press release about Caz's life and death. On my way, I passed the main pool where some sort of contest was being held by our cruise director. Cindy was more casually dressed today in white pants, a blue polo shirt, and a blue and white windbreaker. The pants and shirt were identical to the uniform worn by the mystery witness to Caz's death.

People were crowded all around the pool while a line of people in bathing suits shivered near the diving board. We hadn't hit the Caribbean yet, and the temperature was only in the fifties. Little vapor trails rising from the pool told me it was heated, but I wouldn't want to stand around the pool in my bathing suit.

"Our first contestant is Greg from Goshen, New Hampshire. Let's give it up for Greg!" enthused Cindy into her microphone.

The crowd clapped and roared as Greg mounted the diving board. He was a big guy. I looked at everyone else lined up for the diving board, and sure enough, they were all rather substantial. Daylight began to glimmer.

"Are you ready, Greg?"

"I'm ready, Cindy!"

"Then let's count him down, everybody. Three! Two! One!"

Greg took off running and launched himself into the air, gaining some impressive height. He spread his arms and legs as wide as they could go…and dropped like a rock into the water. Waves rose on all sides, drenching the spectators at the edge of the pool, who screamed with laughter. The belly flop competition was a huge hit.

Luckily, I was far enough away that I stayed dry, but the contestants were doing their level best to soak everyone.

I wandered over to the poolside bar to acquire a pineapple drink and ran into Tom whom I had met the night before at Casimir Koblinsky's Celebration of Death.

"What are you having?" His accent was pure New York.

"A pineapple drink."

Tom laughed.

"It's called Liquid Luck, and it's the ship's signature drink. I created it myself."

"It's very tasty." I pulled out my phone and made a note about the drink in case I wanted to use it in my PR plan.

"Just don't drink too many of them," he warned.

"Seriously? It tastes innocuous."

"Exactly!" He grinned. "I'll make you a fresh one."

"Make it two."

He looked surprised but nodded and got to work.

Tom moved like a cat as he made my drinks. There was an economy of movement about him that attested to many years behind a bar. Somewhere in his thirties, he was tall and trim, with brown hair, tan skin, and dark brown eyes. I couldn't see any tattoos, but he sported a diamond stud in one ear. A cornicello on a gold chain nestled in the open placket of his polo shirt.

"So where ya from, Tom?"

"Brooklyn. You?"

"Queens."

"Not hardly." He paused while coring a pineapple to cock an eyebrow at me. I laughed.

"I live there, but I'm originally from Virginia."

"I been there a few times. I like the beach."

Many people from up north did.

Tom handed me my drinks.

"Don't drink those too fast," he warned.

"Aye-aye, captain."

I edged closer to the pool, and I happily sipped and watched the festivities. I had to step back at one point, as Mona from Ohio made a wave so large that it almost reached my shoes. When the contest was over, Mona was declared the winner, and she and her fans immediately broke into the "Buckeye Battle Cry." Some Michigan fans countered with "The Victors," resulting in some people getting pushed into the pool, but it seemed to be in good fun and not a potential PR disaster. I wandered over to Cindy.

"That was fun." I handed her the second pineapple.

"Yeah, the belly flop contest is a real crowd pleaser." She took a sip and continued. "Usually, I save it for warmer waters, but after last night, we needed something to raise spirits."

"I guess news travels fast aboard ship."

"Like lightning! I heard about it maybe five or ten minutes after Caz died."

"Where were you?"

"Way up on deck eleven setting up trivia in one of the lounges. One of our bartenders came running in with the news."

Deck eleven was four decks up from the promenade deck.

"Well, we missed you at the staff party last night." I threw out the bait.

"I hear it was epic! If I hadn't had trivia, I would have been there. Last night was a night to remember."

Indeed.

Claiming work to do, which was the truth, I took my leave of Cindy and headed for my cabin to write the press release. The internet on the ship was top-notch, so I was quickly able to do some research on Caz. Still, I made a note to run the press release by Mira Koblinsky to make sure it was accurate. Gunnar or Aton could help me track her down. Caz had been profiled in several cruising publications since he held the world record for the number of cruises taken. It seemed like he'd traveled everywhere a boat could take him—the South Pacific, the Galapagos, Antarctica—leaving disaster and disgruntled crew in his wake. That certainly wouldn't be part of the press release, but his cruising "accomplishments" would be. A couple of hours later, the release was finished, and I emailed it to Joseph.

When it was done, I was exhausted, so I lay down to take a nap, except I was also wired. Tired and wired. Not a good combination. The past twenty-four hours had been tumul-tuous. So much had happened, and I was processing. I needed to relax. Then I remembered that I was on board a vessel devoted to relaxation. If I couldn't relax on this ship, then I was a lost cause.

I left the cabin and headed to the spa.

When the receptionist heard my name, she offered me any treatment on the menu, compliments of Mr. Faraday. Yes!

"I'll start with the hot stone massage, followed by the seaweed wrap, and the mani-pedi."

That's how I came to have my feet in a fish tank.

Aton had found a way to apply extreme to the spa treat-ments by having fish nibble the dead skin off feet. Bizarre. And slow. Little fish have little mouths, and the exfoliation part of the pedicure was taking forever! I knew that a pumice stone would have done the job quickly and efficiently, but no! Pumice wasn't extreme enough.

"I'm just surprised they aren't piranha," I mused.

"Oh, we tried that," said the nail technician.

"You're kidding! How'd that work out?"

"Um, I signed a nondisclosure agreement."

I'm sure you did!

It took almost four hours for me to be massaged, wrapped, and nibbled, but I felt so much better afterward. It was worth it, and I told myself that I needed the experience to better represent the cruise line. I would use the same excuse every time I ordered extra dessert too.

CHAPTER 8

When I got back to the room, Liz was already dressed for dinner. It was our first formal night aboard the ship, and she was wearing a gorgeous white cocktail dress with spaghetti straps, a sweetheart neckline, and a full skirt. The dress was made of silk with a lace overlay. She once again had her pearl combs and pins in her hair, and she looked like a dream, almost like a bride.

I quickly pulled out my evening gown for the night. Instead of capable, I had chosen to go glamorous for the first formal night. I so rarely got to dress up in formalwear, and I wasn't going to miss the opportunity. My gown was aqua, a color I didn't wear very often, but when I tried the dress on in the shop, I thought it made my coloring pop. My cheeks acquired just the right amount of blush, and the dress contrasted with my blond hair to great effect. Like Liz's, my dress also had spaghetti straps, but the neckline was straight across. And my dress did not have a full skirt. Instead, it hugged all my curves. The skirt came to below my knee, but there was a slit up the thigh that made it just the right amount of provocative. The instant I put the dress on, I felt like a million bucks, and I knew I had to have it.

Despite my recent success with *The Mr. Snicklefritz Show*, my confidence had taken a bit of a shellacking with the disappearance of my boyfriend. I'd had one horrible date since he ghosted me, and no other dates since that one. I was focused on my career and getting my house in order, and I had done so, quite nicely. Financially, I had never been in a better situation. I'd stuck to my budget, paid off my bills, and focused on my career goals. I felt confident on that front, but where men were concerned, I had no confidence whatsoever. Not that I was looking for a man, but my bizarre encounter with Not-Mike the previous evening, the one where I had acted a complete fool, had shaken my confidence even further and had convinced me that I needed to somehow put that man behind me. I told myself that looking good and feeling great was a strong first step.

It only took me a few minutes to get ready. My hair was still looking elegant in its chignon. I just replaced a couple of wayward pins, added some jewelry, touched up my makeup, and I was ready to go. At my request, we approached the dining room by way of the promenade deck. I paused where Caz had been in his last moments and looked up to where I thought the shot might have come from. I could see the decks above us, including deck eleven. There was even a convenient balcony on which to line up the shot.

But how would Cindy have known when Caz would go outside for a smoke? It suddenly seemed ridiculous, but then I reminded myself that someone HAD known. Someone had either known Caz's habits and waited patiently for him, or someone had been informed of his movements in real time.

I shivered as goosebumps erupted on my arms.

"It's freezing out here," said Liz. "Let's get inside!"

That evening, we would not be sitting at the captain's table.

Guests of the captain's table were rotated every night, and we had been guests of honor the first night. So tonight, Liz and I were allowed to dine in peace, *à deux*. Except we weren't *à deux*. Gunnar was there.

He looked splendid in his dress uniform of navy blue trimmed almost everywhere in gold. The deep blue set off his blond hair and stunning blue eyes. He looked like Prince Charming, and the two of them together, Gunnar and Liz, belonged on top of a royal wedding cake.

The perfect couple sat on one side of a table for four, and I sat on the other. It wasn't quite what I had in mind. I still wanted to talk through some things with Liz, and Gunnar's presence made that very difficult. He seemed like a great guy, and he was clearly smitten with my friend; however, his first loyalty had to be to the cruise line, and I didn't want anyone getting wind of the fact that I wasn't going to let Casimir Koblinsky's death go unmarked. So, as usual, I pasted on a smile and set about choosing my meal for the evening.

"Is this seat taken?" a soft voice asked. I looked up and into the beautiful brown eyes of John Gowdy, my dinner companion from the previous evening.

"Not at all," I managed through a fake smile. As he sat down next to me, Liz kicked me under the table, and I breathed a sigh of exasperation. Here was one more person to get in the way of my investigation, not just by his presence, but by the inevitable matchmaking attempts his presence would cause. At least I would have someone to talk to when Liz and Olaf were picking out baby names.

The waiter came to take our order, and we all chose the lobster, which I'd heard was traditional. Everybody ordered the lobster on formal night.

"I'm sorry, but the lobster is not available," said our waiter.

"Well, that's fine," I said and quickly chose pan-seared duck breast with cherry confit.

"Not available?" asked an incredulous Gunnar. "Since when is the lobster not available?"

The waiter leaned in close to speak to Gunnar.

"Since somehow the freezers housing the lobsters got unplugged. Every lobster on board is spoiled."

Gunnar blanched. He actually turned white as a sheet, which, considering his gorgeous tan, was quite a feat.

"Odin's beard," he whispered. Just kidding. He said, "Oh, no."

"So people can't have lobster," soothed Liz. "There are a lot of other great choices."

"It really is a disaster," John agreed with Gunnar. "I've been on a few cruises. I know how important the lobster is."

"How important?" I asked.

"Lobster is a status item," explained Gunnar. "When people book their cruises, they're thinking about the lobster. They don't have to pay extra for it, and it is perhaps the most sumptuous thing they'll eat the entire time they're on board. If we don't have lobster, people are going to be angry."

Unfortunately, he was correct. The volume of conversation in the dining room had increased over the last couple of minutes as tables were informed that the lobster was not an option. Gunnar excused himself and went off to speak with the kitchen staff and other folks in charge about the situation.

"Cruising is its own culture, isn't it?" observed Liz. "There are traditions and rituals that people expect on a cruise. They're very entrenched in how they think things ought to be."

"It's true," said John. "Cruisers don't always roll with the punches. They roll with the heavy seas, but changes to schedules, menus, internet service? They really can freak out. I've seen some bad behavior on cruise ships."

"So, Casimir Koblinsky wasn't the only passenger who could be obnoxious," I remarked.

John laughed.

"No, indeed. People who are perfectly accommodating when they first board the ship can turn into nightmares when things don't go their way."

Just then, the waiter arrived with our drinks, and the conversation turned to Liz's adventures that day. After the ropes course, she climbed a fifty-foot rock wall and rappelled from the top.

"It was great!" she gushed. "That rock wall was one of the most challenging I've encountered. When you get to the top, it curls over on itself, so you have to hold on if you want to make it. The rappelling was even more fun. I had never tried it, but I felt like a commando. When I got to the ground, I was pumped."

After her extreme adventures, she headed to the hot tub to relax her sore muscles. Then she went back to the room for a quick nap before I showed up.

"And how have you spent your day at sea?" I asked John just to be polite.

"Besides keeping an eye open for you," he smiled and I felt my face get warm, "I spent some time in the business center getting some work done."

Liz beamed at us, and I wanted to kick her under the table. I would have, but I was afraid of kicking the wrong person. People in love always want everyone else to be in love, but I was not interested. Yes, I wanted to completely and thoroughly get over Mike, but I didn't want to take on a new problem, I mean, man. I didn't want to take on a new man.

"Then I went to the movies," continued John, "which is something I never do at home. It felt great to sit in a dark theater and lose myself for a couple of hours."

He had seen the latest superhero flick that had just opened the previous week.

"It was a nice change of pace."

"So, you like movies," enthused Liz as she looked meaningfully at me in a completely unsubtle way. Oh boy.

After that, he tried his hand at skeet shooting.

"But I was awful at it. I missed every clay pigeon. So, what about you, Jill?"

I told him about my meeting with Aton and the captain and that I was helping to repair the damage that Casimir's death had caused to the cruise line's reputation.

"Let's hope he was the Jonah and there won't be any more mishaps," said Liz.

"I'd call the loss of fifty thousand dollars' worth of lobster a bit of a mishap," said John, and he was right.

"But of course, we don't believe in Jonahs, right Liz?" I gave my friend the stink-eye.

"Oh, sure, not really, unless, you know, more bad stuff happens."

Gunnar missed the appetizers but returned in time for the main course.

"No one seems to know who unplugged the freezers. Everyone in the kitchen is afraid of losing their jobs, so they've closed ranks. It's another bad omen." He sighed heavily.

Since there was no lobster, I had chosen a jumbo shrimp cocktail for my appetizer. It was old school, but really, you couldn't beat it. And the duck breast with cherry confit melted in my mouth. For dessert, I decided to brave the baked Alaska. I thought it might give me closure on the previous night's debacle.

The dessert was stunning. Blue flames danced atop a dome of luscious meringue. I thought you had to blow the flames out yourself, but I learned that when the alcohol sprinkled atop the dessert was consumed by the fire, the fire went out by itself. How smart. A self-extinguishing fire dessert.

Anticipating the most glorious thing I'd ever eaten, I dug in and took my first bite.

"Huh," I said. "It's not what I expected."

"What did you expect?" asked Gunnar

Ambrosia. Manna. Something only Willy Wonka could envision.

"I just expected it to be more than…"

"Ice cream?" put in Liz.

"Exactly!" Because that's what it was. Baked Alaska was ice cream covered with meringue and set on fire. It was good ice cream, but it was still ice cream. And the meringue layer turned out to be quite thin.

"This dessert," said John, "is more about the effect."

"Indeed," I resolved not to waste any more calories on showy desserts with no substance. If there wasn't chocolate or custard involved, I wasn't interested.

Dinner alternated between very pleasant and uncomfortable. John was clearly interested in me, and Liz encouraged it when she wasn't lost in a love bubble with her Viking prince.

John was a charming dinner companion, and without a table full of eight other people, I had a chance to get to know him, whether I wanted to or not. His name was John Gowdy. He was forty, single, never married, and an investment banker (already knew that.) He lived on Staten Island (already knew that too), and he admitted he worked too much.

"For several years now, I've been focused on my career," he said. "Things weren't going the way I wanted them to at first, so I decided to knuckle down and keep my mind on the business. I wouldn't let myself get distracted by relationships and other goals."

Hmm. This talk sounded familiar.

"And how has that been working out for you?" I asked.

"Great," he said. "I'm in a much better position with my company. I've made a fair amount of money." His smile was wry and self-deprecating. "And I've accomplished a lot of my goals."

"So you think it's been worthwhile? Because I'm on that same path myself." (Hint, hint.) I told him about public relations and how I wanted to be an account manager or a VP by the time I was thirty. How I wanted to move out of my tiny apartment in Queens. And how I'd had a bad breakup, which led me to believe it was time to focus on myself and my goals and less on romance.

"And how's that working out for you?" He echoed my question.

"So far so good," I smiled.

"That's good." And then he leaned in closer. "But, Jill, future VP, it can be lonely."

"I'm too busy to notice," I lied through my teeth.

"Jill has a lot of friends," added Liz with pride.

She then told John and Gunnar all about our PR Posse, our group of friends in public relations who were my tribe, my besties, my BFFs. We had made a pact to help each other out with our careers to ensure our group's success, and it had worked out great. My posse had even helped me solve two murders, which, when I chose PR for my career, I didn't realize was part of the job description.

When dinner ended, Gunnar and Liz had to say goodbye because he had to work, and John and I watched the two of them kiss. Correction: I looked everywhere except at the PDA in front of my face. So awkward. And I could feel John looking at me, which was equally disconcerting. I didn't want to encourage him, but there was a tiny part of me that remembered toe-curling goodnight kisses and wanted another one. Someday, I thought, but not today, and not with someone I just met.

To break the tension, I pointed at the lip-locked couple and rolled my eyes. In return, John pointed his finger at his open mouth in the universal *gag me* sign. We were on the same page.

Excellent. We continued miming our disgust until Liz and Gunnar came up for air.

"Are you going into Nassau tomorrow?" John asked.

"I was planning on it."

"Then let me show you around. I've been several times, and I know the city well."

I hesitated, and he noticed.

"Just as friends. No ulterior motives. No PDA. We're career-focused, remember?"

I laughed and gave in. We set a time to meet the next day and said goodnight. No spit was swapped.

"Guess what!" squealed Liz after John had left. "Gunnar's taking me to work with him."

"What?"

"He has watch on the bridge, and he said I could come along and keep him company."

My face must have fallen a little because Liz quickly added, "And of course, you can come too…if you want to."

I didn't want to, and I didn't want Liz to go either. First and foremost, we hadn't had a chance to talk about a bunch of things. And second, Gunnar was, you know, helming the ship. Did he need to be distracted by my gorgeous friend? What if he steered us into an island or a reef or a shoal? But I knew deep down that I was being silly.

"No, no, you go ahead. I'm a bit tired."

She giggled. "See you later then." She clasped Gunnar's hand and they were off.

While not really ready to go to sleep, I also didn't want to hang out with the lovebirds. I wanted to take my mind off romance altogether. Since I was dressed to kill, I decided to take a walk around the ship.

I strolled past Mr. Waverly's suite again, but the DO NOT DISTURB sign was still firmly in place. Eventually, I found myself on deck eleven, which was devoted to music and entertainment. There was a huge theater for Broadway-style musicals, enormous dance clubs, and smaller, more intimate music venues. As I walked along the deck, I heard many different kinds of music calling to me from the different corners of the ship, but I didn't want anything too loud and jarring that would make it difficult for me to think. I passed a country bar that advertised a singer named Kenney Rodgers.

How original.

The song emanating from the club was familiar, and even the voice a little bit, but I wasn't in the mood for country—too much heartbreak and Mama. Instead, I followed the tinkling of keys to a piano bar.

When I saw the dueling pianos facing each other, I knew

that normally this club would be crowded and rowdy with singers. But not tonight. Instead, only one piano was in use, being played soulfully by a tuxedo-clad performer. And lying atop the closed baby grand, in a red sequined strapless gown that clung to her like a second skin, was Novette.

She was just beginning Alicia Keyes's anthem "Girl on Fire," which fit my mood perfectly. I sat down at a table and let her voice fill me with girl power, and when the song was over, I whistled the loudest.

As I was taking a sip of my club soda with lime, I heard the opening to Novette's next song and recognized it instantly. "You Don't Bring Me Flowers" is so sad that my fight or flight response kicked in full flight, but I made myself sit still. It was just a song. Nothing to be afraid of. But Novette crooned that homage to dying love as if she had lived it. Novette's rendition was beautiful but devastating—so devastating that all I could think about was the last bouquet I had received from Mike. I wanted to get out of the piano bar before my mascara ran for the second night in a row, but now the entrance was blocked by Novette's growing audience. It was standing room only, so I sat and tried to surreptitiously wipe the tears that trickled down my face.

When the song was over, the applause was thunderous.

"I'm going to take a short break now, but don't y'all go anywhere." Novette left the small stage, and the piano player began some light background music. Then she surprised me by making a beeline to my table and sitting down.

"I'm parched!" she announced, and in no time a server was setting a drink in front of her. "Whiskey sour. Excellent for the throat." Novette took a sip and pegged me with her gaze. "You've been crying."

"That song gets me every time."

"Especially when you've recently been through a breakup."

"It was three months ago."

"Honey, that's nothing. Love time is like…what do they call it? Geologic time? A million years can pass, and you can still be hung up on the same guy. Take it from an expert."

"Who are you hung up on?"

Next door, Kenney Rodgers began singing "Lady," and Novette paused to listen for a moment. It was a night for soulful love songs. Sadly.

"I'm the worst kind of hung up." Novette laughed bitterly. "I'm hung up on a guy who can never be mine."

"Oh, Novette. I'm so sorry. But why can't he be yours?"

"Because he loves someone else."

"That could change."

"And he's married to her."

Ah.

She smiled wryly and took a long pull on her drink.

I studied the singer. She was beautiful and talented and could have her pick of men. But her heart, a traitor just like all the other hearts in the world, had chosen the wrong guy.

"How long? How long have you been pining?"

"Pining. That's a good word. I've been pining over the gentleman for going on four years."

"Four years!" Bad news. If the exquisite Novette couldn't get over a guy in four years, how long was I going to hold on to Mike? A potential future opened up before me in which I spent the next two decades crying over love songs and living for my work. I'd also probably have too many houseplants and yippy dogs. I shuddered.

"It's my own fault. I could have got some distance from him, but every time he changed ships, like a chump, I followed."

"Hold up! He works on this ship? And he doesn't mind that you have feelings for him, even though he loves his wife? Is he leading you on?" Some men just craved attention and would string a girl along to boost their egos.

Novette drained her glass and signaled to the barkeep for another.

"He doesn't know. He thinks we're just the best of pals. Good old Novette. Always there when he needs a listening ear." Another drink arrived. "Cheers!" she toasted mockingly.

So Novette was the author of her own destruction. I couldn't judge her. The adage was true: love makes fools of us all. Still, I had to try to help her.

"Novette, can't you get off this ship? You could go anywhere. Start afresh. Get out from under this man-shaped cloud."

"You say it like it's easy. Once, in a very weak moment, I even considered marrying Casimir Koblinsky, just to get away."

"That must have been some weak moment."

Novette laughed. "I call it rock bottom. But I realized I'd rather be friends with my love and get to be part of his life than lose him completely."

My heart twisted at her words. That was some kind of love. Part of me thought it was beautiful and self-sacrificing while another part thought it was unhealthy and self-destructive. It was certainly the kind of love that would inspire poetry, torch songs, and agonizingly beautiful performances. Maybe, as a chanteuse, Novette had found the right kind of love for her.

Then a third whiskey sour appeared in front of her, and I revised my estimation. Novette chugged the drink and stood with only a slight wobble.

"Time for my next set. Good talking to you, Jill. Let's do it again."

"Yes, indeed." Mentally I added another item to my to-do list. Save Novette from herself.

I gathered my things and made my way toward the exit. As I did, I saw the scarf woman again, sitting at a table just inside the door. She wasn't there when I arrived, so she must have come in after me and sat down.

At least I thought it was the scarf woman. She was now enveloped in a huge orange caftan fringed with blue and green. She wore a floppy sun hat indoors that was a good two feet in diameter and the largest sunglasses I had ever seen. Her glasses from the previous day were Jackie O's. These were Elton John's. She had to be someone famous. Why else would she feel the need to obscure her identity through garish outfits? She was also wearing the most gosh awful fuchsia lipstick I had ever seen, the color many older women prefer but that always seems to bleed into the lines around their mouths. Lucky for me, my mother had instructed me religiously never to wear fuchsia lipstick. I decided I would leave the scarf lady alone and let her enjoy her obscurity.

CHAPTER 10

few doors down, a jazz combo was performing. It was mellow but uplifting, an antidote to Novette's tortured set list, so I slipped inside and found an empty table. A waiter took my order of a club soda and lime, and I looked around the small space. Across the way, at another small table sat Mira Koblinsky. Her red tresses contrasted beautifully with a demure black cocktail dress, and she was sitting with Robin Shelby and his bride. Mr. Shelby wore a classic black tuxedo while Mrs. Shelby wore an ivory lace tea-length gown with a boatneck that contrasted beautifully with her jet-black locks.

I watched them converse. For someone whose father had just passed away, Mira didn't seem too down in the dumps. She chuckled quite often as she chatted with the Shelbys. My drink arrived, and I took a sip and continued to watch the trio across the way.

Mrs. Shelby leaned over to her husband and whispered something in his ear, which seemed to surprise him. Hmm. Had the new missus suggested something sexy? The two were on their honeymoon after all. Get a room!

It was time to go. Confronted by love at every turn, I just

wanted to jump off the ship and swim back to New York. Luckily, I'm practical. I decided on a trip to the coffee bar for a hot chocolate, a good book, and my bed.

But then I remembered that I needed to get Mira to approve the press release. I didn't want to add insult to injury by putting out false information about her father, so I thought I would sidle over and introduce myself, which would allow me to ask Robin about the gunshot, although maybe not. I didn't want to upset Mira with that talk. It could get back to Aton.

Taking a final swig of my drink, I stood up, gathered my purse, and walked calmly across the club.

"Excuse me, Ms. Koblinsky, Mr. and Mrs. Shelby. I'm sorry to interrupt your evening."

The two women looked up at me in surprise, while Robin Shelby downed his drink and signaled the waiter for another.

I introduced myself and explained my role aboard the ship. Then I offered Mira Koblinsky my condolences on Caz's passing.

"You tried to save him." Mira recognized me, clasped my hand, and pulled me down into the seat next to hers. "Thank you so much."

"I wish I could have done more." What else could I say? It was true.

A tearful Mira let go of my hand to dig into her purse for a tissue, but Robin Shelby offered her his monogrammed hand-kerchief instead. While she dabbed at her eyes, I got down to business as gently as I could.

"This must be a terrible time for you."

Mira smiled ruefully.

"When you have older parents, you have to be prepared for things like this. We lost my mother five years ago. I never thought I'd have this much time with my father. He wasn't in good health."

"I have a press release about your father's passing, and I'd like to send it out tomorrow. I was wondering if you would take a look at it. I just want to make sure that it's accurate."

"Sure. That would be fine." She gave me her email address, and I swiftly sent her the release from my phone.

I racked my brain for some way to bring up the gunshot in a way that wouldn't alarm Mira, but I was having trouble. Luckily, Mira herself came to my aid by excusing herself to go to the ladies' room.

"So, you're newlyweds," I began as soon as Mira was out of earshot.

Mrs. Shelby wiggled her fingers to show off her wedding and engagement rings.

"I finally got him to the altar," she laughed.

"And how are you enjoying your honeymoon, Mrs. Shelby?"

"Please, call me Susan. Let's just say it has been interesting."

"I'm sure neither of you anticipated being caught up in a shooting."

Susan looked confusedly from me to her husband and back again. "I'm not sure what you mean."

I looked significantly at Robin Shelby.

"You didn't tell her?"

"Tell her what?" he asked as he met my gaze.

"That Casimir Koblinsky's heart attack was triggered by a gunshot."

"Oh, my goodness!" cried Susan clutching her pearls. "Robby, is this true?"

He turned to his wife and patted her hand.

"Now Su-su, don't get upset. This is just a misunderstanding. There was some confusion when Casimir had his heart attack. We heard a noise of some sort, but we've no way of knowing what it was. It could have been something mechanical with the ship, or someone might have dropped something from one of the balconies."

"But you said it was a gunshot," I countered.

"I was mistaken," he smiled at me. "I'm unaccustomed to the sounds of a ship. It's our first cruise." He turned his smile on his bride, and she put her arm through his and snuggled up to him.

I was about to protest further, but Mira returned.

"What did I miss?"

"Nothing at all," Susan assured her.

Taking that as my cue, I said my goodbyes and left.

I thought I was headed to my cabin and my beauty sleep, but the night wasn't done with me yet. As I left the club, I caught a glimpse of Aton Faraday with John Gowdy. They were about ten yards in front of me and were deep in conversation, so I didn't interrupt. I wasn't loving Mr. Faraday at the moment, and I didn't want to draw his attention. And if John was conducting business with Faraday, I didn't want to distract from that either. If Aton thought I was doing a poor job, and if he thought John and I were connected in some way, it could impact any business dealings. So instead of heading in the direction of my cabin, I turned into another club. It happened to be the country bar where Kenney Rodgers was playing. It was much less formal than the jazz club, so I sidled up to the bar. My friend Tom, the inventor of Liquid Luck, was pouring drinks, and I ordered myself another club soda with lime.

Then I noticed there wasn't a musician on the stage. Hadn't Kenney Rodgers been playing the guitar and singing just a moment before? Movement caught my eye—a door behind the stage closed with an audible click.

"You picked a not-so-fine time to leave us, Kenney *Rrrodgers*," joked a Scottish voice.

"Maybe he felt the long arm of the law," quipped another.

"Or perhaps something's burning," I added without thinking.

Raised by ardent country music fans, I knew my Kenny Rogers, and the song title just slipped out. But every head in the bar turned toward me, men and women, and that's when I noticed that all the heads were attached to bodies sporting bright blue soccer jerseys. Many of the folks were long past soccer playing, so it had to be a fan club. I had wandered into a blue sea of Scottish soccer supporters!

Then everybody laughed, and a pint of beer magically appeared in front of me. I took a polite sip and looked around for someone to thank, but the club had moved on to other matters.

"Since Kenney Rrrodgers has taken his love and his music to town," said a tall Scot with red hair and bright green eyes, "I think it's time we heard from The Legend."

"The Legend!" Cries went up along with glasses.

The person in question was a slight man in his late seventies or early eighties who was sitting at the bar calmly addressing a shot glass of something amber. I could tell he was The Legend because his royal blue trucker cap embroidered with gold lettering told me so.

As the cries developed into a chant, The Legend slowly finished his drink and eased himself off the bar stool. Everyone cheered, and he moved unhurriedly toward the stage and took the mike. He closed his eyes, and a hush descended.

I held my breath in anticipation, and I wasn't disappointed. The Legend opened his mouth and began to sing a cappella, in a rich baritone, "The Bonnie Banks o' Loch Lomond."

Hell's bells. More love.

In an instant, I was swept away on a tide of romance, towed under and out to sea by the sad words sung in a magnificent voice. The Legend finished to thunderous applause, my own included.

Another beer appeared next to the one I'd only taken three sips of. I must have grimaced because Tom leaned in close.

"You passed the test," he whispered. "The beers are just gonna keep coming."

"But I'm not much of a drinker. What should I do?"

Tom winked at me. Then he watched the crowd. When he was certain no one was looking, he swiped the first beer and put it under the bar.

"Thank you! If anyone buys me another, do you think you could put iced tea in a glass without any ice? It should look like beer, right?"

"If anyone asks, you're drinking an amber ale." He winked at me again and was gone.

And then The Legend broke into "My Love is Like a Red, Red Rose" by Robert Burns, and I thought about nothing else.

"O, my love is like a red, red rose that's newly sprung in June; O my love is like the melody that's sweetly played in tune."

My dad had loved this song, especially the Eva Cassidy version, and had sung it to me and my mother many times. I felt the tears welling and dabbed at my eyes with a napkin. Fortunately, I wasn't alone. I caught more than one listener swiping surreptitiously at tears.

On the chorus, everyone joined in, and it became a sing-along.

"Till a' the seas gang dry, my dear, and the rocks melt wi' the sun; I will love thee still, my dear, while the sands o' life shall run."

I sang out with everyone as tears streamed down my cheeks. I didn't care. I was singing to my dad. He was a gambler and a singer and the love of my life.

And I hadn't truly mourned him.

For years I had kept busy—very busy—focused on work and the hustle and bustle of my life in New York. My mom had done the same, and I guess I had followed her lead. She jumped into all sorts of projects back home in Luthersburg, and she embraced the cruising lifestyle, sailing whenever she could. I guess we had both dealt with our grief the same way. Like mother, like daughter. I had cried at the funeral with my mom, and I thought I was done.

Clearly not.

When the song ended, the applause, shouts, and whistles were even louder, and I had three "beers" lined up on the bar. The worst they could do to me was keep me up all night, so I kept drinking.

The Legend immediately launched into another tune, but I didn't know it. It was quick and lively and full of Scottish words. To be honest, I couldn't understand a word, but the crowd knew it by heart and was on its feet clapping. I joined them for the fun of it.

I was raising my glass of "beer" to my lips when someone bumped into me and my drink spilled down my dress. A couple of women rushed to my aid and helped me mop up, while all the men turned to greet the newcomer.

Some greeting. If looks could kill…

Is this a dagger that I see before me?

Why, yes. Twenty of them shooting out of the eye sockets of a gang of Scottish soccer enthusiasts. This guy was toast.

He was also oblivious.

"Two Long Island iced teas," he ordered in an appropriate accent for such a drink.

"Hey, pal," began the tall redhead as he invaded the newcomer's personal space. "Do ye no hear The Legend?"

"The who?" asked Mr. Long Island.

"The man who's singing, you great numpty!"

"Yeah. So what?"

"Haud yer wheesht!"

"What?"

"Shut it!"

"Aye!" affirmed a chorus of Scots.

At that moment, Tom plunked down two Long Island iced teas on the bar.

"I think you should take these to go before I have to clean blood off my brand-new bar."

"Awa' n bile yer heid!" shouted someone from the corner.

"Aye, hit the road, ya eejit!" yelled someone close by.

The interloper sprinted off faster than you could say William Wallace, dribbling Long Island iced tea all the way.

Sometime later, I found myself at a table surrounded by new friends, including The Legend and the chivalrous Scot, whose name I learned was Roddy. I was trying hard to follow the conversation. My favorite time travel romances, set in Scotland, hadn't quite prepared me to translate fully, but I got the gist. I bought a round for the whole bar, charged to my room and thus to Aton Faraday, but I considered it a business expense—market research. I was getting opinions on the ship whenever I could get a word in edgewise.

Kenney Rodgers hadn't returned, but the group hadn't noticed. Once the singalong ended, they were content to drink and talk.

"Did ye no hear boot the ol' yin who deid last nicht?" said my new friend Eileen.

"Och aye!" exclaimed my other new friend Shona. "He was that nasty bugger on the wee scooter."

"He got what was coming to him," proclaimed Tom as he set another round of drinks on our table.

"Well, God rest his soul," said Eileen.

"Where were you when you got the news?" I tried to ask Tom casually. For a second, his gaze turned flinty, or maybe it was my imagination.

"I was prepping for trivia night in Cardsharkey's. That's a lounge and pool hall." He laughed. "I was so surprised I nearly dropped a bottle of O'Sullivan's on my foot. Trivia night is really fun, by the way. You should try it."

Tom headed back to the bar, and I tried to pay attention to the conversation between Eileen and Shona, but my thoughts were racing. Was it a coincidence that Tom and Cindy were working together when Caz was killed? Or was something sinister going on? Probably just a coincidence, but I filed the information away for just in case.

Eventually, not even a gallon of tepid iced tea could keep me awake, and I said my goodbyes to my new Scottish friends and turned to leave.

On my way out, I saw the scarf lady again. She was sitting alone at a small table just inside the door. As I passed, she was re-applying her fuchsia lipstick.

I hadn't gone twenty feet from the bar when I heard the sound of a guitar and the first line of "The Gambler." Kenny Rodgers hadn't left the building.

CHAPTER 11

When I awoke the next morning, we were docked at Nassau in the Bahamas. I looked out our little porthole at our first port of call. The Nassau skyline was primarily made of low buildings in a variety of styles and colors. The harbor was extraordinary, filled with cruise ships, sailboats, and yachts of every shape and size. The view energized me, and I couldn't wait to get off the ship and explore. Liz was already awake and packing her day pack with her bathing suit, mask, and snorkel. She had signed up for the swimming with sharks excursion, part of her research into all the extreme experiences the cruise line offered.

"You know, you don't have to do every dangerous thing offered on the ship, certainly not for me. I just need some of your impressions of the opportunities to be able to write the press materials accurately, but you don't have to risk life and limb."

"Oh, I can't wait to swim with sharks," she cried, and she held up a clear plastic box with something inside it. "I have a new Go-Pro camera, and I'm hoping to get some excellent shark footage."

"Just be careful," I said. "I want to bring you back to New York with all your limbs."

Liz laughed.

"From what I've read, the sharks are mostly nurse sharks. Harmless. Plus, the guides all have shark repellent and know how to deter the sharks, so if anybody gets frisky, they can handle it."

I wasn't so sure, but she seemed excited about it.

"Don't you have a date with John today?" She smiled at me.

"It's not a date, but yes, John's going to show me around Nassau." At the thought, my heart quickened. Today was going to be a fun day full of new sights, smells, and tastes. But first I had some work to do.

From my bed, I grabbed my laptop and checked my email to see if Mira Koblinsky had approved the press release. She had, so I emailed Joseph that he could send it out immediately.

Liz had to catch a launch that would take her to the sharks, so we said goodbye, and I headed for the shower. Before I could explore Nassau, I had a meeting with Aton, and before that, I wanted breakfast.

In a departure from "capable," I opted for a turquoise sundress with a long peasant skirt and wedge espadrilles. Totally tourist, I know, but when in Rome…

I had time to eat breakfast before my meeting, so I headed for the casual dining space on the promenade deck. The place was packed with passengers fueling up before their excursions, and the lines at the buffet stretched almost to the doors. With the clock ticking, I decided to explore the other options. Toward the bow of the ship, I spied a bakery called Le Crois-sant. Perfect. A chocolate croissant would put me in a great mood for my meeting with a potential client who wanted to cover up a murder.

As I approached the café, who should come sweeping out the door but the scarf lady, today clad in a purple caftan with lime green fringe, a black straw hat, and sunglasses shaped like flamingos. And she wasn't alone. A crew member in white pants, a navy blue polo shirt, a baseball cap, and sunglasses was with her. He was tall and slim, with sandy brown hair. They turned left coming out the door of the bakery and soon had their backs to me, but I recognized that crew member's back. He was the mystery smoker from the night Caz Koblinsky died.

"Excuse me," I called out. "Can you hold up for a second?" I hurried toward him, but he sped up. Before I could catch up to him, he popped through a service doorway. I tried the handle, but it was locked, and I would need a magnetic key card to get through it. I turned to the scarf lady to question her about the crew member, but she was gone.

The whole thing was very suspicious. Why would a crew member run away from a guest? Okay, there were a million reasons. He might have thought I was going to make an annoying request. He might have been late for a shift. He might even have been headed for the bathroom. So maybe it wasn't that suspicious. And maybe the scarf lady wasn't really with the crew member. Maybe they just exited the bakery at the same time.

Maybe.

Chiding myself for an overly active imagination, I headed back to the bakery and found Robin and Susan Shelby sitting at a table in the corner. I marched on over.

"Did you see that crew member who was just in here?" I asked without preamble.

"What crew member?" asked Susan without looking up from her chocolate croissant. It looked delicious.

"The one who might have been out on the deck with us the night Caz was killed."

"You mean the night Caz had a heart attack," corrected Robin.

"You heard the gunshot!"

"I was mistaken."

"So what pinged off the side of the ship? A meteorite? A seagull's kidney stone? You know that was a bullet!"

"Enough!" snapped Susan. "Stop harassing my husband! We are on our honeymoon, and Mr. Koblinsky's death has cast enough of a pall. Please let us enjoy the rest of our cruise."

I released the breath I had taken to further my argument. Susan Shelby was right. The newlyweds were supposed to be enjoying a love bubble, unbroken by the cares of the rest of the world. I needed to leave them alone.

But then I saw the coffee cups on their table. Four coffee cups, to be precise.

"Who were you having coffee with?" I demanded. Forget the love bubble.

"No one," replied Robin.

"So you have two extra coffee cups because...?"

"They were here when we sat down."

I looked around at the nearly empty café.

"And you chose the only table in the bakery that had dirty dishes on it?"

"We weren't thinking about dishes!" yelled Susan. "We're in love! We just sat down! For heaven's sake, leave us alone!"

So I did. A shouting match wasn't going to get them to admit they'd been having coffee with the mystery smoker and the scarf lady. I decided on a tactical retreat. Maybe if I got Robin alone I could get some information out of him. After all, we had endured a near-death experience together. That had to count for something. I just needed to get him away from his ball and chain, and I bet his lips would loosen up.

I left the bakery without a chocolate croissant and headed up to Aton's suite to find he wasn't alone. Joseph was there, of course, but so was Carol the Carefree Cruiser, my favorite YouTube star who reviewed all the new cruise ships and dispensed cruising wisdom. Her channel was a key part of my research going into this pitch. True to form, Carol was attired in her signature sailor suit: a navy blue middy blouse, a navy blue skort, and a white dixie cup hat. Her hair and makeup were impeccable, ready for a photo opportunity at a moment's notice. Unfortunately, Aton didn't give me any time to fangirl.

"There have been some new developments," explained Aton. "In addition to Mr. Koblinsky's passing…"

You mean murder, I thought, but kept it to myself.

"…we've had an unfortunate incident with the lobsters, although why anyone wants to eat them I'll never understand. Crustaceans and mollusks are basically the filtration system of the ocean, scrubbing it clean—"

"Aton," interrupted Carol, "let's not get off topic."

"Quite," he acknowledged. "But between the two incidents—"

"And your fiery landing," interjected the Carefree Cruiser again. Aton rolled his eyes.

"Let's just say, the publicity isn't where we want it to be for the inaugural cruise."

"It's in the crapper," pronounced Carol. "There are plenty of videos being uploaded about the great amenities on the ship, but the videos getting all the views are about the things going wrong."

"So, we need to change the narrative," I said. "Let me guess. Carol is going to make some pro-Seaswept videos, and with her immense following, you're hoping they will overshadow the negative reports."

"Exactly!" Aton smiled, which meant his lips went from a straight line to a less severe straight line. "That's why I want you to work with Carol on these videos, Jill. You've done the homework. Steer Carol toward the amenities that are going to have the biggest impact on our target market."

Another test. Great. While I smiled and acted excited about

the opportunity, inside I was seething. If Faraday didn't give Waverly the contract after all the free work I was giving him… well, I didn't know what I would do, but I liked to think it wouldn't be pretty.

I was supposed to join John after my meeting, but now I had to make a video with Carol before I could tour Nassau. Luckily, he was in his cabin when I called, and we agreed to meet in the early afternoon. We wouldn't have much time in Nassau, but it would be better than nothing.

Aton left us to do whatever pajama-wearing futurists do during the day, but he graciously allowed us to use his living room to plan.

"I think we should focus on the thrill-seeking," pronounced Carol. "The ropes course, rappelling, some of the weirder spa treatments and dining experiences. Anything that will give the viewers a thrill, good or bad, will rake in the views. You'll have to change your clothes. Otherwise, if the wind blows when you're on that ropes course, the whole world will know the color of your underwear."

What?

I laughed nervously because Carol had to be joking.

"Good one! You had me going for a second."

"I'm not joking."

It suddenly felt very hot in Aton Faraday's suite. My mouth was also quite dry. I reached for my cucumber water and took a big gulp.

"But your videos are all about YOU experiencing the ship," I finally managed.

"Can't do it." Carol shrugged her shoulders. "I get vertigo."

And that's how I found myself on the ropes course, cursing Liz and all the sharks in the ocean. I had changed into shorts, a Seaswept t-shirt, and sneakers. I was trembling as the attendant fastened my harness and gave me instructions that I couldn't hear due to the rushing sound in my ears. Suddenly it was time to step out onto the course. That's when the trembling turned to shaking.

The first section wasn't so bad. There were boards to walk on and a rope to hold on either side of me. For a moment, my confidence surged. Then I got to the end of that section and discovered it was a fake out. Beyond it was a single wire that I was supposed to traverse and only one rope on the left side for me to hold on to. The shaking began again in earnest.

"Okay, Jill," directed Carol from below, on the safe, firm deck, where she was stationed with her cameraman. "Jim's got a great shot of you. Step out onto the wire."

I closed my eyes, breathed deeply, and took a step. At least I took one in my mind. My foot, however, refused to move.

"Am I on the wire?" My voice sounded funny.

"No, Jill. Take a step. You can't fall. You have a harness and a safety wire."

Made by a human, I thought, and anything made by a human can break! I summoned all my courage and took a step.

"How about now? Am I on the wire?"

"Not yet." Hmm. It sounded like Carol's teeth were clenched.

I tried again.

"What about now? I'm there, right?"

"Get on the *bleep bleep* wire before I *bleep bleep bleep* your *bleep*!"

Well, that did the trick. The shock that Carol the Carefree Cruiser even knew some of those words propelled me onto that wire before she *bleeped* my *bleep*. There I was, standing on a wire thirty feet above the deck. The guide rope on my left was slippery in my sweaty palm. In fact, I was sweating in all sorts of places.

"Just look ahead. Don't look down. You can do this," said a familiar voice. I looked down and into the brown eyes of John Gowdy. He smiled up at me, and I couldn't help but smile back.

"I'll talk you through it."

"Just talk to me about anything but this." I took a step forward.

"Let's compare favorite restaurants."

"Perfect!"

"Let's start with the best pizza."

"Margarita's in Brooklyn. Hands down the best."

"No way! Alfonso's on Staten Island has the lightest crust in the city."

"But Margarita's has a coal-fired oven. You haven't lived until you've had coal-fired pizza."

On went the conversation, and on went little old me over one ropes course obstacle after another. Pizza led us to pasta, which led us to noodle shops, which led us to dim sum, which somehow led us to pancakes, and by the time I had thoroughly defended my favorite diner, The UN ("What a tourist trap," proclaimed John), I had reached The Plank.

It's very telling that a conversation about food could easily distract me from my impending death.

"Okay, Jill," said Carol, trying to wrest control back from John. "Jim has the shot framed up. I want you to walk out to the edge and hold up your arms like you're embracing the abyss."

Poor choice of words. I froze. The calm blue water of the harbor was below me—like a mile below me, or so it seemed. If I fell, it wouldn't be thirty feet to the deck, which I probably would survive with some sort of permanent disfigurement. No, if I fell from The Plank, I would plummet I didn't know how many feet until I smashed against that water like it was concrete. I would die.

"We haven't talked about Greek food." John's voice broke through the vision of my demise looping through my brain.

"Uncle Nick's in Astoria. Don't argue. I'm right."

John laughed, a deep, warm sound, and I felt my shoulders relax a smidge.

"I wouldn't dare argue. Uncle Nick's is legendary. When we're back in the city, we should go there for dinner sometime."

Dinner at Uncle Nick's. My last, horrible date had been at Uncle Nick's, right before my dinner companion turned up dead. I hadn't been back to my favorite Greek restaurant since then, and I missed it.

"I miss the baklava," I said aloud.

John chuckled. "We'll have baklava. Don't you worry."

"Embrace the baklava, Jill. Embrace it!" cried Carol.

Thinking only of flaky, buttery pastry, pistachios, and honey, I stepped to the end of The Plank and raised my arms.

I heard a crack, and then I dropped.

CHAPTER 12

Okay, so I only dropped two feet before the safety cord caught me, but they were the longest and most terrifying two feet of my life since I was dangling hundreds of feet above the harbor.

I was also screaming.

When we reviewed the video later (so glad cameraman Jim was there to catch me at my lowest), it was only a matter of minutes before the ropes course staff reached me and hauled me back onto what was left of The Plank, but it seemed like forever.

Now I was seated once again in Aton's living room, but I was drinking something a lot stronger than cucumber water. The shaking had faded into mere trembling thanks to the scotch, courtesy of Joseph, and John's strong arm around my shoulders. Aton was there along with Carol, Jim, and one of the ropes course technicians.

I hated that all these people were seeing me reduced to Aunt Pittypat having the vapors, but there was a reason I'd invited Liz along to do all the scary stuff. I was not a thrill seeker.

"It's troubling," pronounced Aton. He was staring at a wet board dripping onto his coffee table. Since we were docked, crew members had been dispatched to retrieve the piece of The Plank that had fallen into the harbor.

"To say the least," growled John. "That's a clean cut. Someone sawed almost completely through that board. There's no other explanation."

The board in question did show a very clean cut, leaving only an inch attached to the rest of the piece. It must have been sawn from the bottom to hide the cut, not an easy task, but someone with a lot of courage and a hand saw could have done it.

"How long do you think it has been like this?" asked Aton calmly.

"There's no telling," said the technician. "Days? Not everyone who does the ropes course chooses to walk The Plank. A lot of people are too frightened."

"So, it could have been a manufacturing error," said Aton.

John spluttered, and I froze. A manufacturing error? Thank goodness for Carol the Carefree Cruiser.

"Bilgewater! You lost all the lobsters. Now someone has tampered with your ropes course. You need to consider carefully that someone may have it in for you and your cruise line. This is a cutthroat business, and you're trying to do something new. Do you think Mardi Gras Cruises or Regal Aegean wouldn't stoop to a little sabotage? Think again."

"Yeah," added Jim astutely.

"This is all conjecture!" Aton snapped. "Without evidence, I refuse to entertain the idea of sabotage. We must look at this scientifically. Without evidence to prove that hypothesis, it is simply that, a hypothesis."

He turned to his assistant.

"Joseph, please review all the CCTV footage of the ropes course."

"I've already started, sir. The cameras don't cover The Plank, but they do cover the start of the course. I'll look for anyone there after hours and carrying a tool of some sort."

"Excellent. If we find evidence of sabotage, we'll address it. Until then, it's business as usual."

I felt John stiffen beside me, and I laid a hand on his arm to stop him before he said what we were all thinking—that Aton was an ostrich with his head in the sand.

"Well, I don't think we should ask Jill to do any more extreme sports. The footage was barely usable even before The Plank gave way," remarked Carol.

"That's disappointing," frowned Aton, and he looked at me critically. "Hoss Buckworth led me to believe you took risks to help your clients."

I gripped John's arm even harder because I could feel the anger rising within him.

I smiled at Aton in the best PR fashion.

"Most of the risks you have to take in public relations don't involve danger to life and limb." I added a chuckle, trying to lighten the mood.

"I guess that depends on who your client is." With that, Aton swept from the room, green silk pajamas flapping, with Joseph in his wake.

"I'm getting off this ship," I said before the thought was fully formed. I stood up so fast the room spun, but I didn't let it stop me. I turned to John. "You coming?"

"Absolutely."

CHAPTER 13

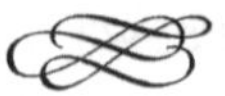

$\mathcal{T}$hirty minutes later, we were strolling down the pier toward the city of Nassau. It felt so good to be in a new place and away from the ship of fools. Still, I was having a hard time letting go of the events of the morning. Honestly, how could Aton Faraday be such a nincompoop? The way he dismissed the idea of sabotage like it couldn't possibly happen to him was just silly. Was complete denial a symptom of being a futurist? Were folks like Aton constantly looking to the future to avoid the realities of today? And how could I be expected to protect the reputation of someone who was constantly making poor decisions? If I wanted to do that, I'd move to Hollywood or Washington, DC.

"If you'd like to be alone to have that conversation with yourself, I can make myself scarce." John Gowdy's voice startled me, and I realized how rude I was carrying on a conversation in my head and completely ignoring him.

"I'm sorry, John. I'm just so mad I could spit."

"Go ahead." He gestured to the aqua water of the harbor.

"If Aton Faraday were in that water, I just might."

"He needs taking down a peg."

I laughed because I remembered saying the same thing about Casimir Koblinsky.

"How would you do it?" I asked.

"Well, embarrassing himself with his jet suit wasn't enough to humble him, so it would probably take something epic, or more painful."

"I don't know how you get more epic than falling out of the sky, but if I get any good ideas, I'll let you know."

We arrived at the end of the pier and the beginning of the shopping district that catered to cruise passengers. We paused at a street vendor who was selling Switcha, a Bahamian lemon-limeade, and while we were waiting for our drinks, Robin and Susan Shelby strolled by. He looked like something out of the PGA with navy blue and pink plaid pants, a belt with whales all over it, and a pink polo shirt. She complemented him nicely in a pink peasant skirt and white peasant blouse. A hibiscus blossom was arranged artfully behind one ear.

I threw up a little in my mouth.

"I know they're newlyweds…," I began.

"But there's something altogether too perfect about the Shelbys?" John finished.

"Let me just say that I would never date a man who wore pink whales on his belt."

"I'm very glad to hear it." He gave me a look. You know the kind. I crossed my arms and gave him a different sort of look back.

"Okay. I get it. Just friends," he gave in, sort of. "But someday when we're done building empires, you might think differently."

I knew that was quite possible, but it wouldn't do to let on. It would be like waving a red cape at a bull.

We continued down the row of shops. I'm usually a sucker for souvenirs, but I abstained from purchasing shell sculptures and vials of beach sand. I was holding out for the souvenir big leagues—the straw market.

John and I arrived at the straw market at the same time as the Shelbys. Robin nodded his hellos to us while Susan linked arms protectively with her husband and glared at me. A laugh bubbled up within me, but I covered it with a cough. As if anyone would have designs on a man in those pants!

Dismissing the Shelbys from further thought, we entered the straw market.

Behold! The mother lode!

Baskets, purses, hampers, bird cages—anything you could make by weaving straw was on sale. John cast a critical eye on the inventory.

"People buy this stuff?"

Because the place was packed with haggling tourists and vendors, I considered his question rhetorical. Besides, I had four friends to buy for. The Posse were all getting presents.

In the end, I opted for brightly colored straw purses decorated with palm trees, swimming dolphins, and "The Bahamas." They were garish and fun, and I couldn't wait to make my Posse carry them to dinner one night. I got one for me too. Solidarity in silliness.

John eyed my purchases skeptically.

"Your friends will like them?"

"They'll love them."

"Why?"

I just laughed.

We left the straw market and continued touring the shopping district, stopping for a lunch of delicious conch fritters. When we came out of the restaurant, who should we stumble upon but the Shelbys again. I waved to them, and Robin Shelby nodded back at me. I'm pretty sure his wife rolled her eyes. What had I ever done to her? I turned to say something to John, but he took the words right out of my mouth.

"Wanna get out of here?"

John hailed a taxi and took me on a driving tour of the island. We started on the coast and made a sort of spiral inward, passing the stunning beaches and resort complexes favored by tourists and the modest neighborhoods inhabited by locals. I was impressed by the variety of sights on the island. For a small piece of land, there was so much to look at. Eventually, we began to climb until the cab pulled up in front of an old stone fort. A historical marker identified the structure as Fort Fincastle, built by Lord Dunmore in the late eighteenth century.

"Not this guy again," I muttered. We Virginians had a hate-hate relationship with Lord Dunmore, who had been the governor of Virginia during the Revolutionary War. Eventually, he fled the colony.

The fort, however, was a charming little example of such edifices. I wasn't surprised to learn from a tour guide that no shots had ever been fired from any of Lord Dunmore's forts, but the views of Nassau were outstanding. I could even see The Lady Luck down at the pier.

"I didn't realize we were so close to the harbor," I said.

"That's why we ended our tour here." John sounded a bit proud of himself. "We can walk to the ship in about twenty minutes."

After taking in the views and listening to the tour guide describe Lord Dunmore's bewildering term as governor of the Bahamas (I wasn't surprised in the least), John led me to the top of a steep but beautiful staircase that descended into Nassau city and toward the harbor.

"This is the Queen's Staircase," he explained. "It was carved by slaves as an escape route from the fort."

Unnecessary forts and escape routes. Lord Dunmore had been more than a little paranoid, but that paranoia had led to some beautiful sights for modern-day tourists. The staircase was green and gray with moss and the pervasive mold of the tropics, giving it a weathered, romantic look. It was also shady as it descended into a canyon of limestone walls on either side populated with tropical plants. The romantic atmosphere certainly attracted couples, who were walking up and down the staircase and promenading through the limestone canyon hand in hand. Therefore, it wasn't surprising when we ran into the Shelbys—again.

They were coming up the Queen's Staircase as we were descending, and I knew the moment Susan Shelby spotted us. She tensed and grabbed Robin's arm.

"Darling," she cooed over loudly. "It's so steep! I'm afraid I'll fall." Then she upped the ante and threw both arms around his waist, which knocked him off balance. For one awful moment, I thought they would tumble down the staircase, but he recovered.

"We will fall, my flower, if you hold me too tightly." His voice was strained.

"Can I help it that I love you so much, my protector!" Susan was talking to him, but she was glancing at me.

I felt the conch fritters coming back for a visit.

"Quick!" I whispered to John. "Hold my hand."

"Happy to, but can I ask why?"

"Susan Shelby thinks I have designs on her new husband, which is ridiculous. I'm sick of her dagger eyes stabbing me whenever I run into her. Just hold my hand so she thinks we like each other."

"I'll do you one better." And then he swept me into his embrace and kissed me but good.

I was of two minds about the kiss. One mind was fighting vertigo from being swept off my feet on a tall, steep staircase. Or was it from the kiss? No, it was the stairs. Definitely the stairs.

The other mind was thinking that if Susan Shelby thought I

had designs on her no-fashion-sense new husband after witnessing this epic kiss, then she should have her head examined.

When the kiss ended, Susan Shelby was still looking at me, staring to be precise, and so was her husband. Message received! I smiled at John and acted completely smitten.

"Well, that did the trick," I whispered. "Let's keep smiling at each other like we're in love. Did you see their faces? They totally bought it!"

He smirked. "Really? That's it? I give you my most romantic lip-lock and that's all the reaction I get? You were supposed to fall madly in love with me, throw away your career plans, and marry me. Jeez! I guess I'll have to try harder."

The laugh that bubbled up out of me echoed off the limestone walls, filling the canyon. I couldn't stop. The situation was so ludicrous and the Shelbys' reaction was so strong that I was just tickled to death. John joined me in a good guffaw. He pulled me into a hug, and we held each other and laughed. At some point, the Shelbys swept past us and continued up the stairs. When the laughs turned to hiccups, we started to pick our way down the stairs again.

"But seriously," said John. "How was my technique? Three out of five stars? Four? Help a guy out!"

And the laughing started all over again.

By the time we returned to the ship, I was happier than I'd been since we departed New York. Sunshine, new vistas, shopping, and good company had worked wonders.

My fabulous mood didn't last. Upon boarding the ship, we were intercepted by Joseph.

"Ms. Cooksey, you have to talk to Mr. Faraday. Maybe he'll listen to you." Normally calm, cool, and collected, Joseph was positively frantic.

"Listen to me about what?"

"There have been more incidents while you were ashore,

but Mr. Faraday refuses to see that someone is sabotaging the ship. Instead, he's blaming the crew, specifically the technicians involved in the extreme sports."

"Wait! What happened?"

"The hoist for the bungee jump jammed, and a passenger was stuck dangling upside down for thirty minutes. Then several of the footholds on the climbing wall separated from the wall itself. It's a good thing the climbers are belayed. No one fell, and it was more annoying than anything else, but it all contributes to reputation, doesn't it?"

"And what does Aton say about all of it?" asked John.

"He says they're just mechanical failures caused by improper maintenance and supervision. He did shut down all the extreme sports temporarily. Now he's gathered all the technicians in the theater, and he's screaming at them. I think he's lost it."

With Joseph in the lead, we raced to the theater. The doors were closed, but we could hear raised voices nonetheless. We cracked a door and surveyed the carnage.

"I want thrice daily safety checks! Morning checks alone aren't good enough. Client use causes wear and tear. We must be vigilant! Yes, our guests are taking risks, but they need to feel confident in the experiences we provide. They shouldn't be taking foolish risks, and if you don't maintain the equipment properly, they will be! Our mission is to help people become more comfortable with risk. Only then will we change society fundamentally! We have a sacred mission to advance humankind! Who's with me?"

Only the crickets were with him. The silence in the face of what Aton must have believed was a rousing pep talk infuriated him. I could tell because his face turned purple.

"If you're not with me, then you're against me! I don't think you understand what I'm trying to do here. Just try, make an attempt, to have just the tiniest bit of vision. Will you? Or is this just a job to you? Are you just here for the money? Because I don't have time for losers like that!"

Okay, time to step in.

I swung the door wide and marched into the theater in an attempt to distract Aton from verbally abusing his staff. It worked, maybe too well.

"Oh yes, Ms. Cooksey. Our PR dynamo." Aton's words dripped with sarcasm as he descended from the stage. "Thrice. Daily. Checks," he told the technicians without breaking eye contact with me. "You're dismissed."

The techs exited the theater like warthogs being chased by a lioness.

Aton leaned against the stage, crossed one sandaled foot over the other, and folded his arms across his chest as John, Joseph, and I made our way to the front of the theater.

"Today was quite a day. We could have used some good PR today. It's a pity you weren't here to help. I hope you enjoyed your tour of Nassau."

"Now wait just a minute." John spoke up before I could. "Jill put her life on the line earlier today, or have you forgotten that she almost fell from the ropes course?"

"Hardly." Aton rolled his big green alien eyes. "The safety cord caught her, exactly as it's supposed to."

"But what if the safety cord had been sabotaged like every-thing else?"

"Nothing has been sabotaged!" roared Aton.

"How did Carol's video turn out?" I inserted myself into the conflict with a businesslike tone, hoping to forestall further shouting.

"Carol backed out after the bungee jumping incident. With so many others posting videos about the problems, she said she would lose her credibility if she posted *propaganda* about the ship. Her word, not mine."

She had a point. Carol the Carefree Cruiser was a trusted

name in the industry, and I couldn't fault her for not wanting to throw away that reputation for a few dollars. Okay, probably a lot of dollars, but reputation is priceless.

"Which is why we needed a PR professional here today." Aton's anger had shifted to pouting.

John opened his mouth to defend me again, but I squeezed his arm. I could take care of myself. Plus, I had a lot of experience in dealing with pouty, butt-hurt, guilt-tripping clients. I wanted to remind him that he hadn't hired me yet and that this was a fact-finding mission, but that kind of reasoning doesn't work with an emotional three-year-old, which is what some clients become when things don't go their way.

The problem was that PR couldn't solve a sabotage problem. No amount of cheerleading could cover up the work of a saboteur, much less stop it.

"As I see it," I began calmly and sat down in the front row. Now Aton was looming over me, which would make him feel good. It did not affect me. I had been loomed over by far more compelling characters than this little alien man. "We have two issues. One is bad publicity from all these cruising vloggers. The other is the safety issues and other problems that have occurred on the ship so far." I avoided the word sabotage because it sent Aton into apoplexy. "PR can help one of these situations, but it can't help the other."

Aton chewed on that for a moment before conceding the point. "True."

"You and your crew have to prevent any future problems."

"I've already spoken to the crew."

Indeed, he had.

"Then you have that situation well in hand." I was using my calmest voice, the one I reserved for irate clients and my mother. "I have an idea to fix the vlogging problem, as well, and it won't cost you a cent."

"You have my attention, Ms. Cooksey."

"And mine," said John as he finally took a seat.

"The solution is simple. Tomorrow, Aton, you will engage in ALL the extreme sports on the ship in front of all the passengers."

The hint of a smile appeared at the corners of Aton's mouth and slowly grew into an alien grin. Shudder.

"I will show everyone how confident I am in the safety of the ship," began Aton.

"And all the YouTubers will post videos of you," continued John.

"Thus, changing the narrative from 'ship of danger' to 'thrill-seeking futurist in action,'" I finished.

Aton rubbed his hands together and looked exactly like a Bond villain. Why did my clients have to be so larger-than-life?

"Excellent!" Aton bounced up and down, just like an excited child. "Joseph! We must monitor the technicians. Everything must be in perfect working order tomorrow. No one sleeps tonight!" He swept from the theater with Joseph in his wake, and the beleaguered assistant shot me a grateful smile.

"Well done, Jill. You certainly know how to handle—"

"Toddlers? Yes, I'm great with the immature set."

CHAPTER 14

$\mathcal{I}$ couldn't wait to get back to my cabin and collapse on my bed. I just needed a few minutes of quiet time to order my thoughts before dinner. John wouldn't be joining us that evening because he needed to work. (Didn't he understand the definition of vacation?) Still, I knew Gunnar would be there, and I would have to use company manners.

Liz was typing on my laptop when I entered the cabin.

"Oh good. You're back. I'm typing up some notes for you about the shark excursion. Maybe it will help with your presentation."

Good old Liz. I couldn't help but smile.

"You should have been there. It was incredible. Reef sharks are quite affectionate."

I had my doubts. Liz, who always looked for the good in everyone, would probably say the same thing about a Great White.

"Tiger sharks, not so much." Maybe I was wrong.

Liz described her shark encounters, which were impressive and would certainly make great copy, while I relaxed on my bed.

"Can we do something different for dinner?" she suddenly asked.

"Sure thing. We have seventeen restaurants to choose from. What does Gunnar suggest?"

"He won't be joining us. He has to work. Aton has some special project going on tonight. Will John be joining us?" She wiggled her eyebrows.

"No, he has to work too."

"Girls' night!" she shrieked. Then she grabbed my arm and hauled me off the bed. "Let's get ready!"

"And here I thought you'd be all mopey because Gunnar has to work."

"It gives him a chance to miss me," she countered pragmatically as she rifled her tiny closet.

An hour later, we were ready. We decided on a more casual approach for girls' night. Liz wore cropped yoga pants and a flowing white shirt. I opted for a pair of vintage navy blue bell-bottom sailor pants that our friend Kate had given me for my birthday and a white blouse with a keyhole neckline. I added a little extra curl to my hair and some red lipstick. It was a fun outfit.

We settled on seafood for dinner and made our way to the restaurant, The Old Chef and the Sea. The play on the Hemingway title didn't work at all, in my opinion, but the place was packed. Even so, we had no trouble getting a table. Aton, or probably Joseph, had alerted every establishment on the ship to who we were.

Feasting on crab, Liz and I finally had a heart-to-heart. I caught her up on all the events of the day and left nothing out. Liz, of course, focused on the least important part.

"So the kiss did nothing for you?"

I rolled my eyes. Saboteurs were wreaking havoc, but by all means, let's talk about kissing.

"I wouldn't say it did nothing. It was a good kiss."

Liz narrowed her eyes.

"The fact that you can speak about it so casually means it did nothing for you. Darn that Mike McCall! He ruined you for other perfectly wonderful men."

Had he? I didn't think so. I was focusing on my career. That's why I wasn't interested in John, and I told Liz so.

"I think you're immersing yourself in work to avoid your feelings, and it isn't healthy. When we get back to New York, I think you should see my therapist."

"What? Liz, I'm choosing to focus on my job and being successful. I hardly think my attempts to be a responsible adult warrant therapy."

"It all comes down to cause. If you're just trying to be responsible, then good for you. If you're avoiding issues, then you need help. Only a therapist can help you discover the truth." She punctuated her remarks by tearing open a crab leg.

"Liz, I'm seeing a different side of you on this trip."

After stuffing ourselves with all the fruits of the sea, dessert was out of the question, so we took off exploring.

We soon found ourselves at the casino. Liz and I wandered through a forest of slot machines. The blinking, flashing, chiming, and, in some cases, yelling machines towered over the patrons who were busy pushing the button to spin the machine over and over again. There were no levers to pull and no coins pouring out of the machines with a satisfying *clinkety-clink*. While the machines would take bills in a variety of denominations, supplied by ample ATMs along the perimeter of the room, the payout was simply a printed ticket. I guess the flashing lights and chimes were supposed to supply the dopamine hit, but without the coins rattling in the trays, I felt that some of the thrills had been lost.

We emerged from the slots into a wide room chock-a-block with gaming tables. On the back wall, flanked by more ATMs, was the casino cage, where players would turn in their slot machine tickets for a payout or hand over cash for chips. Poker, blackjack, and baccarat games were going on all around us. Servers glided from table to table handing out cocktails. I noticed a petite server struggling under the weight of a tray of pints of beer. I followed her with my eyes until she stopped at a blackjack table populated by ladies and gentlemen in blue soccer jerseys. One of the men jumped up to help distribute the beer, and I recognized Roddy from the night before. On the seat next to him was The Legend.

I led Liz over to the blackjack table and introduced her to my Scottish friends. In no time, someone was pressing a beer into her hand.

"Oh. No, thank you. I'm not fond of beer."

Despite the stunned silence and looks of confusion, Liz handed the beer back to its owner. Then she smiled gently at everyone, and the moment passed. Now why hadn't I tried that?

You're a people pleaser, Jill, and you know it.

"Well lass, it looks like you're just plain bad luck," said The Legend.

That's not something you want to hear in a casino.

"It's Kenney *Rrrodgers*, ye ken."

Yes, I kenned Kenney.

"Whenever you show up, he disappears!"

"What are you talking about?"

As it turned out, according to The Legend, Kenney Rodgers was not just a singer. He was also a blackjack dealer.

"He was here a second ago," said one of the Scots.

"He wasn't really running away from me, twas he?" I had never even seen the guy. "Well, maybe if I leave, he'll come back," I joked.

"Here's hoping!" said The Legend. "I was on a winning streak."

Liz and I said our goodbyes and continued through the

casino. We passed a table for five-card draw, and for a moment I was sorely tempted. It had been a while since I'd played poker, but I was good at it, thanks to my dad. Part of me wanted to show Liz what I could do, but the responsible part stopped me at the last second. No sense in wasting money. I was here to make more money, not to lose it.

We seemed to meander forever before we reached the exit on the other side of the casino. Our wandering eventually led us to the music and entertainment deck. The distinctive sounds of banjo and fiddle emanated from the country bar where tonight a trio of bluegrass musicians was holding forth. Fingers and bows flew as they executed the "Orange Blossom Special," so we popped in and stayed for their set before moving on.

Back on the fake street, I heard the sounds of trombone, trumpet, snare drum, and bass. I love Big Band music, so I grabbed Liz's hand and dragged her toward the sound. The musical breadcrumbs led us to a large club with a stage big enough for a full big band and a huge dance floor. The band was playing the Glenn Miller classic "Sing, Sing, Sing," and they were wailing.

A couple was just getting up from a table near the dance floor, and we raced to beat anyone else to it. As we collapsed in the padded armchairs flanking our table, Cindy Helms emerged on stage wearing a forties-era evening gown in red, white, and blue and stepped to the mic.

"Let's give a warm welcome to the Steinway Street Swingers!"

A troop of swing dancers skipped onto the dance floor and started gyrating, pivoting, turning, stepping, and flipping. The ladies wore vintage summer dresses, while the men were dressed as World War II-era soldiers, sailors, and civilians.

One particularly agile dancer sported a teal green zoot suit and the most luxuriant black hair, short on the sides and longer on the top. It practically glimmered in the lights. He turned and I caught a glimpse of his profile.

Suffering Steinway Street! It was my pal Jorge—the proprietor of the Guada-la-car-a car service of Astoria, Queens!

What the heck was my favorite gypsy cab driver doing swing dancing aboard The Lady Luck?

As the song came to an end, all of the gals jumped into their partners' arms and finished with a flourish. Then, as the band struck up "Pennsylvania 6-5000," they trooped out into the audience to find victims, I mean volunteers, they could teach to dance.

Jorge nearly walked past me before he did an honest-to-goodness double take, Looney Tunes style. I burst out laughing, and before I knew it, he was dragging me out of my chair and onto the dance floor where he eyed my vintage bellbottoms.

"Well, you look the part, but can you dance it?"

He took my right hand in his left, planted his other hand on my waist, and began the basic triple step, triple step, rock step of swing dancing. Luckily, I knew that much thanks to my friend Kate, the purveyor of my vintage outfit and lover of all things Forties.

Jorge smiled his approval and, after the next rock step, sent me out under his arm. When I passed that test, he upped the ante again, and I held my own until he tried to teach me the tandem Charleston. I had no idea what we were doing, and we almost ended up on the floor. With infinite patience, he slowly took me through the steps, and soon we were dancing in tandem with finesse.

Jorge dipped me as the song ended, and the band moved quickly into "String of Pearls," a foxtrot, as I'd learned in cotillion, which I could do in my sleep. The slower song allowed for conversation, and boy did I have questions. So did Jorge.

"*Caray!* What the heck are you doing here? I see Liz is here too. Where are the rest of them?"

"Back in New York. Jorge, how on earth did you come to be swing dancing on a cruise ship?"

He laughed, and his eyes twinkled.

"Wouldn't you like to know."

"Tell me!"

He explained that he was in a swing dance club back in Queens, and they had been hired for the inaugural cruise. Then he asked me what I was doing there, and I explained my mission to secure Seaswept Cruises as a client.

"Must be hard to get good publicity for a ship where bad things keep happening," he said.

"You have no idea."

"I thought maybe you were here on a romantic getaway." Jorge wagged his eyebrows at me. "What happened to that reporter?"

"We broke up."

"*Qué va*! I thought you two were headed straight down the aisle."

I didn't know what to say to that. I was shocked that Mike and I had seemed like a sure thing to Jorge, whom I considered one of the shrewdest people I knew.

"I guess it just wasn't meant to be."

"Who broke up with who?" he asked, arching an eyebrow.

"Well, we didn't actually break up. One day he just wasn't there anymore."

Jorge was shocked

"I didn't take him for a low-down dirty dog," is what I thought he said, but the last part was in Spanish.

"I'm not sure what that meant, but it didn't sound flattering."

"It wasn't. So, you seeing anybody new?"

"No, and I'm not going to either."

He looked skeptical. More to the point, he rolled his eyes at me.

"Jorge, I turned over a new leaf. I am simply focused on my career. I'm going to be a vice president in a PR firm by the time I'm thirty if it kills me. That's what I'm all about these days—work, promotion, getting my life together."

"Jill," said Jorge with infinite, annoying patience, "don't you think finding someone to spend the rest of your life with is part of getting your life together?"

Now it was my turn to roll my eyes.

"Jorge, are you a romantic?" That made him laugh.

"One hundred percent! When I find my angel, I'm going to hold on to her and never let her go."

"That's so sweet!"

"Forget sweet. It's true. She's out there, and I'll find her. Great outfit, by the way. Very appropriate for swing dancing."

"I can't take the credit. My friend Kate loves her vintage wear. That's some zoot suit you're wearing. It looks fabulous on you by the way."

"I know," he deadpanned. Then his smile cracked his face wide open. "In all seriousness, Jill, you need to keep your heart open. You never know who's going to show up. If your heart is closed and the right person comes along, you could miss your chance."

I sighed.

"I know it's hard," said my friend. "But all the things worth anything in life are hard."

"String of Pearls" ended, and the band kicked into another fast number. Jorge had to go teach someone new to dance, so we said our goodbyes, exchanged room numbers, and promised to meet for breakfast in the morning.

I looked around to find Liz, and I found her all right—in the arms of Lieutenant Beowulf. He must've finished all his tasks for Aton's big extreme sports showcase the next day because now he was busy swinging and twirling my friend, and she looked like she was having the time of her life. Not wanting to interrupt and also not wanting to watch the romance in action, I quietly gathered my things and left.

CHAPTER 15

Fresh air. That's what I needed. Lots and lots of fresh, salty air that would sting my face and nostrils and maybe provide an excuse for the pressure behind my eyes. I jumped into the elevator and headed up to the promenade deck. When I emerged into the fresh air, the scent of the sea was delicious. It filled my senses. I could smell it. I could taste it.

I strolled and processed what Jorge had said to me. I knew I was having trouble opening my heart to somebody else. Not only was I still slightly hung up on my ex-boyfriend, but I also didn't trust myself. I had made a horrible mistake in judgment. How could I know that I wouldn't do it again, that I wouldn't pick the wrong guy? Clearly, my instincts weren't great. Had there been red flags? I couldn't think of any. Mike and I had played on opposing teams, but in the end, we had joined forces. I couldn't find a single red flag, but there was a huge stop sign —his disappearance. What on earth had happened? I realized that I needed to know even though I'd been avoiding it. I had told myself that he was dead to me and that it didn't matter why he had vanished from my life.

But it did matter. I needed to know what was wrong with me. How was I inadequate? Mike had moved on to someone else, the woman from Central Park, so his heart was open. It just wasn't open to me. Why had it closed? What had I done wrong?

I suddenly, fervently needed to know.

While I was ruminating, I had walked the entire length of the boat and was approaching the stern when movement caught my eye. I looked up and beheld an interesting sight— Mira Koblinsky wrapped in the arms of Joseph, Aton Faraday's personal assistant. Not only were his arms wrapped around her, but his lips seemed intent on devouring her face. The sight brought me up short.

Then Joseph pulled away and looked at Mira with such adoration that my knees nearly buckled. Moonlight bathed the lovers in liquid silver. I stopped breathing. Ever so gently, Joseph caressed her face, and she smiled as she gazed adoringly into his eyes.

I took off running, or as close to running as you can do in heels. Luckily, after my feet hit the deck a few times, I started to breathe again. I may have passed a few people on my mad dash from stern to bow, but I don't remember them. My thoughts were swirling. *Open hearts. Moonlight. Tender kisses. A staircase. A subway station. No. No subway stations. Tropical breezes. The straw market. Brown hair and brown eyes.*

The collision came as I reached the bow, and if John hadn't been so strong, I might not have stopped in time, and I might have carried him with me over the railing.

"Hey, hey. What's the matter?"

Heart pounding and thoughts racing, I looked up into his soft brown eyes and the chaos quieted, not completely, but enough. I kissed him and twined my arms around his neck and kissed him some more.

When our lips parted a considerable time later, John held

me and peppered my face with feather-soft kisses. Then he sighed happily.

"Does this mean—"

"I don't know what it means. I don't. Please don't ask me to figure it out right now."

His lips brushed mine again, ever so gently. "I think I know what it means. It means you're taking a chance. And I'm okay with that."

I looked into his eyes and saw he was more than okay. Desire smoldered in those soft brown orbs, and those sweet, safe windows to his soul suddenly seemed a little bit dangerous. Deliciously so. My breath caught, and he took it for the invitation that, I'll admit, it was. When our lips met again (more like crashed, smashed, collided), it was with a hunger that neither of us knew existed. There in the moonlight, two people welcomed passion back into their lives.

It was quite some time before we could tear ourselves away from each other. I would try, and he would pull me back into his embrace. Or he would try, and my lips would find his yet again.

Heaven.

We did finally part, although we held hands for dear life, and John walked me back to my cabin in silence, although the soft looks and goofy smiles we gave each other were a different form of conversation.

At my door, he safely and chastely kissed me on the forehead.

"See you tomorrow."

And then he was gone.

When I entered the cabin, Liz took one look at my face, and we both squealed like we were thirteen.

CHAPTER 16

"*J*orge!"

I hadn't told Liz that Jorge was meeting us for breakfast. She was delighted to see him and gave him a huge hug, which made him grin. His presence was reassuring, and I felt like we had another Posse member there with us. Over omelets and waffles, Liz and I eagerly filled him in on everything that had happened since we'd set sail, from Caz's death to the most recent sabotage. Thanks to scuttlebutt, Jorge already knew most of it, but the behind-the-scenes details about Aton Faraday's reactions fascinated the cabbie.

"Are you sure you want him for a client, Jill?" he asked.

Was I?

"Because he sounds like a wacko." Jorge forked up some eggs and chewed thoughtfully.

"Jorge is right, Jill," agreed Liz. "I know you want to make vice president, but Aton Faraday might be too high a price."

I sighed because my friends were only echoing my thoughts.

"Well, we have to remember this cruise line is brand-new.

There's a lot of stress associated with the inaugural cruise. Hopefully, things will calm down."

Liz and Jorge eyed each other skeptically, but I tried to ignore it. Maybe Aton Faraday wasn't the only one in denial.

The extreme sports extravaganza was set to begin at nine a.m. After breakfast, we made our way to the climbing wall where Aton would start his demonstration. A sizable crowd had turned up because he was, after all, a bit of a celebrity, and I was happy to see that most of them were holding their cell phones. Why wouldn't they be? One day cell phones would be implanted in us somewhere.

Aton was there at the base of the climbing wall. Instead of his green silk pajamas, I was happy to see that he wore cargo shorts, a Seaswept Cruises T-shirt, sunglasses, and climbing shoes. At nine o'clock on the dot, he grasped the first handholds on the wall and began his ascent. I soon realized that Aton didn't just talk the talk. His movements were unhurried and looked effortless even though they couldn't have been. Aton chose the most difficult path up the wall with the least amount of support. Toward the end, the wall curved to make a ledge, and he hung on by his fingertips and toes. The crowd held its collective breath until Aton made it to the edge and grasped the ledge. He hung there for a moment, playing with the gasping crowd before he pulled himself over the edge with ease and stood up. After an adjustment in ropes, he was ready to rappel back down the wall. Without any fear, Aton leaped backward into nothingness and, in a trice, descended to the ground in front of us. His landing was perfect. Several people clapped but, more importantly, lots of people were taking videos.

From there, Aton moved on to the ropes course. The plank had been repaired, and he clambered up the rope ladders and put on the harness with alacrity. He exuded confidence as he moved from challenge to challenge. When he got out onto the plank, he stood on the edge, and instead of simply holding out his arms and embracing the abyss, he turned to face the spectators on the ship and leaned back so that his safety rope was fully taut and he was leaning out at an angle over the ocean. It was a bold move that spoke of complete trust in the apparatus, and I offered a prayer that there had been no sabotage and that Aton Faraday would live through the morning.

After folks had taken plenty of pictures and video, Aton righted himself and finished the ropes course in no time at all. From there, he moved on to bungee jumping. He sprinted up the stairs of the bungee tower like a kid at an amusement park, eager for the next thrill ride. When he got to the top, it took a few minutes to secure and check all the harnesses and things that were supposed to keep him from dying. When they were done, Aton turned and looked at the now huge crowd that was watching and videoing, their cell phones held above their heads to capture this moment (because they were never going to be able to find a video of it on the internet).

Aton saluted everyone and then executed a graceful swan dive off the platform head first toward the open sea. I watched, biting my nails, as the bungee cord caught and stretched, and Aton, I swear, came a hair's breadth from actually touching the water before he bounded back up. Never once did a sound escape his lips, not even a gasp. He looked completely nonchalant as if this was something he did every single day of his life. Eventually, he stopped bouncing up and down, the cord was hauled to the top, and Aton was retrieved. He turned to the audience below and bowed. The crowd went wild. Everyone clapped, whistled, and hooted their enthusiasm.

Bungee jumping was followed by zip lining, trapeze, and the sky-diving simulator. The crowd grew at each stop and cheered as Aton demonstrated his mastery of all these skills— and the safety of the equipment.

When he had exhausted all the dry activities, he changed

into board shorts with his T-shirt and caught a wave at the surf machine. A strong surfer, he stayed on the board almost indefinitely, executing some tricks. Eventually, as if he'd become bored with it, he hurled himself off the surfboard into the waves, slid down an incline, and glided into a pool below. When he emerged from the water, the enormous crowd applauded him, and Joseph ran up to him with a towel. Aton then spent some time talking to the spectators, making his way through the crowd, shaking hands, and being an ambassador for the cruise line. I had to admit he had done a spectacular job. The narrative would be thoroughly changed, and the trust was now completely restored.

I made sure that Aton's photographer had taken fabulous shots of everything, and then Liz, Jorge, and I went back to our cabins to change our clothes for the next big adventure.

From what I'd read, a keelhaul was an ancient punishment of the navy whereby a sailor was dragged underneath the keel of the ship with a rope. Oftentimes, people didn't live through it. Aton Faraday's version of the keelhaul was completely and utterly different. Instead of being pulled under the ship, participants would be pulled by the ship on a huge inflatable raft capable of supporting hundreds of people. I stood at the stern and watched as the raft was set into the water and then inflated. I wasn't sure of the mechanism, and I made a mental note to ask Aton later for PR purposes. Before long, an enormous inflated raft the size of half a football field was floating behind the cruise ship. I could make out the cables that attached it from various points to the stern. The raft was longer than it was wide, and the end closest to the ship came to a point, like the bow of a boat, which I assumed would decrease drag and enable the ship to pull it at some sort of speed. In just a few minutes, I would be aboard that raft being towed by a cruise ship across the ocean. As extreme sports went, it seemed like my tamest option, and as Aton Faraday had pretty much commanded my presence, I couldn't say no. Liz and Jorge were more excited, and I tried to embrace their enthusiasm.

We made our way several decks down where small motor-boats were beginning to ferry passengers to the giant raft. Some were in their bathing suits while others wore completely normal clothes, minus shoes. Most were carrying cameras or cell phones. Indeed, the raft was so large it was hard to imagine anyone might get wet, although the wake of the ship was going to make for a bumpier ride than some of them imagined. Still, everyone had to wear a life jacket. Soon Liz, Jorge, and I were in a launch and speeding on our way. When we got to the raft, it was much thicker than it had appeared, about eight feet, and we climbed up rope ladders to reach the top. From there, I could see the surface of the raft was covered in handles we could hold onto should things get a little bumpy. I knew from Aton's explanation that the small craft would be traveling beside us just in case someone fell overboard and they had to retrieve them quickly. No problem.

Aton was already aboard, seated cross-legged near the bow of the raft, and we joined him there. I started to get excited. This could be pretty fun. I had been white water rafting before and liked it. I couldn't imagine this would be any more fright-ening than a class four rapid. It took a while to load all the interested passengers aboard the keelhaul raft, but in a little while it was full. Then the ship's engines started up, and the ship began to move forward. It took a moment before our tow ropes became taut, but when they did, the raft jerked and we all fell over laughing. The ship started to gain speed. The ride, which started smooth, suddenly became much more exciting as we came up against the wake of the ship. I found I was very glad for the handles. Some folks were trying to take cell phone video with one hand while holding on with the other and were finding it difficult. More than one phone slipped out of some-one's hands and skittered into the Caribbean. I felt bad for those folks. After the first couple of phones fell overboard, everyone else wisely kept them tucked away.

Suddenly, the raft seemed to be riding lower in the water.

"Oh, that's just water being forced up over the raft because of the ship's wake," proclaimed Aton. "It's nothing to worry about."

Before he had even finished speaking, the raft was further down in the water.

"I think we're sinking," I told Liz.

A moment later, one side of the raft was deflated, like it had just given up and rolled over to die. People were trying to hold on, but the raft sank out from under them and left them bobbing in their life jackets. Our side was sinking more slowly, but the writing was on the wall.

Aton pulled a walkie-talkie from who knows where and shouted into it. "Cut the cable and stop the ship!" Big mistake. Without the momentum of the ship, we sank quickly.

It only took a minute for the shark fins to appear.

Terror isn't just an emotion. It's a force, a substance. I know because I felt a wave of terror wash over the group, starting with those closest to the ominous fins. Terror is ice cold and suffocating.

"Stay together!" Aton yelled. "Get close!"

Panic-stricken passengers fought the water as they tried to get closer to each other to form a human bait ball. (Sorry. Poor choice of words.) To form something larger than the sharks. (Better?) When they could get no closer to each other, adults and children alike burst into tears of horror as they awaited their doom. Aton, Liz, Jorge, and I were on the outer edge of the group. Somehow we had come to a silent consensus to try to shield the other passengers. After all, none of us had kids. At that moment, the chances were good that we never would. A fin emerged about fifteen feet away from me and moved past.

"That's a tiger shark," said Liz calmly. How was she so calm?

Another larger fin appeared, started to move past, then turned suddenly and came within ten feet of us before turning again and swimming away.

"That was probably a bull shark." Liz's voice wobbled a little, and no wonder. *Jaws* fan that I was, I knew that the film was inspired by bull shark attacks.

Liz was teaching Jorge and me how to punch a shark in the nose to discourage it from snacking on us when the small boats arrived, complete with crew members armed with rifles. In the end, no one was hurt. People were terrified and angry, but the boats got everybody out of the water before anybody got bit by the sharks. Personally, I thought it a minor miracle.

CHAPTER 17

When we got back to the ship, I raced to change clothes and get to Aton's suite. As PR nightmares went, Aton was having one of the worst.

I found him with the captain, Cindy, Robin Shelby, and John. Joseph, of course, was in attendance. As I entered the suite, he lay a tablet in front of Aton.

"These are the photos taken by our divers."

Aton perused a photo, then swiped, perused, then swiped.

"As you can see," continued Joseph, "there are large rents in the raft but also smaller slashes. The dive team believes the larger rents are from smaller slashes that expanded due to the pressure when the raft was inflated."

"So it was sabotage," said Robin. I wondered what he was doing there.

"Or faulty manufacturing," countered Aton.

"It's not faulty manufacturing!" protested John. He rolled his eyes at Robin who in turn threw his hands in the air in disgust. So, John and Robin had teamed up to talk some sense into Aton. I knew John was interested in investing, but what was Robin's interest? Was he an investor too?

I was on the verge of offering a public relations perspective on the recent reenactment of the USS Indianapolis tragedy when Aton finally capitulated.

"Fine! It's sabotage! Are you happy?"

He staggered to a credenza and returned with a handful of papers that he tossed onto the coffee table. One fluttered to the floor at my feet. I picked it up and was surprised at the contents.

Sleep shall neither night nor day
Hang upon his penthouse lid.
He shall live a man forbid.
Weary sev'nnights, nine times nine,
Shall he dwindle, peak, and pine.
Though his bark cannot be lost,
Yet it shall be tempest-tossed.

"This is from *Macbeth*," I said incredulously.

"This is from *The Tempest*," said Robin as he held up another page.

"I believe this is *Twelfth Night*, or is it *Comedy of Errors*?" said John. He flipped the page around to show us.

"It's *Twelfth Night*," muttered Aton.

"What am I missing?" asked Captain Staggs.

"It's Shakespeare. All the passages are about ships either in peril or sinking," I explained.

"And they were sent to you?" asked Robin.

"Left for me," replied Aton. "The postal service was never involved, and we could never figure out how they arrived."

"A literary saboteur?" My mind struggled to make sense of it.

"But surely some verses from Shakespeare don't necessarily mean we're being sabotaged," protested the captain.

"The phone calls made it quite clear." Aton grimaced. "They were untraceable. From burner phones. Just in case I wasn't getting the message."

"So, you've known all along?" asked John. "Unbelievable!"

"What do they want?" Robin cut to the chase.

"A cut. Some money laundering. What else? It's a mob shakedown, pure and simple. From what I hear, it's standard when you own a casino." Aton's nose wrinkled in distaste.

"How were you supposed to deliver the money?" asked John. "Wire transfer? Bitcoin?"

Aton laughed bitterly. "Nothing so sophisticated. We were supposed to send it out in mattresses."

A bolt of inspiration struck. "Caz Koblinsky! He had the mattress contract for the cruise line. The shooting had something to do with this."

Aton sighed. "Caz had been doing the mob's dirty work for years in casinos and cruise ships around the world, using his mattress business to ferry cash. To his credit, he wanted out of the arrangement, so he came to me. He wanted to go legitimate for Mira's sake. I guess he had grown a conscience in his old age, but he wanted to leave her something clean. And he knew, with his poor health, he didn't have much time. Someone disagreed with his decision."

So, the infamous Casimir Koblinsky died because he was trying to do something noble for his daughter. That thought warmed me and gave me hope, but Captain Staggs didn't give me much time to dwell on it.

"This is outrageous!" she yelled. "How could you keep this from me? I never would have set sail."

"That's why!" roared Aton. Gone was the eccentric futurist, replaced by a simple man filled with rage. "I wasn't going to let these scumbags win! There's no place in the world for people like these. We can't allow them into our world. If we do, they'll take control. People like this always take control. I won't allow it. Never again!"

"This has happened to you before?" I asked.

Aton wouldn't look at me or anyone else for that matter. He

stared at the floor, but I had a feeling he was seeing something the rest of us couldn't. After a long moment, he snapped out of it and started snatching the papers out of our hands. When he'd gathered all of them, he handed them off to Joseph.

"Just forget about it." Aton's voice was steely. "I have it all under control."

As if to make him a liar, Gunnar burst into the suite.

"People are vomiting!" he cried. "All over the ship! It's probably Norovirus."

Everyone who was sitting stood up, and everyone standing sat down hard. My head was spinning. First hundreds of passengers in shark-infested waters. Now a Norovirus outbreak. The PR situation really couldn't get any worse. This was the moment I knew I didn't want Seaswept Cruises for a client.

"Initiate the Plague Ship Protocol," ordered Aton.

Oh yeah. We were done. No VP position could entice me to work for this ship of fools.

"Sir," began Captain Staggs, and I could tell it took everything in her to address him respectfully. "As we're so close to Isla de Suerte, perhaps we should skip to phase three and offload the passengers, quarantine the sick, and disinfect the ship." Isla de Suerte was the cruise line's private island and our next destination.

"Make it so," commanded Aton. I rolled my eyes because he was no Jean-Luc Picard, bald head notwithstanding.

Joseph then brought all of us surgical masks and bottles of hand sanitizer. "Every surface of the ship will be disinfected, and we'll only be serving prepackaged food and beverages until full disinfection has been accomplished. We should be at the island in a couple of hours."

"I want to inspect the situation firsthand," pronounced Aton. "Joseph, you're with me." He swept from the room with Joseph and the ship's officers in his wake.

"Is it my imagination, or is Aton becoming more imperious by the moment?" I asked of no one in particular.

Robin Shelby surprised me by answering. "He was always that way." I started to ask him to elaborate, but he cut me off with "I have to check on my wife." He hurried from the suite leaving John and me alone.

"I DON'T THINK you should invest in this cruise line," I said over my gin and tonic.

John and I were sitting in a cozy booth in the Crest Club at the top of the ship. From our vantage point, we could see people gathering on the promenade deck with their luggage, eager to depart the ship once we reached Isla de Suerte. I had spotted my boss, William Waverly, in the crowd. He was with a woman, most likely the new Mrs. Waverly, but she was wearing a large sun hat that, from my angle, prevented me from seeing much of her. Still, I could tell they were in honeymoon mode. Mr. Waverly kept ducking under the brim of her hat, probably to kiss her, and he held her hand the entire time. How sweet! Meanwhile, Cindy and Gunnar rushed around in an attempt to keep order. John had suggested we avoid the pandemonium and had led me to our cozy corner. Then he'd hopped behind the bar to make us drinks.

"You think I haven't figured that out?" He laughed. "This cruise has all the appeal of *The Poseidon Adventure*. Please tell me you don't want them as a client."

"Oh no, that ship has sailed."

John winced. "For that bad joke, you get no more drinks." That was fine with me. My head was a little spinny from the gin and the heights, and maybe from the company. I lay my head on his shoulder like a question, and he answered by pulling me into his arms. It was a good place to be, a place where I didn't have to think about the potential client and promotion that I'd just let go of or the wreckage that was the inaugural cruise of the Lady Luck. In fact, John made sure I had no thoughts at all.

The Poseidon Adventure...

Well, almost none.

CHAPTER 18

Sunlight tickled my eyelids and coaxed me awake. The calls and cries of tropical birds filtered in through the soft hum of the air conditioning to second the motion. My eyes fluttered open, and I took in the room around me. White walls and bedding contrasted with mahogany furniture. Above me, a ceiling fan with old-fashioned rattan blades spun slowly, just fast enough to keep the air moving. I was lying in the most comfortable bed I'd ever slept in, surrounded by softness. I didn't want to leave it, but a call of nature soon had me padding across the Spanish tile floor to the bathroom. The word didn't do it justice. It should have been called the bath chamber. Larger than my apartment, it featured every luxury imaginable, from a clawfoot tub to a walk-in shower with a waterfall shower head. The lure of the shower proved irresistible, and I spent quite some time letting the waterfall caress my body. A long time later, wrapped in a soft bamboo cloth robe, I wandered into the open plan kitchen to find Liz seated at the dining table already enjoying a cup of green tea and a fruit plate.

"Morning." I gestured to the breakfast spread arranged artfully on the kitchen island. "Where did this come from?"

"Elves, I think. It was here when I woke up."

I helped myself to coffee, a croissant, and a fruit plate and sat down opposite Liz. We looked at each other and began to laugh.

"How did we get here?"

"It's surreal."

Here was a private bungalow in the village of St. George on Isla de Suerte, Seaswept Cruises' private island.

When Liz and John and I had disembarked the day before, I thought we'd be taken to one of the resort hotels on the north side of the island, where most of the passengers were lodged, some in quarantine. Instead, we'd been driven in golf carts to this luxurious bungalow, and John was given the house two doors down. I didn't know what had prompted our change in status, but I wasn't going to complain. Perhaps Aton was hoping I would help him through the ever-expanding PR crisis, and this was a bribe. If so, he was going to be sorely disappointed. Seaswept Cruises and I were officially over. My only agenda was to enjoy myself until it was time to go home, which wouldn't be for four more days. I had washed my hands of murder, sabotage, blackmail, and extortion. Our cruise had been extended due to the need to disinfect the ship, and Seaswept was going to be out a lot of money in changes to passenger airline tickets. They might also be looking at a lawsuit from passengers who needed to be home by certain dates, not to mention those who had suffered mental trauma during sharkfest. Oh well. Not my problem anymore.

A quick knock sounded on the door. Then it opened slightly, and John poked his head in.

"Anybody home?"

"Come in," said Liz. "There's breakfast."

"I already had mine," said John as he joined us at the table.

He was looking mighty fine in a long-sleeved white linen shirt and blue jeans. With his dark brown hair and black eyes, he took my breath away. I found myself staring, but he was staring right back at me wearing nothing but my bathrobe. I felt my cheeks get hot. I was completely covered up but completely aware that I was wearing nothing under the robe. John seemed aware of that fact too. I could see it in his eyes.

"Anybody up for exploring the island?" he asked.

"Yes, please," I murmured.

"I'm waiting for Gunnar," said Liz. "He said he would have some time this afternoon, so I'm just going to relax until then."

I left Liz and John comparing bunglaows and went to get dressed.

To match John's relaxed island style, I opted for a sundress and sandals, and I put my hair in a simple braid down my back. I loaded up the behemoth straw bag I had purchased in Nassau with my swimsuit, a towel, and sunscreen, just in case. We were surrounded by the ocean after all.

We began by exploring the village of St. George. When Seaswept purchased the Bahamian island, the whole thing had been called St. George, but Aton changed the name to Isla de Suerte, which meant Lucky Island, to emphasize the gambling aspect. The island now boasted the largest casino in the Caribbean, situated south of the town.

St. George wasn't a large village, and much of it was taken up with gorgeous bungalows of varying sizes and degrees of luxury. Some looked original but highly renovated while others were obviously new builds. Most sported wide verandas and huge windows with plantation shutters. The stucco exteriors were painted white or pastel colors. One street led us to a beautiful square featuring a fountain and formal gardens. The bungalows fronting the square were grander, up to three stories, and more elegant. I wondered if anyone lived there full-time, or if they were all for high-paying passengers.

As we strolled around the square, taking in the blooming hibiscus and the playful fountain that featured frolicking dolphins spitting water at each other, movement caught my eye. I looked up and saw Aton Faraday strolling on the veranda of the grandest home on the square. I grabbed John's hand and pulled him behind a bottlebrush tree before Aton could spot us.

"Aton Faraday's on that porch," I explained. "I don't want him to see us. In fact, I hope he forgets that I exist."

"He could use someone like you right now. Don't be surprised if he turns up asking for help."

"What good is helping him when he just keeps making the situation worse? Where does it end?"

"Aton Faraday is an idealist. I see this all the time, the company founder who dreams of a better world and thinks he has the power to create it. A CEO like that means a risky investment because guys like that live in a fantasy world. When the real world intrudes, they can't handle it."

"He should have taken those threats to the police, launched an investigation, and fought back. Instead, he just buried his head in the sand and did nothing, yet he expected everything to turn out okay in the end. That's lunacy!"

"You're right, Ms. Cooksey." I spun around to find Aton Faraday only a few feet away. We were treed like raccoons. "I've been foolish, but no more." Green silk pajamas flapping, Aton turned on his heel and stalked off.

For a moment, I thought about following him.

"He needed to hear it," said John. "Don't feel bad about it."

"I wonder if he'll finally involve the authorities."

"Who knows?" John shrugged.

In silence, we continued our tour of the village. Turning to the east, I caught sight of a beautiful white church with a belfry and a red door. It was a classic clapboard church. The sign in front of it read "St. George's Church, Anglican Communion. Established 1760."

"You're dying to see inside, aren't you?" John smiled.

I nodded my head eagerly, and he took my hand and led me to the church. At the door, I started to knock, but John tried the latch and found it open. The inside was a classic Georgian Protestant church. The pews were wooden, painted white, and formed little boxes. The pulpit at the front of the sanctuary was an elaborate affair with a staircase leading up to an octagonal box capped with a matching sounding board. There was no stained glass in the church, but there were windows on both sides ranging down the sanctuary and a huge Palladian window behind the altar. While we were taking it all in, an elderly priest appeared from a door adjacent to the altar. He wore linen pants, a linen blazer, a light blue shirt, and a clerical collar, and he carried a Panama hat. When he saw us, his eyes lit up, and he made a beeline for us.

"Wait, wait. Don't tell me. You've come to get married. Congratulations! Yours will be the first marriage I've officiated in five years."

"Well," said John, looking at me significantly, "should we take the plunge?"

My mouth went completely dry. Was he being serious? For a moment I thought he was, but then he smiled and let me off the hook. I laughed, slightly hysterically. I would never entertain marrying someone I had known for only a few days; my hormones, on the other hand, were very much in favor.

The vicar looked at us expectantly.

"Maybe another time, father," said John. "We're just exploring."

The vicar's smile faltered with disappointment.

"Well, if you change your mind…"

"Can you tell us something about the church?" I changed the subject.

The church, as the vicar explained, had been built in the 1700s to serve the island of St. George. It had survived countless hurricanes and was mostly still the building from the 1700s.

"Of course, we've replaced siding over the years," said the vicar, "and we lost our stained-glass window not long after it was first installed in 1780, but she's still a gem of colonial ecclesiastical architecture."

"What can you tell us about the village?" asked John.

The vicar sighed.

"The village, as you call it, is hardly a village at all anymore. When Seaswept Cruises purchased the island, they paid off all the villagers to relocate. It was more money than most of them would see in a lifetime, so they all left quite happily."

"But you stayed," I said.

"Well, I have a higher calling than money," smiled the vicar. "I thought there might still be a chance for me to serve the visitors to this island."

"I'm surprised that Faraday agreed."

"He had his reservations," admitted the vicar. "And he made a stipulation."

"Let me guess," said John. "Your church is now a wedding chapel."

I was shocked when the vicar nodded his head. He looked slightly embarrassed.

"As it was explained to me," he said, "Isla de Suerte, as he now calls it, is supposed to be the Las Vegas of the Caribbean. And what's Las Vegas without a wedding chapel? He agreed to let me continue to hold services and minister to passengers who need me as long as I was also willing to perform marriages on demand. While I'm not altogether comfortable with marrying couples who might be making a hasty decision, it's a compromise that my superiors were agreeable to."

"Was there a hefty donation that helped them to become agreeable?" asked John.

The vicar grimaced and nodded.

"You don't have to fill a quota or anything do you?" I asked, remembering his eagerness when we first entered the church.

"Not at all. Not at all," he hastened to assure us. "I was just glad to see people. It's been very lonely on the island while we've waited for the first ship to arrive. You see, there's only a small population that stays on the island full-time. Most of the crew members of the Lady Luck fill jobs on the island when the ship is in port."

"Very efficient," said John.

"And lonely," said the vicar with a rueful smile. "Once all the locals were gone, they completely renovated the village. He kept some of the higher-quality homes and restored them and then built bunches of brand-new bungalows. He also renovated all the stores and businesses to appeal to the tourists. Basically, we are the Disney World of the Caribbean. The only thing authentic on this island is this church."

We let the vicar show us around. We saw pews where famous historical figures sat, including royal governors and even some pirates. We also saw the baptismal font carved out of coral and the churchyard where graves had been lovingly tended over the centuries. The gravestones were well preserved just like the church, and I thought that Aton Faraday probably didn't know what a historical gem he had on his island. If it had been me, I would have made the church of St. George a focal point for visitors.

Eventually, we took our leave of the vicar, promising to return for another visit and to encourage others to see the church.

"And if you change your mind about getting married," said

the vicar with a twinkle in his eye, "I'm always here. You are a lovely couple."

John laughed, but I felt my face get hot. We waved goodbye and headed down the path back into the heart of the village. John slid his arm around my waist and kissed the top of my head.

CHAPTER 19

We found the shops and restaurants that the vicar mentioned closer to the beach. We chose a sidewalk café with a view of the ocean for our lunch. While feasting on shrimp and crab, we watched as the passengers staying at the resort hotels on the north of the island wandered down the main road to visit the village, including Jorge and the Steinway Swingers. We waved to each other, and Jorge's eyebrows shot skyward when he saw I was lunching with a date.

"Friend of yours?" asked John.

"From Queens."

"Small world."

"Indeed."

As far as I could tell, there was only one real road on the island, and it was only traversed by pedestrians, bicyclists, and golf carts. It led from the village north to the resort hotels and south to the casino. To the east of the village was a nature preserve crisscrossed with trails, some of which led to the east side of the island where there were the remnants of an ancient volcano. We still had much to explore, and I couldn't wait. Still,

John wanted to order dessert, and while we were sharing a slice of key lime pie, who should walk by but Robin and Susan Shelby.

"Mind if we join you?" asked Susan, and she slid into a chair before either of us could answer. What the what? Susan generally treated me like I had cooties. Why was she suddenly trying to be pals?

Robin gestured to the server and asked for menus. The server looked at the line of patrons waiting for a table, but she didn't say anything. Once the Shelbys ordered, Robin shared the news.

"We just heard from Lieutenant Halvorsen that they isolated the source of the outbreak. It was Norovirus, and the source was a soft serve machine in the casual dining room."

"What a perfect plan," I breathed. The Shelbys and John gave me funny looks, so I hurried to explain.

"According to Carol the Carefree Cruiser, unlimited soft serve all day long is very appealing to a lot of cruisers, especially families with young children. If you're going to start a Norovirus outbreak, there's no better place to plant it than the soft serve machine."

"Jill, you're positively diabolical," said John. "I'm seeing you with new eyes."

"That's assuming the outbreak was sabotage," said Susan. "It could just be rotten luck."

"It's sabotage," said Robin, more to John than to Susan and me. How sexist. "The perpetrator has continually upped the ante with each act. After exposing hundreds of people to the threat of shark attack, the only worse thing would be to sicken the majority of the passengers."

"Agreed," said John. He and Robin prattled on about ship disinfection, yada yada yada. As I didn't want to talk to Susan, I devoted my attention to my key lime pie and coffee. Luckily for me, Susan didn't want to talk to me either and focused on her salad, or rather, picking things she didn't like, such as lettuce, out of her salad.

If you don't like lettuce, why order a salad?

I was saved from watching Susan dissect her meal by Liz and Gunnar, who came strolling down the road past the café. I practically sprang from my chair and grabbed my purse, leaving John to say our goodbyes.

"Well, I guess we're going," he said to Robin. "See you later."

"Oh, we will," said Susan. "We have the bungalow across the street from yours."

Oh, great.

I gave Liz a big hug like we hadn't seen each other in years, which made her laugh.

"We're headed for the beach," said my friend. "Wanna come?"

I was ready for the beach, but John hadn't brought his swim trunks. He dodged into a souvenir shop to pick up a swimsuit, and twenty minutes later, we were setting up on lounge chairs on the beach and applying sunscreen. I wore a blue halter tank suit cut high on the hips, while Liz showed off a yellow bikini top and boy shorts like a swimsuit model. The guys, well, I can honestly say they were making Liz and me the envy of every woman on the beach. Gunnar was ripped. There was no other word for it. A small tattoo of a trident graced one perfectly formed pec. The rest of him was tattoo free—nothing to spoil the view. John was a bit lankier but equally cut. His skin was tan, and a smattering of dark hair peppered his pecs and formed a trail down to his belly button. He had no visible tattoos, but I noticed a couple of scars that might have been from tattoo removal. Because he'd been forced to buy swim trunks at a beach shop, his were Hawaiian print board shorts, the kind worn by dads everywhere. Except John did NOT have a dad-bod, and he somehow made those garish board shorts sexy as all get out. I knew the chances of the Caribbean water being cold were slim, but I needed something to cool me down.

While I waited for my sunscreen to soak in before I went into the water, I lay back on my lounger and took in the scene. The ocean was almost mint green closest to the beach and clear as glass. The color deepened through several shades of teal as the water grew deeper, culminating in a midnight blue where the shelf dropped off. I couldn't wait to get into that beautiful water and swim. The sand on the beach was not coarse but not fine either, the kind of sand that makes terrific sandcastles. I saw several children and some adults engaged in that activity. Most folks, however, were either swimming or sunning. I looked to my left and saw a woman covered from neck to toes in an aqua caftan with navy blue fringe. She lay back in a lounge chair fully reclined, and a huge white straw hat covered her head and face. Lying on the beach completely covered from head to toe seemed a lot like ordering a salad when you don't like lettuce. While I couldn't know for sure, I'd lay odds it was the scarf lady.

Next to me, John rose and held out his hands. I put mine in his, and he hauled me to my feet. Then he surprised me by throwing me over his shoulder and sprinting toward the water. I squealed when I realized his intentions. Before I knew it, I was sailing through the air and landing in the water with a huge splash, but it wasn't a shock. The warm Caribbean embraced me like a cozy blanket. When I surfaced, John was right there next to me, and he pulled me into his arms for a kiss.

CHAPTER 20

That night we went to the casino for dinner. According to the CCTV network that played on the TV in the bungalow, the casino boasted four world-class restaurants. Liz and I were craving sushi, and John was game. Gunnar, unfortunately, had a shift aboard the Lady Luck, so it was just the three of us…until we ran into the Shelbys.

"What a *coinkydink*?" exclaimed Susan. "Let's all sit together. I'm going to try sashimi for the first time. Do you think I'll like it?"

Like rats abandoning a sinking ship, Liz and John took the chairs farthest from Susan, leaving me to sit next to her. I gave my boyfriend a scathing look.

Boyfriend? I hadn't thought of John in that way until that moment. I guess he had been in the shipboard romance with potential category, but now here he was firmly in the boyfriend column. Well, possum on a gum bush! I wondered what he would think about the label and debated asking him later, perhaps after one of our epic kisses.

The server came to take our drinks order.

"I'll have a Sapporo," said John, "and my girlfriend will have a sweet tea."

Question answered.

I know Liz's eyes were saucers, but I guess mine were, too, because John looked at me and laughed. "Sweet tea is on the menu. Look." He pointed to it. I melted like a pat of butter on a hot biscuit. He had called me his girlfriend AND he'd remembered my love of sweet tea. Could this night get any better?

Liz mouthed a "Wow!" at me, and I winked at her.

"So how long have you two been together?" asked Susan, like it was any of her business.

John and I looked at each other and laughed.

"Forty-eight hours?" he asked me.

"Closer to seventy-two."

Susan made a grunt of disbelief.

"I just assumed you knew each other before the cruise. You seem so close."

John covered my hand with his.

"Sometimes, you just click," he told the annoying woman. "I'm sure you know all about that being newlyweds."

"Yes, but a shipboard romance," she persisted. "Isn't that a bit dangerous?"

"What do you mean?" asked Liz, who had an interest in this topic as well.

"Darling," warned Robin, but his beloved paid him no mind.

"It's just that you can tell each other anything about yourselves, but you have no way of knowing if it's true. You could be dating a con artist!"

"Isn't that true of any new relationship?" I countered. "It's only with time that you come to truly know another person."

"And don't discount instincts," added my potential con-artist new boyfriend. (Insert eye roll here.) "At a certain point, you learn to listen to your gut."

"You certainly do," agreed Robin, prompting a dirty look from his bride.

An awkward silence ensued that was finally broken by the sound of my purse hitting the floor—again. I had slung the bag in question over the back of my chair, but it had a rounded back, so my purse kept slipping off.

"Just put it under the table with mine," said Susan irritably. "It's just going to keep falling off if you don't."

I gave Susan a tight smile— "Thanks for the tip"—and took my time arranging my purse next to hers at my feet. I had found Susan irritating before she pooh-poohed my burgeoning relationship. Now I found her simply intolerable. The thing is, she wasn't completely off the mark, but I didn't need her to tell me what I already knew, especially in such a supercilious way. I was quite aware that I had to take this relationship slowly, chemistry notwithstanding, because I had learned the hard way not to jump in too quickly. I wouldn't be making declarations of love for quite some time, if ever.

Thankfully, the sushi was fabulous, which almost made up for the Shelbys as dinner companions. Robin wanted to pick John's brain about investments while Susan wanted us all to watch her one-woman show: Picky Eater Tries Raw Fish.

"Okay, everybody, here I go! First bite!"

Gag me with an Ahi tuna!

Thank goodness Liz was there. We shared reminiscences of sushi nights with the Posse, like the time Surya ate out-of-date supermarket sushi and we all thought she was going to die. John found it hilarious, and even Robin cracked a smile, but I could tell Susan felt upstaged. Winning!

Another highlight was John's attentiveness. He may have been drawn into conversation with Robin, but he continually checked on me, asked for more iced tea, and best of all, kept his hand on my knee as much as possible. When Susan would say something cringeworthy, he would squeeze my leg. It was our private conversation with the bonus that it kept my blood humming.

After dinner, the five of us explored the casino. John was eager to play blackjack, so we sidled up to a table where I saw some blue jerseys topped by familiar faces.

"Well, ye've done it again, hen!"

"Done what?" I asked The Legend.

"Ye've gone and scared poor Kenney *Rrrodgers* again. The man runs any time you come near."

"It has to be a coincidence! I've never even met him."

"Three times, hen! It canna be a coincidence."

I introduced everyone to The Legend and his pals. Another dealer showed up, and the game began. John and Robin played, but I declined. There wasn't a seat for me, but I'm sure John would have ceded me his if I'd asked. Something else held me back. Memories? Nostalgia? A desire to keep my mascara in place? Blackjack, poker—these were games I had shared with my father, and I just wasn't ready to share them with another man.

CHAPTER 21

aiting until I was sure that everyone was asleep was agony, but I forced myself to read my favorite time travel romance series until two a.m. Okay, forced might be overstating it. But even while I was enjoying a passion that spanned centuries and oceans, part of my brain was whirring and counting down the seconds. At two, I shut off my e-reader and crept out of bed. I had worn shorts and a t-shirt to bed, and now I slipped on my sneakers and tried to creep soundlessly out of the house.

I made it out the front door and down the veranda stairs before I tripped and went sprawling in the grass. My knee hit a sprinkler head, and I clapped a hand over my mouth to keep from shouting in pain. I almost gave up and went back inside. I had a feeling my knee was bleeding, and I was now in worse humor than ever. Hobbling down the sidewalk until I was bathed in the light of an old-fashioned street lamp, I checked my knee. Not bleeding, but I could see a bruise already emerging. I took some deep breaths as the pain receded. Then I dusted myself off and headed across the street.

The Shelbys' bungalow was dark, so I slipped the key I had purloined from Susan Shelby's purse at dinner out of my pocket and opened the front door, which swung open noiselessly and closed just as quietly.

Where the newlywed couple was concerned, something didn't add up. Their hot and cold behavior towards me, sometimes verging on stalking, made no sense at all. That is, unless my guess was correct.

I crept quietly into the living room and took my bearings. The layout of the bungalow was just like mine except reversed, so it was easy to find the bedrooms. The problem was that both bedroom doors were shut. I took a moment to think. Going by my own house, the master bedroom would be on the right and the second bedroom on the left. I took a breath and reached for the doorknob of what should have been the second bedroom.

The room was darker than the rest of the house. I noticed that all the plantation shutters were closed tight. I shut the door as quietly as I could and waited for my eyes to adjust to the dark. When I could see a tiny bit better, I slipped my sneakers off my feet and padded silently to the bed.

Robin Shelby slept on the left side of the bed. I let myself peruse his face. It was dark, but even so, his face seemed thinner. In the shadow of night, his hair was darker, and a moment later, when his eyes fluttered open, they were lighter. Those eyes registered alarm at my presence. Then Robin Shelby rolled out of the bed, crashed into my legs, and took me down. Before I could recover, he was on top of me, pinning my arms and legs as I thrashed underneath him. I heard the door open, and the overhead light was suddenly blinding.

Susan Shelby, in a New York Yankees night shirt, stood over us with a pistol aimed at my head.

I looked from Susan to Robin.

"Robin and Susan Shelby? *The Poseidon Adventure*? Really? You couldn't come up with anything better?"

Mike said a very bad word.

Once he climbed off me and I stood up, my heart rate started to go down. The pistol disappeared, but I figured it was still close by.

"Is there tea?" I asked Mike's putative wife. "What is your name, by the way? I know his, but you and I haven't been properly introduced." I smiled showing all my teeth. I had brushed and flossed exactly for this moment.

"It's Susan to you," she said and stalked off, hopefully to make that tea.

Mike hadn't recovered as well as I had. Granted, he didn't have my rage to fall back on.

I looked at him, but he just stared at his feet. Occasionally he started to speak, but no sounds came out. After five minutes of this hemming and hawing, I'd had enough. I marched out of the bedroom to see what I could get out of "Susan."

At least she was making tea. An electric kettle was just starting to boil. Susan plunked teabags into three mugs and poured water over them. She gestured to the dining table, and I grabbed a mug and sat down.

While the tea steeped, "Susan" and I regarded each other. When I really looked for it, I could see the resemblance between her and the woman I'd seen with Mike in Central Park, but I had to look carefully. With long dark hair, a tan, and false eyelashes, she looked so different from the pale, icy blond of last December.

Eventually, Mike shuffled into the room and took a seat. "Susan" started to speak, but I held up a finger. I rose with my mug and went to the kitchen where I procured a glass, ice from the freezer, the sugar bowl, and a spoon. I poured my cup of tea over ice, added sugar, and stirred loudly. Then I returned to the table fully prepared to have this conversation.

"I gather this has something to do with THE story." The story Mike had been working on when he ghosted me. The story that was supposed to win him a Pulitzer. The story that was going to take a lot of his time. The story he failed to inform me would end our relationship.

Mike nodded, but "Susan" spoke.

"It does."

"Are you going to tell me about it?"

Mike shook his head.

"No," said Susan. "It's better if you don't know."

"Better for whom?"

Mike and Susan looked at each other.

"You want a list?" she snarked.

"What's that supposed to mean?" I gripped my ice tea hard, making the ice clink. I relaxed my grip.

"It's safer if you don't know," Mike managed finally. Except for the spiky blond hair, he looked like himself. I realized that during the day he must have been padding his cheeks and torso and wearing colored contacts.

"Is it related to the sabotage?"

No one spoke.

"It has to be. Is your story about the mob? Is that why you're in disguise?"

Silence.

"Answer me!"

"Let's get one thing straight," seethed Susan. "This man owes you nothing. Do you hear me? He has been through hell—"

"Susan!" Mike shut her down. He shook his head, forbidding her to say more.

I took a very deliberate sip of my tea while I figured out what to do next.

"So," I asked, "is there anything you CAN tell me?"

Susan and Mike looked at each other for a long time. These long looks were really getting on my nerves. Finally, Mike spoke.

"Trust no one."

"Well, great. That's not obscure at all. Clear as dishwater that is."

We sat in silence for a few more minutes, and I sipped my tea as if it were the only thing keeping me alive. The sugar hit with every sip helped me keep a rein on my emotions, which were all over the place. After a while, Susan excused herself.

"I'm going back to bed." She gave Mike another of those seriously annoying long looks and left the table.

"Well, the missus seems awfully nice." I let the sarcasm flow like honey on a warm day. "How did you two kids get together?"

Mike sighed.

"Jill."

Hearing my name on his lips sent a fresh jolt of pain right through my heart.

"Please keep this a secret."

"Come again?"

"Please keep this to yourself. If you blow our cover, some really bad stuff could happen."

I looked at him hard. His mouth was a grim line, and his eyes looked tired and lifeless. Whatever path he was on, it was taking a toll.

So what? My anger spoke up. *He chose this path, over you I might add. He made his bed.*

I couldn't disagree with myself. Maybe if he had offered up some answers I might have felt kinder to him, but I was as much in the dark now as I was last November.

"I'll think about it," I said and casually sipped my tea. Mike's eyebrows rose. At least I'd finally gotten a rise out of him.

"Just be careful."

"Look, I've got a good thing going right now with John. You just stay out of my way, and I'll stay out of yours." I swilled the last drop of tea, plunked the glass on the table, and rose to leave.

As I opened the front door, Mike joked lamely, "So we should have gone with Belle and Manny?"

Considering Belle died in *The Poseidon Adventure*, it wasn't a bad idea.

CHAPTER 22

I slept in the next day. When I awoke, I took a long shower and did a full beauty routine, so I didn't expect anyone to be in the bungalow when I finally emerged from my room. On a subconscious level, I was probably avoiding people to give myself some time to process the events of the previous night.

No such luck.

"Sleeping beauty has arisen," cried John as I entered the kitchen to find him, Liz, Gunnar, and the Shelbys sitting around the kitchen table enjoying brunch.

I pasted a smile on my face.

"Coffee," I murmured before spending an inordinate amount of time pouring myself a cup and adding cream and sugar. I stirred the heavenly liquid for a ridiculously long time, long enough for me to gird my loins and turn to face the crowd. I was not allowed to deal with my demons that morning. I'd just have to put it off for later in the day.

John eagerly patted the seat next to him, so I sat down. He leaned in and kissed me on the cheek. I felt my face get hot. I looked at Mike. He was looking everywhere except at me, which somehow made it worse.

I needed something to do, so I started filling my plate with food I had no appetite for. I made polite chitchat with everyone, but I caught Liz and John giving me speculative looks. I would have to try harder.

"So, what's on the agenda for today?" I asked overly brightly.

"How about a tour of the nature preserve?" suggested Gunnar. "The variety of wildlife is impressive."

Everyone agreed, and the Shelbys left to get ready for our hike, leaving me with some breathing space.

"How did you sleep?" asked John as he caressed my cheek with his thumb.

"Pretty well," I lied. I had slept fitfully and not deeply. "You?"

"Like a baby."

"That's good," I said rather lamely, causing John to look at me quizzically.

"Are you feeling okay?"

"I was wondering the same thing," piped in Liz unhelpfully.

"I'm just hungry," I lied again. Such a liar this morning! I tore a hunk off a croissant and stuffed it in my mouth. It tasted like paper.

"Well, eat up," directed Gunnar. "We have a lot of walking ahead of us."

After forcing myself to clear my plate, I went back to my room to get ready for the nature preserve.

The closest entrance to the preserve was behind the Church of St. George. As the six of us passed, the vicar waved, and I wondered if he was looking at us as three potential weddings. If so, he'd be sorely disappointed.

Directly behind the church, a trailhead heavily framed by

vegetation led into one of the darkest forests I had ever seen. A cheerful sign next to the trailhead welcomed us to the St. George Blackland Coppice Forest and provided a guide with a map.

"Are you sure we're supposed to go in there?" asked Susan with no little trepidation. Was she really afraid, or was yellow-bellied ninny her cover persona? I walked over to the sign to read the guide.

"Certainly," urged Gunnar. "I've walked all the trails. It's a magical place."

It certainly seemed like one according to the write-up on the sign.

"It says here there are rare trees and orchids in the forest," I relayed to the group. "It sounds interesting."

"Then let's do this," pronounced John. "After you, Gunnar."

The sailor-cum-park ranger took Liz's hand and led her onto the trail. The Shelbys followed, and John and I brought up the rear. In no time, we were plunged into deep shadow, and it took some moments for my eyes to adjust. When they did, the sight took my breath away.

We had stepped into another universe. The ground beneath my feet was black with eons of decomposition and dotted with delicate ferns. Lacey under canopy trees added texture and a hundred shades of green and black at eye level, and far overhead stretched the canopies of mahogany, red cedar, and many other trees I couldn't identify. The air was cooler and more humid in the forest, and from somewhere I could hear flowing water.

In many ways, it reminded me of home, of hiking in Shenandoah National Park, although at home we didn't have the glorious orchids or the wild parrots. Still, this forest gave me a sense of peace, and I felt myself relaxing in the hyper-oxygenated air as the shade engulfed me like a quilt.

I traipsed happily along behind the others, going slowly so I wouldn't miss any of the flora and fauna.

At one point I stopped to watch a plump little bird that was something between a quail and a dove. I strained to make out his coloring in the darkness of the forest—gray breast and teal head. He seemed like such a gentle creature. After watching him for a moment, I turned to catch up with the others and found John watching me, a bemused smile on his face.

"You seem very happy." He held out his hand to me, and I took it.

"I am."

The others had paused to wait for us, so it took only a minute to catch up with them. We continued until we came to the source of the running water, a spring that came cascading out of a rock formation into a pool as black as midnight. The pool had been carved out of the rock by the water pummeling it from above for millennia, and there was no way to know how deep it was without getting into it. Mist rose from the pool, feeding the orchids and bromeliads that clung to the rocks and nearby trees. At the edges of the pool, rivulets trailed off in different directions to feed the forest. This place felt special, sacred, like the beating heart of the forest. I closed my eyes and offered a prayer of thanks for the opportunity to see such a special place, and I prayed that tourism wouldn't destroy it.

After a time, we moved on, but I promised myself that I would come back before we left the island.

We emerged from the forest on the north side of the preserve near the resort hotels. Directly in front of us, I could see a lazy river and a swimming pool flanked by two of the four enormous hotels. Families were enjoying the amenities. There was laughing and shouting and splashing…and I just wanted to go back into the forest. After the dark green serenity, a beach resort was more than a little jarring.

"There's more to the nature preserve, right?" I looked to Gunnar.

"There is," he said, "but I thought everyone might like lunch. There's a seaside grill one building over that is excellent."

Gunnar led us over a bridge that spanned the lazy river. From atop the bridge, I could see that the artificial river circled the entire resort complex—four different hotels! I'd have to check if there was a longer lazy river at any other resort in the world—this one had to be a mile long—because Aton would want to promote that.

Except I didn't work for Aton. I had given up on Seaswept Cruises, but it was practically impossible for me to turn off my PR brain. Maybe I could just send him an email to let him know my thoughts.

Snap out of it, Cooksey! Aton Faraday isn't your client because Aton Faraday is crazier than an outhouse rat!

I had to agree with myself. Anyone who was being extorted by the mob and didn't go to the police was nuts. Anyone who took risks with his passengers' lives rather than facing the truth of sabotage was criminally negligent.

But there was so much going for Seaswept. The ship was magnificent. The island was full of delightful surprises. The whole enterprise had amazing potential.

"I know that look," said Liz. "Don't even think about it."

"Think about what?" asked John, and everyone else turned questioning looks toward me.

"Nothing," I replied quietly.

"Nothing is right," affirmed Liz as she took a firm grip on my hand and pulled me along. "Absolutely nothing."

After crossing the lazy river, we headed straight between two of the hotels, skirting a beautiful pool elaborately landscaped with tropical foliage and featuring a water slide. Then we were on the other side of the complex, and the ocean was in sight. We turned left and followed a path that ran along that side of the resort, following the lazy river. To the left of the path, in front of the hotels, was a series of restaurants, clubs, and music venues. As we passed one of the venues, I spied Novette sitting at a piano in close conference with a man—a thin man with sandy brown hair. I only saw him from the back, but that was all I needed.

"Hey, y'all go on ahead," I said to the group. "I'm just going to say hi to Novette. I'll be along in a minute."

Liz gave me a curious look, John kissed my cheek, and the party moved on. When they were gone, I squared my shoulders and headed for the club.

The place was closed until the evening, and a placard by the entrance read "Tonight: Novette and Kenney, Duets for the Ages." Ignoring the closed sign, I went in. Novette was alone at the piano.

Of course she was.

"Hey, Novette!"

She turned and gave me a sweet smile that didn't reach her eyes.

"Hi, sugar! I haven't seen you in donkey's years."

"I'm staying in the village. How are things?"

"They could be worse," she chuckled. "I'm just going with the flow because that's all I can do."

"So, where's your duet partner?" I smiled at her benignly.

"My duet partner?" Novette's eyes grew larger.

"Yes. Kenney Rodgers. Wasn't that him sitting at the piano with you a minute ago?"

Novette took a beat to recover. With her heart of gold, lying must have been a strain.

"Oh, right, Kenney. Yes, he had to leave. We finished rehearsing, and he has another shift to go to."

"Oh? Where else does he work? Another club or restaurant?"

She forced a laugh. "I honestly don't know. Everything has

been so confusing, what with coming to the island earlier than expected. It's been so crazy."

"The thing is," I began as I perched on the piano bench next to her, "I've been trying to talk to Kenney for several days, but I think he's avoiding me."

Novette looked very carefully at the sheet music in front of her.

"Avoiding you? Now, why would he do that?"

"I'm wondering the same thing. I was hoping you could shed some light on it. I just wanted to ask him about the night Casimir Koblinsky died. You know he was there, right?"

"No, he didn't tell me." She flipped the page and stared hard at the bars of music.

"I just wanted to get his opinion on something that happened that night. Do you think you could get him to talk to me?"

Novette picked up the book of music and began leafing through it vigorously.

"I don't know what he could tell you. He was just having a smoke."

"I thought you didn't know he was there when Caz died."

The singer became very still.

"Well, I just assumed he must have been having a smoke if he was out on the promenade deck," she whispered.

"Oh."

"Sugar, I hate to do it, but I need to rehearse this song," she said more firmly as she replaced the sheet music on the piano. "You understand, right?"

"Sure, Novette." I moved to leave but she grabbed my arm. I turned back to her, and she finally looked me in the eye.

"Kenney is a good man. An honorable man. Any woman would be lucky..." She swallowed the rest of the thought. "He's a good man." Then she turned to the piano and began to play.

As I exited the club, Novette's sweet voice began the first

verse of Patsy's most famous song, "I Fall to Pieces." As always, she sang that paean to being friend-zoned like a woman who had lived it, and I started to wonder. Was Kenney Novette's forbidden love?

$\mathcal{I}$ was distracted all through lunch.

"Jill! Are you listening?" Susan Shelby clapped her hands, snapping me out of my reverie. I hadn't heard a word she'd said, but I suspected it was no great loss.

"Not really," I admitted. Susan's eyes narrowed. Next to me, I thought John turned a chuckle into a cough.

"She's not listening," said Liz, "because she's about to announce that she still wants Seaswept Cruises for a client." She smirked at me and cocked an eyebrow, essentially daring me to contradict her.

"You're joking!" scoffed John. "There's no way! After what Aton Faraday pulled?"

"I have to agree," said Mike in his most condescending Robin Shelby manner. "It wouldn't be prudent to take on a client knowing he has been involved in covering up criminal activity."

"It would be lunacy," agreed Susan, making me more determined than ever.

Gunnar kept quiet. I think he was ashamed of what Aton had done, but it wasn't his fault. He had no reason to feel bad.

"Look," I tried to explain, "this cruise line has a lot going for it, this island for one. It's a paradise. And if Aton Faraday contacts the police and starts making things right, there's still a chance this cruise line could be wildly successful."

"But what makes you think he'll do the right thing?" asked Mike.

"John and I ran into him yesterday. Some words were exchanged. Basically, he gave us some reason to believe he's going to do things differently."

"Well, I wouldn't hold my breath," said Liz as she stabbed a shrimp more violently than it deserved. "I'd want some assurances."

"And I'd demand to know exactly what he's doing before I would commit to him as a client," added John.

"I wouldn't consider it!" pronounced Susan. "I'd give Aton Faraday a wide berth." She glared at me.

"I must agree with my wife," said Mike right before he lifted her hand to his lips. "She always gives excellent advice." I threw up a little in my mouth.

When lunch ended, the group broke up. Mike claimed he had some emails to return, and Susan had an appointment for a manicure. Surprisingly, John also had to work. He jumped in a golf cart with the Shelbys that would take them back to the village and the bungalows, but not before he kissed me properly.

"Come by my bungalow in a couple of hours," he whispered to me. "I'll try to get through my work as fast as I can. I want to be alone with you."

Alone sounded nice. I was tired of the crowd, specifically the Shelbys and Gunnar, because I couldn't speak freely in front of them. Truthfully, I couldn't speak freely in front of anyone without blowing Mike's cover. I wanted to tell Liz, but her closeness with Gunnar gave me pause. But when John and I were alone, it was like none of the drama existed. I could use a couple of drama-free hours.

"I can't wait," I whispered back and kissed him softly. I was rewarded with a dazzling smile.

After they left, I walked with Liz and Gunnar down the beach to the pier where the ship's launch was moored. Mira Koblinsky was being helped aboard. She took a seat under the canopy, and I imagined she, a redhead, was trying to avoid a sunburn. But why was she heading back to the ship? Were passengers even allowed on board while the disinfecting was happening?

Then Joseph came strolling down the pier and hopped aboard the launch, as well. I watched as he walked right past Mira without acknowledging her and sat down near the bow. Interesting. Were the lovebirds fighting? Or were they keeping their relationship a secret? Mira no longer had an overbearing father keeping a tight rein on her. She could date anyone. Why the subterfuge? I watched Mira for any sign of acknowledgment of Joseph. She looked everywhere but at him, which was itself an acknowledgment of sorts. Then I glanced back at Joseph to find him looking straight at me. Busted! I hastily looked away and pretended to be watching another boat moored nearby. Joseph hadn't looked pleased.

Liz interrupted my speculation.

"Gunnar only has an hour or so before he has to work, so we're thinking of renting a kayak."

"Sounds like fun. Y'all go ahead. I'll catch up with you back at the house."

"Are you sure you're okay on your own?"

I was more than okay, but I only said, "Absolutely."

As soon as Liz and Gunnar walked off, I turned and headed back the way we had come. As I passed the club where I'd spoken to Novette, I happened to glance up. Perched on a balcony several floors up was the scarf lady, and I would swear she was watching me. I was distracted from my counter-surveillance when the sliding glass door one balcony over suddenly opened, and an object flew out to land at my feet. It shattered into brown shards, scattering little blue pellets all over the sidewalk. I looked again at the balcony, but the door was now closed. On further inspection, the mess on the sidewalk seemed to be a prescription bottle, but there was no label on any of the pieces, just some residue where the label had been torn off. Little blue pills. Interesting. An employee from one of the cafés came running over with a broom and dustpan.

"I'll take care of this, ma'am." Soon all traces were swept away.

Whatever was going on in that hotel room was none of my business, so I kept going, past the restaurants, past the pool, and over the bridge until I came to the trailhead for the nature preserve. I hurried into that cool, green, darkness and sighed as it enfolded me. Inhaling the fresh, clean air, I slowed my pace and gave myself time to take everything in.

The flora was varied and stunning. I paused to admire some wild orchids with bright pink centers, and that's when I heard the sniffling. It seemed to be coming from further down the path around a little bend. I crept in that direction until I caught a glimpse of a man and a woman in an embrace. It was Tom the bartender, and in his arms he held a crying Cindy Helms, our cruise director. Her back was to me, but I could see Tom's face full of concern. Before I could jump back and give them privacy, he saw me, his eyes going wide as shot glasses. I silently mimed, "Is she okay?" Tom nodded reassuringly and went back to stroking Cindy's back. I waved farewell and hastily retreated.

Now what was that all about? Were Tom and Cindy an item? Just friends? And why was she crying? Was she feeling guilty about something?

I chastened myself for jumping to conclusions. People cried

all the time for lots of reasons. Maybe she and Tom had been dating but they were breaking up. Maybe she had received a distressing call from back home. Maybe she was stressed out from trying to soothe grumpy passengers on a cruise plagued with problems. She might have been crying about anything.

In my haste to give Tom and Cindy some space, I took a wrong turn, but I didn't mind the result at all. I found myself standing on a rock formation overlooking the sea. I could hear waves thunderously crashing, but I couldn't see them because they were crashing into a cave right under my feet. Every so often, a wave would be strong enough that it would come shooting out of a hole in the rock like a whale's blowhole. That's what it was called, according to the informational sign posted where the trail emerged from the forest.

Wanting a closer look, I crept toward the blowhole. Because the large waves gushing up through it were frequent and regular, I assumed it was high tide. If I wanted an up-close look, I would have to get wet. Accepting my fate, I crept even closer. I felt the wave crash below my feet as a fifteen-foot-high geyser spouted up through the hole. As the water fell, it soaked me instantly. The force of the blowhole wasn't as strong as I'd expected, and I soon found out why. Between large waves, I managed to look down the channel in the rock. First, it was larger than I expected, about eight feet across. Second, the sea in the cave below was very far down, maybe fifteen or twenty feet.

Suddenly, my vision was obscured, and I ducked away just in time as another wave hit the cave below me, and spray and mist jetted out of the blowhole and drenched me. I looked around, but I saw no other tourists enjoying the spectacle. Did people prefer the lazy river and swimming pools to nature's majesty?

Calm down, Wild Kingdom. It just needs promoting.

I moved out of the line of fire and sat down on the volcanic rock to observe the blowhole for a while. The power of the sea was thrilling and energizing. The rhythm of the waves breaking and blowing seemed to contain a message for me, but I couldn't make it out.

After a while, my blood humming from the awesome spectacle, I rose to my feet and plunged back into the forest.

This time I didn't take a wrong turn, and I found myself exactly where I had intended, at the spring at the heart of the forest.

Instead of an incessant pounding of the surf, here there was a gentle patter and tinkle of flowing waterfall and streams. Again, I looked around for signs of other humans, but I saw none. I was completely alone, thank goodness.

Normally, being alone in the woods might unnerve me, especially back home where I could easily run into a venomous snake or a bear. But I knew from my reading that there were no dangerous snakes in the Bahamas and no bears. The most threatening creatures in the Bahamas (if you don't count humans) were spiders, but I wasn't worried about them. I was just glad to finally be alone with my thoughts.

I found a nice flat rock overlooking the waterfall and the deep pool beneath it, carved out of the rock over millennia, and plopped down crisscross applesauce. Then I did a little yoga breathing, and I started to think.

Everything had started with Caz Koblinsky. He had wanted to go straight for Mira's sake, so the mob had fired a warning shot with unintended consequences.

Who had fired that shot? Who was the mob's representation on board? Was there more than one person? I felt in my gut that there had to be. Otherwise, the shot that scared Caz to death would have been a one-in-a-million. Somebody was acting as an informer, and someone else was acting as a hitman. Of that I was sure.

I was sure of nothing else.

Thousands of people, both passengers and crew, had the opportunity to shoot at Caz. I might have met the killer already, but most likely I hadn't. How would the police go about finding a shooter among thousands of people on a ship? Interviews? Checking movements and alibis? CCTV footage? First, they'd have to determine the angle of the shot to know which CCTV cameras to check. A ricochet made that a lot harder, I supposed, not that anyone on the Lady Luck had even made an attempt.

The whole situation was impossible!

Go with what you know.

Go with what I know? Did I know anything?

I knew that Caz was dead.

I knew that many people wanted him dead, but the mob probably only wanted him scared.

I knew that Aton was desperate to succeed on his terms.

I knew Kenney Rodgers was avoiding me.

I knew there was a lady in disguise who was watching me.

I knew Mike and Whatshername were undercover.

I knew Liz liked Gunnar a lot.

I knew John was a fabulous kisser.

I knew Joseph and Mira were in love and keeping it a secret.

I knew Cindy and Tom were friends and maybe more.

Did I know anything else?

Yes. I knew some people knew a heck-of-a-lot more than I did, and I needed to know what they knew.

Say that five times fast.

With a clearer mind than I'd possessed since walking up the gangway of the Lady Luck, I stood up. That's when someone pushed me, and I tumbled head first into the pool below.

CHAPTER 24

When I broke the surface, I struggled to take a breath. Whoever had pushed me had hit me so hard they'd knocked the wind out of me. I told myself not to fight the water, to roll onto my back and float while I regained my breath. After what seemed like forever but was probably only a few minutes, I started to catch my breath. But then it occurred to me that my assailant might still be up there waiting to finish me off, and a fresh wave of panic had me flailing and thrashing.

"Jill!" I heard my name and felt the reverberation as something large hit the water next to me. Was someone throwing rocks at me? Was this how I would die?

I felt strong bands encircle me and propel me forward. I didn't stop thrashing, but a minute later, I felt the cold granite ledge at the edge of the pool. The strong bands, now recognizable as arms, gave me a push upward so I was now half in the water, half resting on the ledge. Breath finally entered my lungs, and I wheezed and gasped until I had taken in all the air I could. Then I opened my eyes.

A beautiful pair of eyes looked back at me, one green and one blue.

Mike.

"Your eyes are two different colors," I croaked.

"I lost a contact when I dove in."

"Did you see—"

My breath was knocked out again as Mike crushed me in an embrace. On the plus side, his warmth stopped my shivering. After a moment, he relaxed a bit, and I could breathe again. Now I was warm and breathing. Two thumbs way up.

"How could you be so careless?" he whispered frantically in my ear. "You could have been killed."

"I wasn't careless!" I couldn't quite shout yet, but he got the picture. "I was pushed."

"Are you sure?"

I pulled away and gave him my *Are you kidding me?* look.

"You're sure."

I tried not to roll my eyes, but I don't think I was successful.

Then Mike yanked me back into his arms and showered my face with kisses.

"What (kiss) are (kiss) you (kiss) even (kiss) doing (kiss) here (kiss)?"

Inadvertently, I laughed, which made Mike grab me by the shoulder and give me a little shake.

"You're supposed to be safe at home in New York! Of all the cruise ships in all the world, you had to stroll onto mine."

I laughed harder. Or maybe I sobbed.

"My client, my cruise ship," I hiccuped.

"My case, my cruise ship," he countered.

"Our case, our cruise ship?" I bargained.

"No dice." Mike let go of me and pulled himself clear of the water. Then he helped me do the same because I was still a tad short of breath. Soon we were sitting cross-legged, facing each other, dripping onto a slab of rock in what felt like our own secluded grotto. Except I knew that anyone could be out there watching us.

"This time, it's too dangerous."

"Because I've never been in danger before." Acid dripped from my tongue. "Oh, that's right, you weren't there the last time."

Mike sighed.

"This is a different level of danger. The things these mobsters could do to you, to your family and friends...I don't have the heart to describe them. They're ruthless. Money is the only thing that matters."

I started to protest, but he cut me off.

"I couldn't live with myself if anything happened to you. Do you hear me?"

"Does your girlfriend know that?"

"Karen's not my girlfriend."

Karen? It figured.

"Do you and Karen know who shot at Caz? Do you know who the saboteurs are?"

Mike hesitated. "No."

Crap.

"That's why you must keep your head down and get home safely. Anyone could be involved, even your...boyfriend." Mike grimaced with distaste.

"I highly doubt that."

"Trust no one. Not even him."

"Don't worry," I said as I rose to my feet. "I stopped trusting men about three months ago."

With that parting shot, I picked my way carefully around the pool, climbed up to the path, passing a beautiful boa constrictor along the way that hurried me right along, and took off for the bungalow.

CHAPTER 25

Now that I knew that Mike knew next to nothing, it was time to get close to someone who did. I was still dripping when I arrived at the bungalow, but the first thing I did was head to the phone and call Aton Faraday. He was unavailable, so I left a message asking for a meeting. Then I jumped into the shower. When I emerged, I threw on a bathrobe and went in search of Liz. I found her sipping green tea in the living room and looking at her phone, which she turned away from me when I entered.

"Is there anyone else in this house?" I asked without preamble.

"No," she replied uncertainly.

I stalked off to the front door to make sure the deadbolt was thrown. I marched back through the living room to make sure the patio doors were bolted. I went through the kitchen to the utility room to make sure that door was locked and the safety chain was engaged. Then I marched back to the living room, plopped down on the sofa next to Liz, and dove in.

"First, Mike is here."

"He's Robin Shelby, isn't he?"

"Shiitake mushrooms, Liz! How did you know?"

"Well, he does look like Mike."

"Why didn't you tell me?"

"I'll answer that question!" boomed Surya's voice from Liz's phone. She turned the screen to reveal the rest of our PR Posse on a Zoom call. "Liz had strict instructions to help you get over poop-for-brains. Why would she bring him up?"

"Maybe because he's been in disguise the entire time and that's incredibly fishy!"

Pause.

"True," admitted Surya, "but we've been rooting for John."

"Team John all the way," pronounced Kate.

"I made shirts," boasted Anupa.

"He's a terrific dresser," said Kate.

"And he cut a fine form at the beach," added Surya. "Hubba! Hubba!"

"And I liked the way he held your hand in the forest," Anupa sighed. "He's pretty dreamy."

"Have you been filming me?" I screeched at Liz.

"Calm down. It was for your own good. We're not there. How else could we put our two cents in?" Kate was very matter-of-fact.

"Ladies, we need to talk about healthy boundaries."

"I only want to hear about healthy boundaries from someone healthy." Surya's comeback stung. I couldn't even respond.

"Girls, give us a minute," said Liz, and she muted the phone and put it face down on the coffee table. Then she turned to me and took my hand. I had half a mind to pull away, but this was Liz, who didn't have a mean bone in her body.

"I'm sorry," she said. "I never—we never—meant to hurt you. We just wanted the best for you. You were so hurt when Mike broke your heart, and you've been so happy with John on this trip. I just wanted the girls to know how happy you were."

"Did you send a video of me on that ropes course? Did Jim give you the footage?"

"Well…"

"Cause if you did, I'm not sure I can forgive you."

"Then I didn't."

I gave her a long look.

"Fine. Unmute the phone."

I spent the next several minutes filling in the Posse on everything I knew and didn't know, including being pushed into the pond and Mike's rescue.

"Why couldn't it have been John?" complained Surya. "This complicates the storyline."

"Agreed," said Anupa. "This opportunity was wasted on Mike. He's yesterday's news. A brush with death might have induced John to share his deep and abiding passion for you. Then you could have had a *From Here to Eternity* moment."

"That was on the beach," I countered. It was a favorite movie of mine.

"Water is water."

"The point is," I attempted to redirect the conversation, "Mike doesn't know who the crooks are."

"Does anybody?" asked Kate.

"Maybe Aton," replied Liz. "He has been slow to share what he knows."

"That's putting it mildly," I snarked, remembering the threatening letters he only revealed to us AFTER people had almost died. "The only other person I can think of is the singer-slash-blackjack dealer Kenney Rodgers. He was there when Caz died, and he's been avoiding me ever since."

"That's funny," said Liz. "When I left Gunnar, he was going to fire Kenney Rodgers. Something about canceling a show tonight after consistently disappearing from his shifts."

"What? He's firing Kenney right now?"

"It might be a done deal," shrugged Liz.

"But if he gets fired, Kenney might go back to the ship! How will I track him down then?"

"Well, Gunnar was going to the casino to fire him. He might still be there."

I leaped off the sofa and ran for the front door.

"Uh, Jill," I heard Kate say. I spun impatiently.

"I don't have time! I have to get to Kenney Rodgers!"

"You have time for clothes."

I looked down. Bathrobe. Yikes! I sprinted for the bedroom and threw on the first clothes and shoes I found. When I sprinted back through the foyer, the front door was open, and Liz was ready to go. We raced from the house and leaped from the front porch.

"We need a golf cart!" I scanned the street. "There!"

A cart had pulled up to a bungalow two doors down, and a housekeeping attendant hopped out carrying a stack of towels and headed for the front door.

"I'll drive," said Liz.

Moments later, we were careening down the road toward the casino taking turns at speeds I didn't think golf carts could do. My thrill-seeking friend was a speed demon, but I held on and said nothing, my focus solely on getting to Kenney. When the cart took to two wheels on a particularly bad turn, Liz must have noticed my white knuckles.

"I'm just channeling *Six Pack!*"

"Appropriate."

We dumped the cart in front of the casino and took off running through the front doors and into the foyer, only to come to a screeching halt. The casino was enormous. How would we find Kenney?

"I think we should split up," Liz and I said in unison.

"I'll go right," I said.

"And I'll go left." Liz held up a fist, we bumped, and then she was gone.

I race-walked toward a room full of slot machines and ATMs. There wouldn't be a musical venue here. Too much noise. I passed through the room into a sort of vestibule. A grand curved staircase tempted me toward the second floor, while another archway opened onto a gaming room full of felt-covered tables. I took the stairs.

It was the right call. The second floor was partially open to reveal the gaming floor below. Up here, ringing the open view of the first floor was a series of intimate bars. In the recesses of the first bar I passed, I spied a small stage with a mike. Musicians played here. Kenney would be here somewhere, but the place was enormous, like an airport terminal lined with bars and restaurants. I'd have to check them all.

Then I saw Gunnar emerge from the next bar over. Jackpot. He saw me and jogged over.

"Kenney Rodgers?" I asked without preamble, which threw Gunnar a bit.

"I…I just left him."

"Great. Liz is that way." I gestured distractedly toward the direction from which I'd come. I felt like a heat-seeking missile locked onto my target. It was only a matter of moments before I would strike.

And then countermeasures appeared in the form of the scarf lady. Of course! Wherever Kenney had been, the scarf lady had hovered. What was their connection? And would she get in my way? Worse, would she warn him off?

I grabbed Gunnar's arm to prevent him from racing off to his lady love.

"Wait, who is that woman?" I gestured to the scarf lady, again sporting one of her caftan-sun hat-sunglasses combinations.

"Oh, that's Dahlia."

"Come again?"

"Dahlia. Dahlia Parden. She's a cruising fixture. I've seen

her on a bunch of ships. Normally she isn't dressed like that. I can only imagine she's had a skin cancer scare or gained some weight."

"Dahlia Parden," I repeated dumbly. "And Kenney Rodgers. Are they close?"

"I guess. They know each other from other cruises. I've seen them together a few times."

"And Dahlia and Kenney together doesn't seem odd to you at all?"

"Why would it?"

Why, indeed. Why would a thirty-something Norwegian get the joke? Because I was certain there was a joke being played here. But why? And on whom?

"Thanks, Gunnar." I patted his arm, and he headed off in Liz's direction.

Now I had a dilemma. I had to get past Dahlia. If she saw me, she would certainly warn Kenney, and he would disappear yet again into the bowels of the casino.

I ducked into the nearest bar for some reconnaissance. Dahlia was standing outside the bar Gunnar had just left. She seemed to be looking for something, or someone. Me, perhaps? She scanned the casino floor below and then turned her attention to the avenue of bars and restaurants on the second floor. I had no chance of getting past her and into Kenney's bar before she spotted me. I needed a diversion.

A middle-aged couple sat nearby at a small table counting gaming chips and sipping fruity drinks. Matching Hawaiian shirts and shorts told me these were serious cruisers having a seriously good time. Perfect. I approached them.

"Good afternoon! I'm Jill, a PR representative for Seaswept Cruises. How are you enjoying your day?"

"We're good," replied the woman as she raked me with her gaze. Good thing my hastily donned clothes matched.

I asked them their names and learned they were Lois and Bill Hotchkiss from Cincinnati, Ohio.

"Lois and Bill, do you see that woman over there?'

"Yeah."

"That's Dahlia Parden," I said very quickly in an attempt to slur my words.

"You're kidding!" exclaimed Lois.

"That's not Dolly Parton," said Bill.

"It is Dahlia Parden. I swear it."

"She doesn't look like Dolly," mused Bill.

"How could you tell? She's all covered up," protested Lois.

"I can tell."

"How?"

"You gonna make me say it?"

"How?"

"She's missing the boobs, all right? Are you happy?"

"The boobs are there," I said, technically not a lie. The woman had boobs.

"They look smaller," said Bill, now turning scarlet.

"He has a point," admitted his wife.

"They only look smaller because she's not on TV," I argued. "The camera adds twenty pounds, and when you're not on camera, you look smaller."

Lois was nodding her head emphatically.

"That's so true! Our son's wedding video made me look at least twenty pounds heavier. She has a point, Bill."

"So not being on camera is kind of like going on an instant diet. And where do you lose weight first when you go on a diet?"

"Your boobs! Bill, it's her!"

Bill still looked skeptical. I only hoped he wouldn't examine my air-tight logic too carefully.

"Now," I whispered, "Dahlia likes to meet her fans, but she doesn't like to be mobbed by them, which is why I'm reaching out to you. I could tell you were Dahlia fans. Do this long enough, and you get a sixth sense about these things. If you ask her, she'll pose for photos and give you her autograph."

"Let's do it, Bill! It's Dolly Parton! When will we get this chance again?"

"And you're sure about the boobs?" asked Bill.

"I'm sure."

Bill, who was hoping to be convinced, rubbed his hands gleefully.

"Let's do this, Lois!"

"Thanks for the tip," said Lois as Bill dragged her toward Dahlia.

I wasn't sure the two of them would be enough, so I turned to another table of bar patrons and said, "They're getting their photo with Dahlia Parden." I pointed in the scarf lady's direction. This table didn't need convincing, probably because someone else had already taken the initiative, and soon the bar cleared as a crowd headed toward Dahlia.

She was thoroughly distracted as I slipped by and made a beeline for Kenney. Lois was gushing, while Bill was attempting to aim his selfie-stick just so.

I entered the bar on tiptoe lest I should alert Kenney to my presence. If he slipped out another door, I would be back at square one. The bar was deserted, which I expected. I doubted Gunnar ever fired someone in front of a crowd. Kenney sat at the piano, his back to me.

I was in mid-tiptoe when he began to play. The opening was familiar. I froze. Then Kenney began to sing that old Tom T. Hall classic "I Love."

I couldn't breathe. Something was stuck in my chest.

He sang about baby ducks, Sunday school, puppies, and onions.

My face was wet. Why was my face wet? I struggled to understand what I was hearing and what I was feeling. The song was an old one from before I was born, but I knew it by heart.

"And I love you too," sang Kenney.

"Daddy!" The sob tore loose from my chest. Startled, my father turned to face me, and the music trailed off.

"Jilly Bean." His eyes were shining with unshed tears.

I threw myself into his arms and cried my heart out.

That's where Dahlia found us. She looked a bit different. Her fuchsia lipstick was smeared and her hat had disappeared.

"Hi, Momma," I hiccuped between sobs.

My mother sighed in resignation, a sound I knew so well. Then she smiled and wiped her eyes.

CHAPTER 26

"That song was a dead giveaway. How many times have you sung it to me?"

Calvin Cooksey, my father, was alive and sitting on a stack of tablecloths. He looked good, thinner but in a healthy way. His gray hair was dyed sandy brown, but it went well with his tan. He looked younger like he did when I was a child. It was a bit surreal.

"Well, I was thinking about you, Jilly Bean, and it just came out. I thought your Momma was keeping watch, or I never would have played it."

"I was trying to keep watch," replied my mother tartly, "but a certain someone sicced a crowd of Dolly Parton fans on me."

"Look, my little islands in the stream, if you're going to tell people your names are Kenney Rodgers and Dahlia Parden, you have to live with the consequences."

"Living is what I've been trying to do," said my father.

The overwhelming joy of discovering that my father was alive had up until now saved my parents from my wrath, but a reckoning was in the offing.

We were now seated in a storage room somewhere in the

bowels of the casino. It had no security cameras, my father assured us, although I wasn't clear on why he thought that was important.

"Yes," I replied drily. "I believe it's time for an explanation."

"Don't take that tone with your father, Jilly." My mother tried to wrest the upper hand from me, but I had no plans to relinquish it.

"I'll choose my tone, Momma, since you and Daddy clearly faked his death." A thought occurred to me. "Does Jeremy know?" Jeremy was my brother. If he knew my father was alive and I didn't, there was going to be hell to pay.

Momma gave me her *Oh, please* look.

"Your brother would have gone right to the police," sputtered my father, "which would have been counterproductive."

Jeremy was a minister and very righteous indeed. I had a lot of respect and love for my brother even though I didn't like him very much.

"So," I began, "how we did get to this place?"

Daddy sighed and closed his eyes. "It all began with a poker game."

Calvin's Tale

"It was at Dud Scott's cabin near Charlottesville, and it was my last professional game, although I didn't know it then. I won big that night against some of the regulars: Dud, of course, Lester Tidwell, and Hi Graham, and some boys from out of state called Tommy, Johnny, and Frank. I hadn't played them before, but they'd heard about me from some of their friends I'd played in Atlantic City. They seemed nice enough for Yankees. Dud even loaned them the cabin for the weekend. Tommy was a decent player but not as good as he thought he was. Johnny was slightly better, but Frank was easy pickings. When the game ended, I went out on the porch for a cigar."

My mother cleared her throat, but Daddy ignored her.

"Stupid mistake. When you win big, it's always best to leave quickly."

"Know when to walk away?" I couldn't resist.

Daddy grinned, and my heart constricted.

"Something like that. I guess I was smoking for a while. Dud, Hi, and Lester had left, and Tommy must have thought I had left, too, because out the door he came holding Frank at gunpoint. Now Tommy had lost money that night, but Frank had lost big time. Frank was apologizing and pleading for his life. It turned out that Tommy had staked Frank after he claimed to be a cardsharp. For the record, he wasn't.

"I was in the shadows, so they couldn't see me. I contemplated running around the cabin to my truck to get my gun, but there was no way I could do it undetected. I hoped Tommy was just trying to scare Frank, but he marched him out into the woods. The gun was silenced, but I could still hear it. It sounded…"

"Like a staple gun?" I put in.

"Exactly. Before you could say Flatt and Scruggs, Tommy came strolling out of the woods with a smile on his face. Chilled my blood. Then Johnny came out of the cabin.

'Well?' he asked.

'Death, a necessary end, will come when it will come.' That's Shakespeare. I looked it up later. That was all Tommy said, and they went back inside. I'm not ashamed to say I was shaken. I crept around the cabin to the driveway, and I was just about to run to my truck, jump in, and drive like the devil when Tommy came out the front door. He saw my truck and stopped. I guess he realized I was still somewhere around there. He ducked back into the cabin, and I ran faster than the time the copperhead got into the house. I screamed out of the driveway with a tidal wave of gravel behind me, and I didn't stop until I got to Luthersburg. But I didn't go home. I knew that psychopath could find me, so I went to Dud's house and called your Momma from there.

"She lit out of the house and joined me at Dud and Shirley Scott's. We laid low there until we figured out what to do. Dud put out some feelers in law enforcement. Come to find out, Tommy was a gangster named Tommy Tantrum. Nasty feller."

"WAIT!" I interrupted. "I know that name." Worlds were colliding. I turned to my mother. "That's the gangster that shot Mike when he was trying to extort money from some of Mike's friends."

"The very same," said my dad.

"What? How do you know?" My gaze swiveled between my parents as I tried to discern an explanation. How did my "dead" father know Mike?

"They met when we joined forces," replied my mother calmly.

"What?"

As my mother explained and would continue to remind me for many years to come, she had spotted Mike immediately.

"Really, Jill, that you could be fooled after dating the man has me thinking you need an eye exam. Cotton in his cheeks? Padding around his middle? Blond hair? But he couldn't hide his brow, chin, and nose, could he? He could use some tips from the theater teacher at the community college."

I did some deep breathing.

"When I cornered Mike and threatened to alert you to his presence," she continued, "he had to come clean. I quickly real- ized that he was looking for the same gangster that wanted to kill your father, and when he told me Tommy Tantrum was on the ship, everything got real serious real fast. The four of us had a council of war."

"So that's what Mike's doing here!" I exclaimed. "He wouldn't tell me."

Mike, according to my mother, was trying to bring down Tommy Tantrum by catching him in the act.

"That woman, Susan—"

"Her real name's Karen," I interjected.

"Of course, it is. I think she was his partner in law enforcement."

Things were finally starting to make sense, but I still had questions.

"Not so fast. Daddy, finish your story."

"What's left to tell?"

"Oh, I don't know. Maybe the part where you faked your death."

Momma sighed and rolled her eyes, but Daddy grinned and rubbed his hands together fiendishly.

"A masterpiece of deceptionary practices, if I do say so myself."

My turn to roll my eyes. Daddy ignored me. He had a lot of practice at ignoring eye rolls.

"I knew I had seen enough to put me in mortal danger. Worse, now your Momma, you, and Jeremy were in danger too."

"Why didn't you go to the police?" I couldn't resist asking.

"Because of what I just said. You were all in danger. If I had gone to the police and become a witness, Tommy Tantrum could've come after y'all to put pressure on me. Even if I had gone to the police, he would've taken me out as a preventive measure. You were especially at risk since you insist on living in a city run by gangsters. Easy access!"

More eye-rolling.

"I had no other choice—"

"He really didn't," echoed Momma.

"So, I called on the Woodboogers."

The Concatenated Order of Woodboogers was Daddy's lodge. The Woodbooger is the southwestern Virginia version of Bigfoot. Why the lodge chose that mythical beast as its mascot is a story lost to history.

"My doctor, the sheriff, the coroner, and the undertaker are all Woodboogers, so it made the plan simple."

"Daddy, the entire male population of Luthersburg is in the Woodboogers. Are you telling me they all know you're still alive?"

"Calm down. Only half the male population is in the Woodboogers. The other half are Ruritans. So that's, what, a quarter of the population of the town that knows since one-half are women?"

"Surely some of the wives know," put in my mother.

"I reckon so." Daddy nodded.

That's when my head popped off my body.

"So, hundreds of people in my hometown know my father faked his death, but you failed to tell me, your own daughter? You let me grieve! You let my heart break!"

"Okay, Loretta, I owe you twenty bucks."

"I told you she'd react this way."

I screamed. Sometimes it was just too hard to be the daughter of such cold-bloodedly pragmatic people.

"Keep your histrionics to a dull roar!" hissed Momma. Daddy chose a different tack and wrapped me in his arms.

"Jilly Bean, I had to protect you and your brother. You're my babies."

As quickly as my anger flared, it dissipated. I hugged my father back for a long time.

"How did you end up on a cruise ship?" I asked when we finally let go of each other.

"Your mother's brilliant idea!"

"Thank you, Cal." Momma looked pleased with the compliment.

"It all started with the country music cruise," explained Daddy.

"The one you took for your anniversary?"

"The very same."

They had adored every moment of the cruise, my father reminded me. The exotic ports of call, the music, the casino, the food. Dad had joked that in another life, he would have worked on a cruise ship. He was a fabulous singer and a whiz at cards. Mom had joked back that in another life, she would have lived aboard one. Someone made your bed every morning, you never had to cook, and you could see the world.

"So, when Calvin Cooksey died, Kenney Rodgers was born." I had to hand it to my parents. It was an ingenious and enjoyable way to stay alive.

"Don't forget Dahlia Parden." My father chuckled. "We chose the names so it would be easy to find each other."

In the last few years, my parents had cruised the Caribbean, Mexico, Central America, Hawaii, Alaska, and the Mediterranean. They had also crossed the Atlantic and transited the Panama Canal. In a way, Tommy Tantrum's death threat had given them a new lease on life.

"So, what's the plan?" I asked when we finally let go of each other. My mother's disguise was back in place. A gaudy scarf covered her head, her fuchsia lipstick was pristine, and her sunglasses made her resemble a colorful housefly.

"It hasn't been finalized yet," Momma pronounced.

"What are the options? A trap? Surveillance? Have you found any witnesses who are willing to rat on him in exchange for immunity?"

"We had one," began Daddy. Momma shook her head ever so slightly, and he clammed up.

So that's how it was going to be. Even though I had discovered my very-much-alive paterfamilias, they were going to keep me in the dark, probably "for my safety."

"You mean Caz Koblinsky?"

Daddy sighed and looked at Momma. Finally, she shrugged.

"Fine! Mike approached Caz in the hope he would turn against Tommy Tantrum, but you know how that ended."

"Tommy shot at Caz to scare him into obedience but accidentally scared him to death," I summarized. "What about Mira?"

"Mira knows nothing," said Daddy. "Mike and Karen sussed her out. She seems completely ignorant of her father's business practices, and she wants to sell the company."

"Well, that should put an end to Tommy Tantrum's extortion schemes," I mused. "And to Mike's story. He'll have to track down another of Tommy's schemes and start all over again."

"That's why Mike has asked Mira not to go public with her plans," countered Momma. "He's even told her that he, Robin Shelby, is interested in purchasing the company. That should keep her quiet until the cruise is over."

"So, he hopes to expose the criminal activity in her company that she knows nothing about and that will probably damage the company at a time when she's trying to sell it. That feels more than a little underhanded." Mira had already lost her father, and I didn't like the idea of kicking her when she was down.

"What's more underhanded than murder?" asked Daddy pointedly. "If Mira's company has made money through criminal practices, it's not her fault, but the company still has to be held accountable."

He had a point. I just wished there was a way to protect her from the coming retribution.

"Maybe Joseph could help."

"Aton Faraday's assistant?" asked Momma. "What could he do?"

"Well, he and Mira do appear to be dating. Maybe he could

act as moral support or use some of Aton's resources to shield her from the prying eyes of the press. If Tommy Tantrum goes down and Cashmere Dreams goes with it, the press is going to rake the mattress heiress over the coals."

"Mira and Joseph are dating?" my parents squawked in unison.

So I knew something they, and probably Mike, didn't. It felt really good.

"If they're not dating, they put on a good front. I witnessed an epic kiss aboard ship."

Momma and Daddy had one of those telepathic conversations, just like they'd had my whole life. Dang it, it was good to have my father back!

"We can't approach Joseph," said Momma.

"Why not?"

"Because Joseph might not be Joseph," said Daddy.

"Come again?"

Daddy explained. The problem that underlay Mike's investigation and gave it the foundational equivalent of shifting sands was that nobody knew who Tommy Tantrum was. Yes, he was supposedly aboard the ship and now on the island, but he hadn't been seen by anyone in years. After Mike was shot and Tommy got off with no jail time whatsoever, explained my father, he had gone to ground. He was "disciplined" by the mob, whatever that meant, and basically had to work his way back up from the bottom. Along the way, it appeared he may have changed his appearance with plastic surgery.

"Everyone's picture is taken when they come aboard," explained my father. I remembered the process well. I had just lost a favorite hat. "I've managed to look through all the photos on the computer, and I can't find him."

"Mike has kept an eye out, too," said Momma, "with no luck."

"So Tommy Tantrum could be anyone at all. Do you have

any suspects?"

Momma and Daddy eyed each other nervously.

"Well," said Daddy, "we have a couple."

"The first one being your boyfriend." Momma ripped off the band-aid.

"You've got to be kidding? John Gowdy?" Momma had lost her mind.

"He's from Staten Island, and everyone knows that Staten Island is ground zero for the mob," said my mother, whose knowledge of the mafia came from *The Godfather* movies and reruns of *Mob Wives*.

"But if he was a mafioso in disguise, why would he tell everyone he was from Staten Island?"

"A double blind."

I sighed and successfully resisted the urge to roll my eyes.

"He was at the captain's table when Caz died. He couldn't have pulled the trigger."

"That just means he has an accomplice."

It was quite a stretch.

"Who else is on the list?"

"Tom the bartender," said Daddy. "He's newish to the cruise industry, and his name is Tom."

"You're suspicious just because he's the new kid on the block. Why would Tommy Tantrum use the name Tom if he was in disguise?"

Both of my parents rolled their eyes at ME. I decided not to hold back on the eye-rolling from that point forward.

"Double blind!" they said in unison.

Oh, for the love of Pete!

"So, what happens now?"

"Now," pronounced Momma, "you go back to your bunga-low, your father goes back to work, and since I no longer have to run interference between the two of you, I'm going to the spa."

CHAPTER 27

"Did you find Kenney Rodgers?" asked Liz when I tracked her and Gunnar down. They were sitting on a sofa in the lobby holding hands, the picture of lovebirds.

"I did."

"Why did you need to see him?" asked Gunnar.

I had no answer. I stood there with my mouth gaping.

Gunnar's eyes narrowed suspiciously.

"He's bad PR." Liz came to my rescue. "He keeps disappearing. As you said, guests have complained."

I grabbed the lifeline Liz had thrown. It was a flimsy lifeline, but it was better than nothing.

"Another complaining video is the last thing we need right now." In truth, one more critical YouTube video couldn't hurt us. Since the Norovirus outbreak, countless videos had been uploaded. At this point, Seaswept was notorious in the industry. I just hoped Gunnar wasn't monitoring YouTube.

"Well, I already told him he wouldn't be returning to the Lady Luck after this cruise." Gunnar had bought the story.

"Maybe I broke the news prematurely. Now he has no reason to do a good job."

I sincerely hoped Daddy wouldn't be returning to the Lady Luck or any other cruise ship for that matter, although the hope was slim. If we couldn't identify Tommy Tantrum, my father would continue to hide in the cruise industry. Still, I preferred a seafaring father to a dead one. Speaking of Daddy, I needed to fill Liz in on his return from the dead.

"Gunnar, do you mind if I speak with Liz privately for a minute?" Thor looked at me suspiciously, like he thought I might be Loki, but he gave us the room.

"Well, that all makes sense now," Liz said after I filled her in on the story of my resurrected father. Then she added, "You might need some family therapy."

Understatement of the year.

I left Liz at the casino so she could hang out with Gunnar since I was heading to John's house. Our golf cart was where we had left it, so I climbed aboard and took it back to the bungalow. When I reached our street, there was no sign of housekeeping, so I left the cart right where we stole it and tried to walk nonchalantly down the street. I walked past my bungalow and continued two doors down to John's. The idea that mild-mannered John Gowdy could be hot-headed gangster Tommy Tantrum was laughable to me, but I needed to eliminate him as a suspect.

When John answered the door, he was grinning from ear to ear. I had never been in his cabin on the ship or in his bungalow. He had always come to me. I supposed my showing up on his doorstep was a sign of my interest, which delighted him.

"Hi, gorgeous."

He was wearing reading glasses and had a pen stuck behind his ear. These little nerdy touches only enhanced his good looks. I told myself my mother was crazy. Gangsters didn't look like this.

His bungalow was similar to mine but not an exact copy. Where mine was all about stark whites and dark woods, his was all about peaches and cream, warm and inviting.

He showed me into the living room where the coffee table was covered with a laptop, papers, and books. I glanced at some of the titles: *The Future of Finance*; *Global Markets in the Twenty-first Century*; *Work-Life Balance*; and *The Life of Benjamin Franklin*. If a to-be-read stack could eliminate someone as a suspect, this one would be a prime example. I highly doubted that mobsters read about work-life balance. I wasn't sure they read at all.

I relaxed and joined John on the sofa.

"I'm sorry to interrupt your work."

"I'm not sorry. Thank you for interrupting my work." He extended his arm along the back of the sofa and began playing with my hair.

Now that I was in his bungalow, I wasn't sure what to do. I had come to eliminate him as a suspect, but he probably thought I had amorous intentions. Romance was the last thing on my mind. I had just reunited with my dead father and learned he was on a mob hit list. I had bigger fish to fry.

"Tell me about it, your work. I don't know much about finance, but I have a friend who specializes in PR for finance."

"You'd probably find it pretty boring. No sabotage. Just moving money around and lots of research."

"There must be something you find interesting about it. Otherwise, how could you do it?"

"Well, it's a little like gambling, but you're better informed. The satisfaction comes from watching a client's balance rise and knowing you made the right decisions. When that happens, you feel a little like a hero, at least to your client."

The gambling remark put me on alert, but everything he said afterward calmed me down. It was all perfectly reasonable, and I supposed most people in his field felt the same way. Heck, I felt that way when I garnered lots of great PR for my clients. We all want to feel like heroes sometimes.

"Tell me about your family."

John laughed.

"You're full of questions today."

"I just want to get to know you better."

"We have lots of time to get to know each other." He very solemnly took my hands in his. "If you're wondering if this ends when we get back to New York, I'm telling you right now, it doesn't."

His brown eyes radiated warmth. John was telling me the truth.

Or he thinks he's telling you the truth.

I had experience with men telling me something that I'm sure they believed in the moment.

But Mike came back.

Did he? If we hadn't been aboard the same cruise ship, would I have ever heard from him again? And why was I thinking about Mike during this incredibly romantic moment? *Argh!*

John was waiting for a response, but I was caught up in my head instead of the moment. I nodded and squeezed his hands because I didn't trust myself to speak. Thankfully, it seemed to reassure him because he smiled and caressed my cheek.

"I can see that I'll have to prove to you this isn't just a vacation fling, and I look forward to convincing you." He leaned forward and brushed his lips against mine. The whirlwind in my mind calmed. This man affected me.

"But right now, I have to get this work done. It's going to take me a while, probably through dinner time. How about we meet up at the casino for some slots and some music, say nine o'clock?"

"Sounds good." That would give me a chunk of time in which to sort some things out.

I left John, feeling much better about his potential for criminal activity. He seemed like a normal workaholic New Yorker.

CHAPTER 28

The only person I could think of who might have a bead on the identity of Tommy Tantrum and his associates was also the person I sort of wanted to have as a client. Not for the first time I shook my head at myself. Glutton for punishment. PR patron saint of lost causes. That's me. I headed for Aton Faraday's house.

A butler answered the door and ushered me into the foyer once I'd introduced myself. Then he disappeared, presumably to tell Aton I was there. I hardly noticed because I was gaping at my surroundings.

While Aton's house looked like a traditional low country mansion on the outside, the inside was quite a different affair. In walking through the front door, I had stepped from the old Bahamas into, I don't know, the starship Enterprise? The futuristic design of the interior was jarring, to say the least—all whites and grays with nontraditional shapes, rounded edges, and light coming from unknown sources.

I peeped into the rooms on either side of the foyer. One had to be a living room because there was seating. It was all connected and curving and looked truly uncomfortable. The wall it faced pulsated with light that changed hue almost imperceptibly over time. Was the entire wall a screen of sorts? The room on the other side of the foyer was even more of a mystery. There were places to sit, I think, but for what purpose? Some of the seating seemed to face the wall. Other seats were at ledges that could be desks. Still other seats were reclined and canopied by arches, making a sort of egg shape.

"How do you like my library?"

I jumped, and Aton smiled his creepy smile. Clad as always in his green silk pajamas and surrounded by Tomorrow Land, he looked more like a Bond villain than ever.

"Where are the books?"

"Paper is a thing of the past." Aton slithered (or was it just my imagination?) to one of the seats and sat down. Immediately the wall in front of him lit up to reveal a touch screen.

"What would you like to read?"

"*Thunderball*," I replied without thinking. Me and my big mouth.

Get a grip, Cooksey. No need to let your potential client know you think he's Ernst Stavro Blofeld come to life.

Aton's jaw hardened.

Too late.

"I've never read it," he replied flatly as he rose from the seat.

Liar.

Daddy had a collection of Ian Fleming paperbacks, and I had read them all. I felt a sharp pang of joy mixed with pain. Daddy was alive, and I would do whatever it took to keep him that way.

"Now what can I do for you, Ms. Cooksey?"

I started with flattery. It always works best with clients.

"I want to work for you. This cruise line has so much to offer, and I want to promote it."

"Even though you think I'm negligent? Even though you think I've got my head buried in the sand?"

"But you're taking steps, right?"

"I am."

"Then let me tell you what I have in mind."

I took him through my plan, how I wanted to promote the island and its rich history and ecology along with the exciting cruising experience.

"It's the total package. Positioned correctly, your cruise line could be the go-to for Bahamas cruising."

"You know I'm not one for looking to the past," replied Aton, "but I can see how the history of the island could appeal to some passengers."

"Lots of passengers. And preserving an ecosystem has nothing to do with the past. That's all about saving valuable resources for the future. There's nothing backward about saving the planet."

"I'm intrigued, Jill." I was Jill again. *Whew!* "But are you really back on team Seaswept? You seemed so adamant about not working for me."

"To be honest, it depends on your response to the sabotage and extortion. If you can reassure me that the end of this crisis is in sight, then I'm all in for Seaswept Cruises."

"I can assure you that I am taking every necessary step to be rid of these gangsters once and for all."

"So you've called in law enforcement?"

Aton paused for a fraction of a second, or was it my imagination again?

"Law enforcement is on the case, rest assured."

I breathed a sigh of relief.

"That's wonderful news. Does that mean you've identified the criminals?"

"Not yet, but we are in contact with them, and it's only a matter of time before this distasteful situation comes to a close."

Beyond that, I couldn't get Aton to specify. He was being

cagey, but I was just a PR professional. I wasn't law enforcement, and he didn't have to tell me specifics about the operation. In fact, if the identities of the gangsters were still in question, it behooved him not to tell me just in case I let something slip to the wrong person.

That didn't mean I wasn't going to try to find out.

We parted with renewed promises—that the sabotage of Seaswept Cruises was nearly over and that I would prepare a fresh PR proposal. My heart felt lighter. Soon Tommy Tantrum would be in custody, my daddy could come home, and Mike could put the past behind him. Would he get his story? Who knew? It would serve him right if he didn't.

Speak of the devil, I passed Mike and Karen, or rather Robin and Susan, who were arriving as I was leaving.

"You'll never get anything out of him," I whispered. "Trust me."

"I'm a journalist," whispered Mike. "Trust ME."

So smug, just like a reporter. I rolled my eyes as the Shelbys vanished into Aton's spaceship disguised as a mansion.

CHAPTER 29

It was well past dinner time, and I needed to find my parents and Liz and bring them up to speed. I knew my dad was supposed to have a concert with Novette. Since I had blown his cover, he had no reason to cancel. Hoping the concert was back on, I headed up to the resort area, and I texted Liz and suggested she meet me there for dinner.

By the time I reached the venue, the sun was setting. The club, which had been closed earlier that day, was open and packed, but the sign advertising Novette and Kenney: Classic Duets, had a banner across it that read "Canceled." I walked into the club looking for my father, but I found The Legend and his crew. They wore black tie—kilted black tie—and they cut quite a swath among the more casually dressed passengers. Short, fitted black jackets over white tuxedo shirts and black bowties, a plaid rainbow of kilts, white socks with flashes and little knives stuck in the rolled tops, and black leather shoes that laced up the ankle. Roddy was particularly dashing, with his height and broad shoulders.

"Och, if it isnae the wee besom herself?" cried The Legend.

"It's no wonder you've pitched up. Kenney's done a runner again!"

"He's canceled the concert," clarified Eileen. "And it's no yoor fault. Dinna fash."

"I know it's not my fault. The concert should be back on. Where's Novette?"

I scanned the crowd and finally found her luxuriant blond curls.

"Novette!" I cried. Her curls vibrated as she scanned the room. I waved my arms, and she soon spotted me and trotted over. She was concert ready in a purple sequined halter-style gown and platform heels.

"Sugar! Kenney told me. I'm so happy for you." She called him Kenney, not Cal, and I wondered if she knew his real name. What had Daddy shared with Novette?

"Have you known he was my father all this time? Since the first night of the cruise?"

"I did. I wanted to befriend you, to know what Kenney's daughter was like. Of course, you're wonderful, just like your daddy."

"He's the man you're in love with, isn't he?"

"It doesn't matter, sugar. All that matters is you know he's alive. It must have been agony when you thought you'd lost him. And soon, your family will be back together." Novette smiled at me, but the tears trickling down her cheeks told the real truth.

The space around us had grown eerily quiet. I looked around and found a gaggle of Scots hanging on our every word.

"So Kenney Rodgers is your da?" asked The Legend. "And you thought he was deid?"

"And he's been hiding from you all this time?" asked Eileen.

"But you're in love with him?" Shona pointed at Novette.

Novette blushed.

Roddy tapped me on the shoulder. "What does your ma think o' that?"

Heavens! What did Mom think of it? Did she know? For that matter, did Daddy even know that Novette loved him? My guess was no. Men are often oblivious.

"Don't ever tell him." Novette grabbed my hand. "Promise me."

Winner, winner, heartbreak dinner.

"Cross my heart and hope to die."

For years, Novette had suffered in silence, and soon my father would leave the cruise world behind. I prayed that she could move past Daddy and find someone who could love her the way she deserved to be loved.

"So, if Kenney doesnae have to run away from you, where is he?" The Legend had a point.

"Well, he was fired today. Maybe he took them at their word."

"I'll see if I can reach him." Novette pulled a cell phone out of her cleavage and started tapping.

"Jill!" Liz burst into the club with Gunnar and Jorge on her heels. "We just saw something strange."

"What?"

"Well, we were in a golf cart on our way here, and we ran across Jorge, so we stopped to invite him to join us for dinner. He hopped in, and as we started to move, along came this... this...THING out of a science fiction film."

"It had huge wheels and some serious suspension, and it was going at least sixty miles an hour," said Jorge. "It was out of this world, literally. Like you could explore Mars in that thing."

"It's a souped-up golf cart," clarified Gunnar with a slight eye roll.

"Maybe for golf on the moon!" protested Jorge.

"Let me guess. Aton was driving?"

"Not only that," panted Liz. "Mike and Karen were in it with him."

"Where were they going?"

"They veered off the road and took off around the lake, headed for the nature preserve," said Gunnar.

"Who are Mike and Karen?" asked Novette.

I looked at Liz. Liz looked at me. Our panic had a playdate.

"Did I say Mike and Karen?" Liz tried to cover the gaffe. "Silly me. I meant Robin and Susan Shelby. I'm so bad with names." Liz smiled sheepishly.

"Oooookay," said The Legend. "So why is that important?"

"I'm not sure," I said, but I had a bad feeling.

Aton had assured me he'd been in contact with law enforcement, but what if that was only technically true? What if his law enforcement contact was an off-duty cop trying to restore her and her former partner's reputation? What I had hoped was cooperation with a law enforcement agency, leading to the arrest of Tommy Tantrum and his associates, might simply be Karen and Mike recreating the sting operation that had landed them in trouble in the first place.

Or maybe Aton was just showing them the nature preserve.

Fat chance.

CHAPTER 30

*L*iz, Jorge, Gunnar, and I stood at the entrance to the nature preserve. Aton's souped-up golf cart, which did indeed look like something out of a science fiction movie, was parked nearby. The last rays of the sun were slipping over the horizon, but a full moon was rising. Inside the jungle, under that canopy of trees, the moon wouldn't be of much help.

"I hope everyone's phones are fully charged."

They weren't, but they would just have to do. We switched on the flashlights and entered the forest.

"Anybody else having Scooby-Doo flashbacks?" I asked to break the tension. "Just me? Okay, then."

"If I admit to it, do I have to be Shaggy?" asked Jorge.

"You can be Fred," said Liz.

"Not with the Viking around, I can't."

"What are you even talking about?" asked Gunnar, and I laughed.

"What's so funny?" Liz stopped and shone her flashlight in my face.

"The whole situation. We're going to search a nature

preserve in the pitch black using only our phone flashlights, which are going to run down sooner rather than later. I think this right here is the definition of foolhardy."

"So, what are we supposed to do?" asked Jorge. "Leave Mike and Karen to their fate?"

"Who are Mike and Karen?" asked Gunnar.

"Robin and Susan," I corrected.

"So why are you calling them Mike and Karen?"

"Long story."

"And why is it so urgent that we find them? I don't understand why Mr. Faraday can't show some guests the nature preserve if he wants to."

"Jill, I think we should tell him," said Liz with a sigh. "After all, he's about to go into a potentially dangerous situation. He should have all the facts."

Liz had a point, but what if Gunnar was involved? What if he was one of Tommy Tantrum's henchmen? If Mike and Karen were trying to catch Tommy, and my gut told me they were, Gunnar could blow the whole operation with a text message.

Of course, if he was part of the operation, then he most likely already knew about the meeting, and he had probably already texted his boss to tell him we were on our way. My stomach heaved over at the thought. If that was the case, we were already in trouble, and Mike and Karen were in danger. All things considered, it didn't seem to matter if we clued Gunnar in, so we did, starting with who Robin and Susan Shelby actually were and their purpose in being on the cruise. I then told him about my meeting with Aton that afternoon and the vague reassurances he had given me.

Gunnar took a minute to absorb the information. Then he spoke.

"Let me get this straight. This Mike and Karen, along with

Mr. Faraday, might be attempting an undercover operation to trap the saboteur, this gangster, Tommy Tantrum."

"Correct."

"Or...not."

"Also correct, although my gut tells me it's happening. Why else would they come to the nature preserve at night?"

"Well, the blowhole is supposed to be beautiful by moonlight," said Liz out of the blue. "I read about it in the cruise literature."

The blowhole.

Secluded because it was as far as you could get from the resort and still be on the island.

Well-lit by the full moon.

"That has to be where they're going!"

"I know the way. Let's go." Gunner took Liz's hand, and they sped off down the trail.

Jorge and I looked at each other, and I could tell we were thinking the same thing. Gunnar the affable Viking might be leading us into a trap.

I remembered the way from my first trip to the blowhole, but this hike, lit only by bobbing flashlights, had a horror-movie quality that ratcheted up my nerves with every step. Liz's phone was the first to die, followed by Jorge's, then mine. Soon Gunnar's was the only source of light.

Suddenly, Gunnar stopped and extinguished his phone, and we all bumped into each other.

"There's something large ahead of us on the trail," he whispered. "I think it's coming this way."

We all strained to listen, and soon we could hear footsteps and snuffling sounds.

"What do you think it is?" asked Jorge.

"I don't know," said Gunnar.

"The Bahamas have no large predators," said Liz. "Although

a few islands have wild pigs. I don't know if this is one of them."

Before the conversation went any further, the "wild pig" in question picked up speed and charged in our direction. Gunnar fumbled with his phone trying to get the flashlight back on, while the rest of us braced for impact. The light came to life at the last moment, stopping our assailant in her tracks.

It wasn't a pig, although I might have described her as such in my less charitable moments.

It was a woman with leaves and twigs in her bleach blond hair, dirt under her ruined manicure, and rents in her couture dress.

"Jill…Isn't that your boss, Pamela?" asked Liz in amazement.

It was. Pamela Van Princis, the never helpful, always aggravating, bane of my existence stood before me on a trail in a Bahamian forest looking like something the cat dragged in.

"Mrs. Waverly, I presume?"

"Jill!" she cried and threw herself into my arms. "It's awful Jill. It's not worth it. It's just not worth it. I thought, he's eighty-five. It'll be a piece of cake. But it isn't! There's no cake, Jill. No cake!"

I thought of all those times in old movies when a slap to the face was a cure for hysteria, and I was sorely tempted.

"He's after me. I got away, but he's on my trail. I slipped out the door when he went to run us a bubble bath. I don't want to take a bubble bath with a husband who's already got pruney skin!"

"Did you by chance throw a bottle of Viagra off the hotel balcony?"

"I did! But he has a never-ending supply. There's Viagra in every nook and cranny of his luggage! Every nook and cranny! Oh, he knew what he was doing. Got me to sign a prenup and everything. I thought he was frail. I thought he would pass on in his sleep and leave me the company."

She desperately clawed at my shirt.

"He's going to outlive me! I swear he is!"

"Liebschen! Turtle dove! Where aaaaaare you?" cried a voice that was too close for comfort.

"How do I get out of here?" asked Pamela as she came close to choking me with my shirt.

We sent Pamela on the right trail toward the Church of St. George where I told her she could ask for sanctuary. I didn't know what else to do. We had bigger fish to fry. I only knew one thing. The return to the office was going to be interesting.

Not thirty seconds after Pamela raced off, William Waverly came staggering down the path. He was bedraggled, but his eyes shone with excitement. Someone enjoyed the chase.

"Which way did she go?"

We all pointed in the other direction, and he passed us by without batting an eyelash.

"Pammy-whammy! Willy-boy is going to catch you! Run, run, run!"

Silence.

"Shall we move on?" asked Gunnar.

"Yes, I think so," I replied. Without another word, we continued down the trail.

When I thought we were getting close to our destination, I sprinted ahead to catch up with Liz and Gunnar and silently signaled for them to stop.

"We need another way out of the forest," I whispered. "If we come barging out of the trailhead, we could mess things up. We need to stay hidden until we assess the situation."

"Let's get off the trail," suggested Gunnar. "We're close enough now. We can pick our way through the forest."

"And just what will we run into off the trail?" asked Jorge. "I'm a city boy and not afraid to say it. Cockroaches and rats I can handle. Snakes and spiders? *Dios mio.*"

"The Bahamas have no venomous snakes," said resident

encyclopedia Liz. "And you're very unlikely to run into a venomous spider."

"But you might walk through some webs," added Gunnar. I shuddered. "These tropical spiders, while not dangerous, do make some huge webs." I shuddered some more.

Gunnar volunteered to go first, and we all found some sticks to use like machetes to knock down any webs that got in our way. Unfortunately, there was a spider attached to the one Jorge picked up, which caused mild hyperventilation. I was seeing a very different side to the tough cabby who roamed New York with a Town Car and a Smith and Wesson.

Speaking of Smith and Wesson, we had no guns. It was very difficult, not to mention very illegal, to get a gun through the TSA and aboard a ship. I was sure gangsters had other means, as demonstrated by Caz Koblinsky's death. I don't know why it took me until that moment in the forest to realize that we were unarmed, but Tommy Tantrum and company wouldn't be. I shuddered for a new reason, and I offered up a silent prayer for everyone's safety. Even Karen's.

The going was pretty easy until Gunnar's phone died. Plunged into near-stygian darkness, we crept along for a while. But as we neared the forest's edge, it became easier to see as moonlight began to penetrate the canopy.

By the time we reached the edge of the forest, we were filthy and scraped up from tree branches that came out of nowhere in the darkness. We got down low in the ferns that lined the forest floor and peered out.

It was like watching a play. The flat, rocky terrain around the blowhole made for a perfect stage brilliantly lit by the full, liquid moon. The scene was composed of two characters. Aton Faraday's green silk pajamas were the color of jade in the moonlight. His back was to us, and he was talking to another man whose face was in full view.

Son of a biscuit! My parents had been right. Double blind indeed.

Tom the bartender was still wearing his uniform. He was talking to Aton, but I couldn't make out what he was saying. While the absence of waves spurting up through the blowhole indicated low tide, the sound of the surf combined with their distance from the forest still managed to cover their voices.

"Aton must be wearing a wire," I whispered to the group. "Mike and Karen must be hiding somewhere."

"What do we do?" asked Gunnar. He hadn't run into the scene to alert Tom, so I was feeling more and more confident that he was on our side.

"We watch and wait," said Jorge. "If it goes according to plan, Mike and Karen will get the evidence they need, everyone will go their separate ways, and they never need to know we were here."

"Wouldn't that be nice," breathed Liz.

"Boy howdy, it would," I agreed.

Could it be that simple? Could Mike and Karen get their evidence? Could Tom be arrested and brought to justice? Could my father come home and the cruise line recover? Could Mike and I, I mean John and I, ride off into the sunset together?

I got my answer when Mike and Karen marched out of the woods with their hands up followed by cruise director Cindy Helms holding a gun.

"I should have known," I muttered. I had seen Tom and Cindy together. It should have occurred to me the moment I'd seen Tom that Cindy was somewhere in the vicinity. And if Cindy was armed, chances were so was Tom.

"I can't believe it," murmured Gunnar. "I simply can't believe it. I've worked with her for years."

"What do we do now?" whispered Liz.

"We need to get closer," I said. "We can't hear anything, and we need to be in a better position to rush Tom and Cindy."

"Agreed," said Liz.

"Hold up!" said Jorge. "Rush Tom and Cindy? You know what they have? Guns! You know what we don't have? Guns!"

"It's okay," said Gunnar. "You can hold back if you're afraid. I will lead the charge and protect the ladies." Gunnar's teeth glinted in the moonlight as he grinned at Jorge.

Jorge sputtered. "You may have brawn, Thor wannabe, but I have street smarts and lightning reflexes. You ever been in a gang? I thought not, son. I'LL protect the ladies."

"No one is going to need protection if we can take out Tom and Cindy quickly," I put in before the peacock feathers grew any larger. "If Tom has a weapon, it's probably in the waistband of his pants. We could get to him before he has a chance to draw."

"Cindy's the greater danger," said Liz. "But she seems like a sensitive soul. She might not have the nerve to shoot."

I remembered how shaken she was by her encounters with Casimir Koblinsky.

"Do you think she's the one who shot at Caz?" asked Liz, reading my mind.

"Even if she did, I would bet my life that Cindy would never shoot me," said Gunnar firmly. "We've been through a lot together."

Gunnar was going to get a chance to take that bet, but first we had to get closer.

Between the tree line, where we were hiding, and the blowhole, where the drama was unfolding, was open ground. But the rocky area enclosing the blowhole was roughly circular, which made the tree line circular. To the left, it curved around until it ended in a low rock formation a good twenty feet closer to the action than where we were currently. It was cover and it was closer. I conveyed the plan to the group, and we inched back into the forest and headed left. Trying to move silently, it probably only took us five minutes to change positions, but it felt like an eternity.

Emerging behind the rocks, we were rewarded for our efforts with the sound of voices. We could hear everything.

"You've miscalculated, Tommy," said Mike.

"Not me, man," said the gangster-turned-bartender. "Not me."

"Alvin, why aren't you saying anything?" demanded Mike.

"Who's Alvin?" Liz mouthed, but I could only shrug.

"Answer me!" Mike reached out as if to shake Aton, but Cindy jammed her gun into his back.

"Easy. Easy," Karen cautioned. "Mike's not going to move anymore."

"No, he's not." Aton snapped out of his stupor and fixed Mike with an icy stare. "And he's not going to tell me what to do, either."

So Aton was really Alvin? What in tarnation was going on?

"You were so smug in school. Mister popularity. Captain of the football team. Voted most likely to succeed. But which one of us has truly succeeded? The newspaper reporter or the billionaire futurist who can influence the global economy with a snap of his fingers? I've made myself all by myself, and I won't let anybody destroy what I've built. That's why I've just made a deal that will keep interfering parties out of my empire forever."

Shades of Lando! The situation was far worse than I'd thought. Aton (or Alvin) Faraday had gone over to the dark side. I looked to my compadres to see if they were taking it all in. Their shocked expressions showed me they were.

"Alvin Faherty was a nice kid," said Mike. "He might have been president of the chess club instead of captain of the football team. He might never have been picked first for dodgeball, and he might have rubbed his good grades in people's faces, but he never would have betrayed a friend."

"A friend? We were never friends. I was your math tutor, and in return you kept the bullies at bay when you were around. But when you weren't? Let's just say I know the taste of toilet water."

Ew!

"And those guys who gave me swirlies and wedgies, not to mention bruises and bloody lips, THEY were your friends."

"And that's all that matters?" demanded Karen. "The past? Our lives don't matter at all?"

Aton took a deep breath and pulled himself together. Alvin Faherty, who had made a brief appearance, vanished, and Aton Faraday reemerged.

"Not in comparison with the greater good. Your deaths are but a sacrifice on the altar of progress. Unhindered by the pressures of organized crime, I will accomplish things that will advance humanity. Alvin Faherty was another necessary casualty, but I'm fast learning that progress necessitates collateral damage. Maybe when I've perfected the world, that will change."

Unhindered? More like unhinged.

Gunnar gestured for us all to get closer, although huddling together behind a boulder, I wasn't sure that was possible. Jorge had bony elbows.

"We can still take them," he whispered. "Aton is never armed. He doesn't believe in guns. I just have to get between Cindy's gun and Robin, I mean Mike. Whatever he's called. She won't shoot me."

"You should distract her," hissed Jorge. "If she's not expecting you, you might surprise her long enough for Mike and Karen to get out of the line of fire. I'll take Tom. I'll launch myself over these rocks and take him down."

"And Liz and I will go for his legs," I added. "Between the three of us, he doesn't stand a chance."

"Gunnar, just promise me you'll be careful," whispered a tearful Liz.

Well, that ship had sailed. The SS Careful was over the horizon, but I kept that to myself. No need to make things worse.

But then something happened to make things worse.

Aton was still ranting about his vision for the future. He put the raving in raving lunatic. But behind his monologue, I began to make out something else. Something musical.

"Hold up!" I hissed. "Listen!"

Something, something "summer's eve." Something, something "nowhere." Something, something "gambler."

My heart sank like a stone.

Daddy.

"Louder! It's your anthem, isn't it? Aren't you the gambler?" shouted a malevolent voice, malevolent but familiar, and my sinking heart rolled over and died.

Daddy sang louder as ordered. His song became clearer as they came closer, and soon he and Momma stumbled into the clearing followed by a pair of lips I'd been kissing just that afternoon. I clapped both hands over my mouth to silence the cry that welled up from the depths of my soul. Then Liz was enveloping me in a bear hug and whispering in my ear.

"It's okay, Jill. It's all going to be okay. Hold it together, girl."

For a brief moment, I succumbed to silent sobs against Liz's shoulder, but her words hit the mark, and I quieted quickly. An eerie calm descended over me. I had lost my father once. I wouldn't lose him again. Boyfriends come and go, but Daddies are forever.

Momma and Daddy were holding up better than I was. Their posture was defiant. Even at gunpoint, they didn't look defeated. Their courage inspired me, and I vowed not to let them down.

"Mike McCall, let me reintroduce an old friend of yours," announced Aton with undisguised glee. "Tomaso Giovanni Gaudiano."

"Please, the name is John Gowdy now. Tommy Tantrum is a thing of the past."

"Looks like reinvention is all the rage," sneered Karen. "Maybe we should reinvent ourselves, Mike. I think I'll be a fairy princess. Who do you want to be?"

"Elliot Ness."

John laughed.

"Mock all you want, but I AM a different person. After the fiasco at Meehan's pub, I was finished in the organization. I hit rock bottom. Family ties were the only things that kept me alive. I had to change to survive, so I got therapy."

I did not see that coming.

Mike snorted. "A regular Tony Soprano. I wonder what the diagnosis was. Psychopath or sociopath?"

John just smiled.

"I also got an education, and I became someone much more valuable to the organization. I'm a rational man now, and I like working with rational people, like Mr. Faraday here. He understands that business is transactional. He gives me something I want. I give him something he wants. In this case, he gives me you, and I give him a successful cruise line." He turned to Aton. "You've sweetened the deal with Calvin Cooksey. What are you hoping for in return?"

"Assurances that you won't have a change of heart in the future."

"As long as our ATMs stay in place for money laundering, you will never hear from me again."

"And what will the mob think about you giving up a gold-mine in exchange for settling some personal scores?" Mike interjected. "I think they'll take a dim view."

"As I said, I'm very valuable to the operation now, and my

superiors aren't fond of loose ends. They like things tidy, and I'm about to clean house."

"And what will Jill think of you murdering her parents?"

"My bride-to-be will never know. Oh yes, we will be married. I'm sorry none of you will be able to attend the wedding. That's a lie. Relieved is more like it. Soon I will add domestic bliss to my list of accomplishments. The boss loves a family man." He turned to Daddy and Momma. "Be comforted in the knowledge that I truly love your daughter, and I will protect her with my life."

"You're a monster!" screamed my mother.

"Well, it's good to know we'll be avoiding scenes like these during the holidays." Then John looked to the skies.

Frozen in horror at the drama unfolding before me, it took me a moment to recognize the *whump-whump* of helicopter blades, but when I did, hope surged through me. Could it be law enforcement?

"Right on schedule." John's grin widened, and my hope evaporated. He and Cindy herded everyone closer to the blowhole.

The clearing became a tornado as the helicopter descended and landed. Palm fronds and other foliage were still swirling when the blades finally stilled and the pilot and a passenger got out. Joseph and Mira.

"You remember Johnny Fingers, McCall." John was enjoying himself immensely. "Although he looks a little different. We both do."

"Nip tuck," chuckled the man we'd all known as Joseph.

"And his beautiful bride-to-be, Mira Koblinsky. What do you say to a double wedding, Joseph?

"They murdered your father," my mother screamed at Mira. "Doesn't that mean anything?"

"It means I'm finally free." Mira's voice was steel. "Free of embarrassment. Free of the mattress business. Free of cruise ships."

"She's selling the company to me," boasted John. "It will be business as usual at all our other cruise lines and casino hotels. No inconvenient pangs of conscience to get in the way."

Aton, who had been vibrating with rage, finally exploded.

"Joseph! How could you? My most trusted lieutenant. Spock to my Kirk. Riker to my Picard. How could you betray me?"

"Wrong franchise," laughed John. "He was always Luca Brasi to my Vito Corleone."

"Well, we all know what happened to Luca Brasi," scoffed Karen.

John and Joseph looked at each other and burst out laughing.

"I love irony!" roared John. "The only people who are going to sleep with the fishes are the four of you. Now move!"

He and Cindy ushered my parents, my erstwhile boyfriend, and his partner to the edge of the blowhole.

"This island has everything. Even the perfect way to dispose of enemies and inconveniences. In a tragic sightseeing accident, four tourists drowned. So sad."

Time stood still except for my pounding heart, which echoed painfully in my years. My prayers were wordless now, pure expressions of agony as I faced losing my stalwart mother, my resurrected father, my overprotective ex-boyfriend. And Karen.

"Take me instead!"

I don't remember moving, and it wasn't a conscious decision, but suddenly I was there. I fell to my knees in supplication as I looked into the faces of my nearest and dearest, now distorted with horror. They'd thought I was safely out of it. Well, if they couldn't be safe, then I didn't want to be safe either.

The color drained from John's face.

"Jill…you weren't supposed to know."

"It doesn't matter, John. I'll marry you. I'll be a wonderful wife to you. We'll have as many kids as you want. We'll go wherever you want. Just please, spare them."

"They'll dog our footsteps. We'll never be free."

"No, they won't." I looked to the three people who meant the most to me. And Karen. "If I ask them not to, they will respect my wishes."

"Like hell I will!" shouted Mike and my father in unison.

"Oh Jill, you inspire so much love. You have enchanted me from the first moment. I must possess you. Come away with me, my darling."

"As you wish."

Keeping his gun trained on my loved ones, John took my arm and steered me toward the helicopter.

This was it. Once we were airborne, there was no turning back. I would become a mob wife to save my family. In my darkest nightmares, I could never have predicted this scenario. I desperately tried to find a bright side to quell the panic welling up inside me. How bad could it be? It was the mob, so there was a good chance John would be killed at some point. Then I'd be free.

Don't kid yourself, Cooksey.

Shaking uncontrollably, I climbed aboard the helicopter followed by John as Joseph and Mira took their places at the controls.

"What about us?" yelled Tom. "You can't leave us here. If they live, the whole deal goes south. We'll go to prison."

"This wasn't the plan," said Aton.

"Never fear. As soon as we're in the air," said John, "dump them in the blowhole."

"No!" I screamed and tried to launch myself from the helicopter, but John blocked my path.

Then Mike and my father did the unthinkable. They rushed the chopper.

John opened fire, and I saw Mike push Daddy to the side and out of the line of fire even as he kept coming. A bullet tore through his arm, spinning him around, and he fell to his knees.

Then the forest began to move.

Was I going insane? Had the stress of losing my loved ones finally broken me?

"Great Birnam Wood!" exclaimed my Shakespeare-loving mobster fiancé.

The movement in the forest was really more of an undulation, as if something big, like a T-Rex, was headed our way.

Distracted by the quivering jungle, John stopped firing, and I changed plans. Instead of flinging myself from the helicopter, I leaned back on the seat and used both legs to kick John as hard as I could. He fell from the opening and dropped the gun just as a mass of kilted, knife-wielding Scotsmen came shrieking like banshees out of the forest.

You've been reading too many time travel romances, Jill.

When they rushed the chopper, joined by Liz, Gunnar, and Jorge, I knew they were real. They extracted Joseph and Mira and disarmed Cindy, who, as predicted, had never fired a shot. Roddy's face loomed in the doorway.

"Allow me, mistress." And he scooped me up.

Way too many time travel romances.

So much was happening around me. Aton, John, Tommy, and Cindy were being forced to the ground at knifepoint. Shona and Eileen were wrapping Mike's wounded arm with their tartan sashes. Liz, Gunnar, and Jorge were tending to my parents. Or were my parents tending to them? It was hard to say.

And on the periphery, observing the scene and wringing her hands as if she didn't know what to do next, was Novette.

"Take me to her," I whispered to Roddy.

He put me down when we reached her, and I threw myself at her in a hug that probably hurt.

"Sugar?"

"You did this," I said, somewhere in the vicinity of her ear. So many golden curls. "You saved us."

Novette hugged me back.

"Och, aye," said Roddy. "She's a braw lass, oor Novette!"

"Jilly Bean!" I heard my father cry.

"Go to him," said Novette, so I ran.

There's something about a hug from your dad. It just makes everything right again. I pulled Momma into the hug, and the three of us just held each other for a long time. We didn't say anything, although I knew there would be lots to say later. For the moment, all that mattered was that we were alive and together.

When we finally parted, I went in search of Mike and found him on his feet conferring with Karen and The Legend. I was a jumble of emotions where Mike was concerned. Part of me wanted to hug him and part of me wanted to slug him. I compromised with a handshake.

"Thank you for what you did," I said as I offered him my hand and tried to look anywhere but at him.

"You've got to be kidding me," I heard Karen mutter.

"Uh, you're welcome," said Mike as he awkwardly took my hand and shook it. "It's just a scratch." I saw The Legend watching our interaction with undisguised amusement and Karen rolling her eyes. I'm surprised they didn't get stuck up in her skull. More's the pity. The handshake went on way too long, and extracting my hand from it led to an even more awkward moment that I'll probably cringe over at three o'clock in the morning for the rest of my life. When it was over—sweet relief—I hurried to find Liz and Jorge. They were chatting with Gunnar (of course), Shona, and Eileen. Was it my imagination, or was Shona giving Gunnar the stink-eye?

Liz threw herself on me in a Posse hug for the ages, and Jorge decided to join in. Strangely enough, I started to shake. The adrenaline was abating, and shock was surging to the fore.

"What possessed you to do such a crazy thing?" demanded Liz.

"Seriously! You were there and then poof, you were gone." Jorge grabbed his gorgeous hair with both hands in frustration.

"I don't know. It wasn't a conscious decision." I laughed shakily.

"I would have taken your place," said Gunnar solemnly. I didn't point out that John wasn't in love with him so it probably wouldn't have worked. Jorge, however, did.

While they were sparring verbally, I suddenly got goosebumps and felt eyes upon my back. I turned and looked straight into the eyes of John Gowdy. He was several yards away, sitting on the ground, staring intently at me, but, unexpectedly, his gaze held no hate.

"Excuse me," I said to the others and walked toward John. I heard Jorge whistle softly in disbelief.

"Closure is good," murmured Liz.

John was seated on the ground with Aton, Cindy, Tom, Joseph, and Mira. No one was talking, although the two couples were sitting close. The gang of villains was encircled by Scots wielding knives and the guns that had been confiscated. There on a rock by the ocean, I was witness to a kilted *Lord of the Flies*. That thought almost made me chuckle. Almost.

"Have you read *Lord of the Flies*?" asked John. Darn him for reading my mind! I tried not to show my surprise but failed utterly. John smirked knowingly. "I double majored in finance and literature."

"That explains the Shakespeare quotes."

"There's a lot of wisdom in Shakespeare."

"Especially the tragedies."

"I love you, Jill."

"I believe you." I did.

"And you love me."

"No, I don't. You tried to kill my mother and father. Any affection I had for you died when you held them at gunpoint."

"I can't believe that. Juliet loved Romeo even after he killed Tybalt."

"Juliet was thirteen and hopped up on hormones. She was an idiot."

He laughed. "While you, my love, are not thirteen and not an idiot."

I thanked him for the compliment.

"Well, we'll always have Nassau." He sounded resigned, and I was glad. I didn't want to be anyone's fixation while doing life in Rikers. "See ya around, Jill."

I nodded in reply, turned, and walked away. I didn't cry, despite the lump in my throat.

"Okay, on your feet," ordered Gunnar. "Time to head back to civilization. Captain Staggs has been notified and the authorities are en route."

Cindy Helms started to cry as Tom helped her stand up. Gunnar gave the orders as the captives lined up two-by-two and the Scots formed a phalanx around them, only the Scots were slow to form up, giving John his opportunity.

He darted out of formation and headed, not to the jungle where he had a hope of survival, but to the blowhole.

He perched on the edge, rimmed in moonlight, and smiled at me.

"Farewell! Thou art too dear for my possessing."

And he dropped.

We raced to the edge and peered into the abyss, but the moonlight couldn't penetrate that stygian darkness. The water was black and boiling. Cell phone flashlights were deployed to no avail. Of Tomaso Giovanni Gaudiano, also known as John Gowdy, there was no trace.

I did cry then and found my way to my mother's embrace.

"He's not worth your tears, baby." She stroked my back and made calming noises.

He wasn't, but the man who courted me and protected me, though fictional, was worth my tears. I wasn't crying for Tommy Tantrum. I was crying for a modern-day Mr. Darcy who was too good to be true.

I soon quieted. After all, even I knew I was mourning someone who never existed, and soon we were marching through the coppice forest.

And the Scots were singing.

And so was my dad.

And mom, and Liz, and Jorge, and Gunnar, who possessed a delightful bass voice.

And Karen.

The only people not singing were our criminal captives.

And Mike.

And me.

But he was keeping close.

CHAPTER 32

I didn't wake up until sometime the next afternoon. The previous evening was a fever dream that still didn't feel real.

When we arrived back in St. George, the Bahamian police were there to greet us. Interpol arrived soon after.

Two different law enforcement agencies made for infinite, headache-inducing questions. At first, they kept us all separate until we'd given our statements, I guess to see if we were all on the same page and therefore telling the truth. But the tale was long and took time to tell. By the time they were done with us, we were all exhausted. Thankfully, the bungalows were just a golf cart ride away.

Momma and Daddy stayed with Liz and me, so I let them have my room and bunked in with my friend. We crashed hard, and for my part, I didn't even dream, which for me was very strange.

I awoke to murmurings from the other room. Thinking it was only Liz and my parents, I padded out of the room in my t-shirt and sleep shorts. I made a quick about-face when I saw Jorge, Gunnar, Novette, Karen, and Mike.

Reemerging fully dressed, I found everyone at the dining table polishing off a very late brunch.

Everyone was very solicitous of me. Gunnar held out my chair, Liz and Momma filled my plate, and Daddy fixed my coffee just the way I like it. They were treating me like a china doll, and I hated it. I'd had quite enough of that.

I focused solely on the coffee and getting answers.

"So, who wants to go first?"

"Don't you want to eat something?" urged Liz.

"I want to drink my coffee while someone tells me what in blue blazes happened yesterday that nearly led to four deaths?" I fixed my gaze on the four people at the center of the story and calmly sipped my coffee.

"I'll start," said Mike unexpectedly. "Karen and I went to Aton to get his help in trapping Gaudiano, but you know that. What you don't know is that he and I have a past. I knew him before he was Aton Faraday, when he was little Alvin Faherty, the nerd of my high school class. He tutored me through calculus, and I thought it was my in. I didn't know he was so bitter. Karen and I revealed our identities and that we wanted to help him bring down his saboteur. He jumped at the idea, so I revealed your parents' identities, as well—"

"With our permission," interjected my mother.

"To show him that we had even more ammunition to use against Gaudiano. He agreed to wear a wire and meet with Tommy Tantrum under the guise of solidifying their business relationship."

"Unbeknownst to us," put in Karen, "he made a different deal. Us in exchange for no interference moving forward. He took a risk, but it worked. Gaudiano jumped at the chance to even old scores and tie up loose ends."

I turned to my parents. "So how did you two wind up on the wrong end of his gun?"

"He told us you were eloping at the Church of St. George,"

said Daddy. "But he wouldn't feel right if we weren't there. He said he wanted to surprise you."

"And you believed him?" I was shocked.

"It seemed like the sort of hare-brained thing you might do," said my mother, ever kind and supportive, "so we went along to talk you out of it."

I tried to form a response but only managed some incoherent noises.

"She's choking!" cried Liz right before she pounded me on the back.

"I'm (pound) not (pound) choking (pound)."

"Well, you do an excellent imitation," said Karen.

"Just go on with the story."

"Well, when we got to the church, he pulled a gun on us and marched us into the jungle. And he made your father sing 'The Gambler.'"

"Sick son of a gun! I'll never sing it again, I can assure you!"

Despite everyone's best intentions, it had been easy-as-pie for Aton and Tommy Tantrum—I refused to call him John anymore—to move everyone around like chess pieces.

"So, Joseph, Cindy, and Tom the bartender were the saboteurs," I thought aloud.

"It looks that way," said Gunnar. "Between the three of them, they could go anywhere on the ship and do anything they wanted to."

"But why Cindy?" asked Liz. "She's worked in the industry for years. Surely she couldn't have been with Gaudiano's organization."

"I think it all goes back to Caz Koblinsky," said Gunnar. "I was there when he got her fired from her last job. She was afraid of him, and she probably jumped at the chance to frighten him instead. And Tom went along because he loved her. That's my best guess. But once she was involved, she couldn't walk away. I bet Joseph wouldn't let her."

"I'm sure you're right," said Novette. "Cindy was always a sweetheart. She just got in over her head because of Casimir and couldn't get out."

I traded glances with my mother, and I knew we were thinking the same thing. Cindy Helms had come very close to being an accessory to murder before I had intervened. "Sweetheart" didn't seem like the right word, but I wasn't going to mention it. Instead, I asked the next pressing question.

"Novette, how did you get the cast of *Braveheart* to save the day right in the nick of time?"

Dressed down today in white pants and a Seaswept Cruises polo, and with her hair in a ponytail, Novette looked younger and more vulnerable. She blushed prettily at my question.

"After you left, I finally heard back from your daddy. He texted that he couldn't do the concert because he was trying to stop you from eloping. Well, I had just seen you, so I knew that wasn't true. I tried to warn him."

"But by that time, Tommy Tantrum had already pulled a gun on us," said Momma.

"I knew something was very wrong," continued Novette, "so I told The Legend, and he rallied the troops to save Kenney Rodgers and his family." We all laughed. I could imagine the scene perfectly. Nobody says no to The Legend.

"So, what happens now?"

"The authorities are searching for Gaudiano's body," said Karen. "So far, there's no trace. He most likely drowned."

"There are a lot of sharks in these waters," added Liz.

"That would be a fitting end," said Daddy.

I shuddered. If he'd been taken by a shark, I prayed he had drowned beforehand. I wouldn't wish that on my worst enemy, and I guess he fit the bill.

"What will happen to the others?" asked Jorge.

"Cindy and Tom are fully cooperating with the police," said Mike. "Tom has even confessed to pushing you into the waterfall, Jill. Joseph and Mira, on the other hand, have clammed up. And Aton's not going down without a fight. He has lawyers for days."

"But we have a recording," grinned Karen. "Aton did wear a wire to trick us into trusting him. The whole thing was recorded. He must have thought the recording would never see the light of day once we were disposed of. He thought wrong."

"Don't forget our testimony," put in Liz. "We were all witnesses to the double cross."

"Yeah, but don't underestimate the ability of a billionaire to weasel out of prosecution," said Jorge. I prayed he was wrong. Aton Faraday was brilliant, but he was also mad as a hatter.

"Now I have a question," said Mike with a hard edge to his voice that got everyone's attention. He fixed me with a gaze of steel. "Why did you offer yourself up to a murderer?"

"That's an excellent question," said Daddy. "I'd love to hear that answer."

Time froze for an instant while I struggled to understand how the people I had tried to save could be angry with me.

"Seriously? You're asking me why I jumped in to save the people I love?" I wouldn't look at Mike. I would NOT look at Mike. Instead, I focused on Daddy. "Here's another question. Why did you keep me in the dark? Why didn't you trust me? Why did you push me away?" I stood up. "You know what? It doesn't matter. I'm going for a walk." I headed for the door. Mike followed.

"I'm going with you."

"Like hell you are!" But he kept following.

"Finally!" I heard someone at the table say.

I slammed out of the house and took off in no particular direction. Mike kept pace with me, although he didn't try to overtake me. That was good because I probably would have decked him.

Walking is normally a way to let off some steam, but in this case, my steam was only building. With every step, I got angrier. My feet pounded the pavement, the grass, the cobblestones, and the sand as I marched around the village of St. George. I saw nothing except red, and I only stopped when I encountered the ocean and could go no farther.

"How could you?" demanded Mike at my back. "How could you offer yourself up to that psychopath?"

I rounded on him with a fury I didn't know I could muster.

"I HAD TO SAVE YOUR HIDE! Maybe, just maybe, if you had included me in your plans, it wouldn't have come to that. Did that ever occur to you?"

"I was trying to protect you! We all were!"

"I don't need your protection!"

Mike scoffed. "You got involved with a gangster, Jill. You might need more protection than you think."

"I wasn't the one about to sleep with the fishes. I saved you, dumbass."

"Yeah, you had no trouble throwing yourself at Gaudiano. Maybe part of you was more than willing."

Crack! I felt my tingling hand and saw the scarlet mark erupt across Mike's cheek. I had slapped him silly.

His nostrils flared, his blue eyes burned, and I thought he might slap me back.

Instead, he yanked me off my feet and into his arms. His lips clamped violently down on mine, stifling any protest, not that I was protesting. He still smelled like a camping trip, but now there were notes of coconut and suntan oil. That heady combination was oxygen to a smoldering fire that I thought had been extinguished.

I thought.

Now it roared to life in a conflagration that consumed us. I heard nothing, felt nothing, saw nothing, tasted nothing except Mike.

Dagnabbit! I was still crazy about him.

Eventually, my senses recovered. I could hear the pounding surf. I could feel sand against my skin and realized that we were now lying on the beach. When did that happen? I pulled away slightly and gently punched his good arm.

"I'm still mad at you."

"Back at you." Mike tightened his grip on my hip. "Seriously. Why would you sacrifice yourself for us? How could you think that would be okay?"

I just glared at him. I wasn't going to say it. I would drop dead before I said it first.

"Why did you shut me out? Why didn't you include me?" I said instead.

"Because I wanted to protect you."

"Have I needed protection? Haven't I proven myself? Not that I need to prove anything. Why leave me out?"

"Because I love you!"

I closed my eyes and exhaled, and it felt like my first exhale in a long time, like I'd been holding my breath for hours, days, months.

When I opened my eyes, I could smile again. And then Mike smiled. And the sun came out. The world made sense again.

"Now it's your turn," he said.

"My turn for what?"

"You know, to say it."

Was Mike blushing? Evidently, he needed to hear it too.

So darn cute.

"I."

Smooch.

"Love."

Smooch.

"You."

And I was about to go in for the mother of all smooches when...

"*Ahem*. In that case, maybe you'd like to make it official."

I looked up and into the smiling eyes of the vicar. I wondered just how long he'd been standing there and if he was a fan of *From Here to Eternity*.

Then I looked at Mike. His eyes held a challenge that made my pulse race.

"Well, Cooksey, what do you say?"

CHAPTER 33

Reader, I did NOT marry him.

Although it was tempting.

But really, how could I? We had been apart for almost three months, and I had only known him for six. And in that time, he had pushed me away in order to protect me.

We couldn't have that.

Mike needed to prove that we could be partners in everything, including danger. And I looked forward to the proving.

I explained it to him as we watched the sunset, hand in hand, from the promenade deck of The Lady Luck as she steamed homeward to New York, and he took it with good grace…almost.

"I will try," he said and kissed my fingers.

"Plus…"

"Plus what?"

"Technically we've only dated for two and a half months."

"But we've been in love since September."

"Cocky! You act as if I fell in love with you the moment I met you."

"Didn't you? I know I did." He was nibbling on my pinky.

Then he nipped the inside of my wrist. What were we talking about? "When you fell into my arms in Central Park, I knew it was destiny. I should have kissed you like this." He pulled me roughly to him, dipped me slightly, and captured my mouth which promptly surrendered, white flag and everything.

"*Hmph.*"

Startled apart, we looked up to see Daddy and Momma watching us from nearby.

"If you want dates, you got 'em." Mike picked up the thread as he set me back on my feet and we started moving toward the door to the dining room. "Dinner, dancing, games, movies, museums—"

"Broadway."

"Musicals?"

"You betcha!"

"You're going to make me pay, aren't you?"

"And you're going to enjoy every minute of it."

The door slid open and we glided through, the full skirt of my evening gown making a susurration as it brushed the frame. Momma and Daddy followed, and the four of us rejoined the party in the main dining room. Captain Staggs had ordered a gala to celebrate the return of The Lady Luck to the high seas after the Plague Ship Protocol, not to mention the capture and arrest of the saboteurs, minus one. We were also celebrating the fact that Seaswept Cruises was soon to be under new management. After the investors were informed of what went down, Hoss Buckworth called to let us know he would be buying out Aton's shares and I would be working for him. I was so thankful I almost cried. The odds I would have to become an astronaut to do my job were now about a million to one.

But there were even more important things to celebrate, my father's return most of all. I had been robbed of four years with my dad, but four years compared with a lifetime was something I could live with. He and my mom were now inseparable, and it felt just like old times. Mom had shed her caftans and fuchsia lipstick in favor of a pink cocktail dress with a boat-neck that made her look like a young girl again. And Daddy had somehow borrowed a kilt from one of the Scots. He was strutting about, squiring my mother, and looking very pleased to be alive. I imagined Easter, the Fourth of July, Thanksgiving, and Christmas all with my dad present and accounted for. What a gift! I offered up yet another silent prayer of thanks. Who could say? Maybe my brother would even come home for Christmas this year. The Cookseys reunited at last.

I was celebrating another reunion too. Mike and I were back in business. Cooksey and McCall. I understood now why he had pushed me away, although I still didn't like it. And if he ever tried to do it again, he'd be sorry. But it was a relief to have answers to my questions and assurances that his affections had never swayed.

Which really couldn't be said for my own. John Gowdy, the biography-reading workaholic financial adviser from Staten Island, had held a lot of attraction for me, but he wasn't real. Well, maybe part of him was. I wondered if Tomaso Gaudiano would have become John Gowdy if he'd had a different upbringing or different influences in his life. The question was moot anyway. Tomaso Gaudiano had been a gangster and a murderer, education notwithstanding. And now he was dead, and it was too late for redemption.

Was it?

Okay, his body hadn't been found, but the chances he was alive were incredibly slim. Like the width of a human hair slim. Still, if he had somehow survived, I hoped he would turn his life around, for his sake. Certainly not for mine. His red flags, when they'd finally appeared, were blood red and the size of football fields.

And I loved Mike. Pure and simple. He was the Benedict to

my Beatrice. The peanut butter to my chocolate. The Bogey to my Bacall. Or was I the Bogey to his McCall? YOU KNOW WHAT I MEAN.

He was my other half.

Not that I would tell him that. Not yet.

A stage had been erected in the dining room and a dance floor laid. The orchestra was wailing, and the Steinway Street Swingers were tearing up the floor. Jorge, in zoot-suited splendor, swung his partner around his back and through his legs and never missed a beat. While the dance troupe had pride of place on the dance floor, some brave couples were dancing on the periphery. That's where I spotted Novette and Roddy. I sucked in my breath as she rolled into his arms, and he held her there, nuzzling her neck before he sent her out again. Novette and Roddy? Could it be? No one deserved a happily-ever-after more than Novette.

And between his kilted good looks and her golden ringlets, they'd make a terrific cover for a time travel romance.

I searched for Liz and found her seated with the Scots at a table to the right of the stage, her back to Gunnar who was sitting on the other side of the dining room looking grumpy, probably because of the breakup that had happened earlier in the day.

I was chatting with Shona and Eileen over lunch in the casual dining area when Liz arrived with tears streaming down her face.

"You won't believe what just happened!"

"Lieutenant Halvorsen just broke up with you," said Shona with a sympathetic smile.

"Wha…Yes! How did you know?"

"You weren't the first, and you won't be the last," said Shona as she squeezed Liz's hand. "Have I mentioned this wasn't my first cruise?"

"Did he tell you what a great gal you are? That you'd make a wonderful life partner, but his first love is the sea?" asked Eileen with a twinkle in her eye.

"YES!" Liz was gobsmacked.

"Let me get this straight," I said because I couldn't believe my ears. "He broke up with you using the lyrics to 'Brandy'?"

Liz's eyes were the size of dinner plates.

"That RAT! He couldn't even be original. And now I find I'm just the latest in a string of women he's dallied with! I thought he was a Captain Wentworth, not a Bluebeard! I'll kill him!"

She raced off before we could stop her.

"Are we aboot to have another murrder?" asked Shona.

I shook my head. "No. At worst it'll be a black eye. Maybe a bloody lip."

"She seemed such a gentle wee lassie," said Eileen.

"Oh, she is. Liz is the sweetest friend there is, but she has no tolerance for bad boy behavior."

Shona raised her glass of soda. "Well, good for her. To Liz! We could all take a page out of her book."

Now Liz and her Scottish pals were living it up while Gunnar looked miserable. I wondered if this would be the time Lieutenant Halvorsen came crawling back. If anyone was worth crawling back to, it was Liz.

"May I have this dance?" Mike offered me his hand, and my mouth fell open in astonishment.

"I seem to recall someone telling me that he doesn't dance."

"That was before he almost lost the thing he treasures most in the world."

"And what was that? His story?"

Mike shook his head, pulled me close, and began a slow dance, even though the beat was driving. I chuckled to myself as I lay my head on his shoulder. Mike was dancing but on his terms.

"Besides," he whispered in my ear, "we need to try out some songs for the first dance at our wedding."

"Don't get ahead of yourself," I whispered back. He'd been making wedding remarks ever since the Vicar interrupted our reunion on the beach. Clearly, the man had missed me. "By the way, what happened to your limp? Robin Shelby didn't limp, and now you don't, either."

"Intense physical therapy. It was my tell, and I had to get rid of it once and for all so I could go under cover."

"Congratulations. It certainly fooled me." I thought back to that first night in the dining room when Robin Shelby's lack of a limp had convinced me I was hallucinating. What would have happened if I had trusted my instincts?

We danced for two songs and headed back to our table to find Novette and Roddy in conversation with my parents. The chanteuse was radiant, and Roddy, who held her hand, was smitten. My heart almost burst. I'm a sucker for a happy ending.

"Roddy here was just telling us about Scotland," said Daddy while absently shuffling a deck of cards. "I've always wanted to visit. You know, my mother was a Buchanan."

"And my mother," said Momma, not to be outdone, "was a Kincaid."

"That's wee Andy Kincaid over there." Roddy pointed to a short man with blond hair talking with The Legend. "Maybe you're related. When did your family emigrate to America?"

"Around 1750."

Roddy pursed his lips. "Maybe not."

"How about you go home to Luthersburg first?" I put in. "You can tell my brother that you're alive. How's that for a next step?"

"Keep your britches on," soothed my father. "We're headed home as soon as we dock in New York."

"Good."

"Well, we've still got tonight," said Mike. "How about a little five-card draw?"

My mother laughed drily and shook her head. "Bless your heart."

"Son, I'd take you to the cleaners," said Daddy. "Besides, I've given it up. That's how I got into this mess in the first place. But you should play Jilly. She's the second-best card player in the family."

Mike's eyebrows shot up. "Really?"

I crossed my arms and cocked my head. "Really."

Mike took the deck from my father.

"What should we play for?"

"Well, not for money," I said. "You need to afford all those upcoming dates. Broadway isn't cheap."

Novette hooted and leaned over Roddy to give me a high five. Roddy didn't mind at all.

"I was thinking bigger stakes," drawled Mike, and the wicked gleam in his eye sent a frisson of fear down my spine. What was he up to?

"Woo-hoo!" Daddy grinned ecstatically. "The game is afoot."

"What did you have in mind?" Whatever Mike was thinking, he was going to lose. Big.

"If you win…I will stop pestering you about marrying me. I won't bring it up again until you do."

The table was silent.

"And if I lose?"

"You have to marry me before the end of the summer."

Roddy looked at Novette who looked at my mother who looked at my father who looked at Mike, but Mike only had eyes for me.

I uncrossed my arms and cracked my knuckles.

"Deal the cards."

Jill Cooksey will return in *One Bigfoot in the Grave.*

ACKNOWLEDGMENTS

A book, like a person, needs a support system, and this book is no exception. I owe a huge debt of gratitude to my family near and far who somehow get me and make allowances for my writerly ways. They want the books to keep coming, and their confidence and support mean the world to me. A special shoutout goes to my husband, Matthew, who not only has to endure the teacher/school-year cycle but also the publishing cycle. Great will be your reward in Heaven.

Thank you to my alpha reader and oftentimes therapist, Melissa Carothers, and my beta readers, Elizabeth Berry, Samantha Bowles, Cate Newlands, Sarah Seager Stewart, and Stephanie Thames. They are Jill's guardian angels, and they make sure I don't screw up her life too badly. Cate also made sure I wouldn't offend the Scottish people. As a rule, I try not to cause international incidents, so I appreciate her help. Thanks also to my assistant Isabella Da Cunha.

I'm also very grateful to those stars of the cozy world Scarlett Moss and Molly Burton. Scarlett is always there for me when I'm having a publishing crisis, and Molly isn't afraid to tackle my crazy cover ideas. Thank you, ladies.

One of the most important people to this book is Novette Lewis. Last year, she won my contest to become a character. Looking back, I can see it was divine intervention because without Novette, there is no *Cruising Toward Death*. Thank you, Novette, for lending your name and your curls to my character. She's one of my favorites.

Galations 6:9

ABOUT THE AUTHOR

Lesley St. James began her career in film and television before moving to public relations and then to education. A devoted, lifelong reader of mysteries, she always knew the kind of books she would write. When she's not writing or teaching writing, Lesley enjoys traveling, movies, and genealogy. She resides in Virginia with her husband, Matthew.

For more books, newsletters, and information,
please visit www.lesleystjames.com.

The Sweet Scent of Death
Death of a Dolly Waggler